KT-545-553

Alison Jameson studied English at University College Dublin and worked in the advertising industry for many years. She is now a full-time writer. *This Man and Me* is her first novel.

THIS MAN AND ME

Helen Wilton used to be Hélène Fournier — until her French father walked out of her life . . . Given a new name, she also gets a lesson about the unreliability of love. Helen grows up to become a mass of contradictions: as warm-hearted as she is sharp-witted, as steadfast in her friendships as she is eclectic in her loves. And when life and love cause her to trip, Helen picks herself up and gets on with it. But could facing the loss of her father and finding the inner Hélène be the keys to her future . . . and to finding real love?

ALISON JAMESON

THIS MAN
AND ME

Complete and Unabridged

ULVERSCROFT
Leicester

First published in Great Britain in 2006 by
Penguin Books Ltd
London

First Large Print Edition
published 2007
by arrangement with
Penguin Books Ltd
London

British Library CIP Data

Jameson, Alison, 1966 –
   This man and me.—Large print ed.—
Ulverscroft large print series: general fiction
1. Fathers and daughters—Fiction 2. Young women
—Psychology—Fiction 3. Large type books
I. Title
823.9′2 [F]

ISBN 978–1–84617–631–9

Published by
F. A. Thorpe (Publishing)
Anstey, Leicestershire

Set by Words & Graphics Ltd.
Anstey, Leicestershire
Printed and bound in Great Britain by
T. J. International Ltd., Padstow, Cornwall

This book is printed on acid-free paper

For Mum and Dad
And for Grace

1

He can only say no

December 1980

There are three red spots on the kitchen floor. Rue wipes them away with a cloth and leaves a newspaper flat on the stone flags. For two days our turkey has hung by his feet from the rafters. My father carried it up the kitchen stairs and then leaning out over the banister hooked the rope on to a nail. It makes the meat lean and when a drop falls now it makes a 'tap' sound on the paper and they have argued over this. Rue does not like any kind of bird inside the house. 'Especially one that is dropping blood,' she says. She shakes her head and says it's bad luck — but I don't want to think about that; today I am happy about all sorts of things. I stand in my slot — a warm place between our red Formica table and the Aga — and talk to her while she works. We have always called my mother by her first name which is Rue. A nickname given to her because of the colour of her hair. It is still red, but there is some grey in there now as well. She wears faded jeans and an old pair of green sneakers and her hands and feet move quickly all the time. In the middle of telling me something she will hand me a jug or a cup and say, 'Put that away,' or she will point at a drawer and say, 'Get me a spoon,' and I do all of these things and we talk all the time. Rue is always busy and sometimes when she crosses the kitchen floor she shuffles in time to the music from the radio.

I am happy because it is Christmas and that means our guesthouse is closed for two weeks. It is just us like a real family. My father, my mother and my little sister Beth. My father is French by the way and his name is Jacques, although we have never called him that.

There is Martha Penrose too. She is my mother's best friend and she is nearly always here. And Jacob who is older than any of us. He lives in a cottage near the green swamp and he comes here every day to help Rue with the gardens and the house. After that we have one dog, a Jack Russell called 'Mr Chips', and that is my normal family.

I am also happy because there is a new boy in our class called Leo Adams and because my mother and father are not fighting today. They have not had a fight for two weeks now. In fact, they haven't really spoken to each other much since then. After that fight Rue sat outside on the kitchen windowsill. It was cold and she had no coat on and she was wearing a nice dress and her gold hoop gipsy earrings. When she saw me she wiped her nose on her hand and then sat looking down at the ground.

'I can't take any more,' she said, shaking her head, and when she looked up she had to catch another tear quickly with her thumb. That was the first time I had ever seen a grown-up person cry. Until then I didn't know they could.

My father is a very tall man with black hair and a slow easy walk. He wears brown leather shoes that leave a little grind print on our carpets. When he comes home from work he is usually in a bad mood. Sometimes I run out and open the gate so he can drive in, but usually I just keep out of his way. He doesn't like it when Rue reads the newspaper before him and he also doesn't like it when children answer the phone.

★　★　★

When Leo Adams walks into our classroom everyone goes quiet. We watch in silence as he takes out a new copybook and opens it on his desk. He is sitting beside Birdie in the front row and I am in my usual spot at the window beside Brendan Farrelly. Brendan's father owns the chipper in our village and sometimes he brings in a bag of Rancheros and shares them with me. He slides one across the desk now and watches me as I hold it to my lips.

'Body of Christ,' he says, and I say, 'Amen.'

He has already asked me to meet him behind the coal shed, but I don't want to.

'It's because of the Rancheros,' Birdie says. 'You've eaten them. You have to kiss him now.'

Leo is taller than the other boys and he has dark curly hair and green eyes. He takes a pair of glasses from his bag and puts them on and the other children nudge each other and whisper about this. I just watch him, and when Brendan nudges me I look into my book. I have a pair of glasses in my bag too and until now I have been afraid to put them on. The first time I wore them Rue said I looked like Nana Mouskouri and I haven't put them on since.

When we rehearse the Nativity play, Leo sits at the back of the room and smiles. I walk with the Virgin Mary to the cupboard and open the door and ask if there is any room at the inn. Mary is a small, thin girl with pink glasses and a short square haircut. Last year she had ringworm on one side of her head and I don't really like being Joseph to this kind of Mary. I'm afraid of catching ringworm and I also know that she came to school once without any pants on. We carry a small cardboard mushroom basket and knock on imaginary doors, and when I look around Leo is trying not to laugh.

At lunchtime I sit near the cypress tree with Birdie and we eat our sandwiches and talk. When Leo comes outside we start running around. I am wearing the red-and-yellow kilt Rue made for me. There is a small leather belt on one side and a big silver pin on the front. We start to chase each other up and down the hurling field and this is just because he is watching us and then out of nowhere the kilt just comes off. It seems to unwind itself and there is no warning and suddenly it's at my feet. Birdie doesn't even see and Leo just looks and then he turns and walks away quickly. When Birdie runs back I am sitting on the wooden logs near the tree.

'Brendan Farrelly says Leo's mother died suddenly last year. Found dead in her bed,' she announces and then she says, 'What's wrong with you?'

'My skirt fell off,' and we both know that this is much worse than anything she has said.

★ ★ ★

My name is Hélène Fournier. I am twelve years old and the 'H' in Hélène is silent. We

7

live in a village called Laytown, which is on the East coast, and our guesthouse is called 'Sea Breeze'. There are two lawns at the front and eight stone steps that lead down to the beach. It is a big grey house and from a distance it looks like a giant rock in the sand. The windows look dark and cold from the beach, but inside there are corridors that twist and turn and rooms that open into other smaller rooms. Sometimes the guests get lost and the kitchen door opens suddenly and they are standing there looking in at us as if they have no idea who we are. Usually we are just eating macaroni cheese and watching *Star Trek* on TV.

When I walk home from school with Birdie we always go by the beach. Sometimes we stop and study a shell or a rock and sometimes Birdie spins around and around and then lets her schoolbag fly into the air. If we find a jellyfish we kneel beside it and cut it up like a cake. Once we found a pair of bedroom slippers and we sent them floating out to sea.

'I dare you to kiss Brendan Farrelly,' I say.
'I dare you to kiss Leo Adams,' she replies.
'OK.'
And we walk on kicking into the sand with our feet. There is a cold East wind and it gets in under the hoods of our duffle coats and

makes our noses and ears ache. The bigger dunes are covered in green sea grass and today it is flattened in the wind.

'I dare you to run in your togs on the beach tomorrow,' I say.

'I dare you to run without your togs on the beach tomorrow.'

'OK.'

And then she says, 'Tomorrow, after school,' and I nod, not really knowing if I have agreed to ask Leo for a kiss or run without any clothes on the beach.

When we pass the nuns' bungalow we slow down. Sometimes they walk in twos with their rosary beads in their hands. Rue says they are 'on retreat' and I think that means they are hiding from something.

In the distance I can see my father's car parked at the side of our house and it makes me want to slow down and stay with Birdie on the sand. Sometimes I bring her in and Rue gives us hot apple tart and cream. She admires Birdie's auburn hair, her curls and the colour of her eyes. It is different when my father is at home and I am afraid to ask her inside.

'See you tomorrow,' I call, and she trudges up the side road into the village with her curls blowing around in the wind.

'Don't forget your tea towel!' she shouts

back over one shoulder.

These are our costumes for tomorrow's Nativity play and I will be wearing my new glasses with mine and I'm already worried about this.

Beth is waiting for me at the front door. She is only six and she has red cheeks and blonde hair. Today she is wearing a camel coat and short red Wellingtons.

Mr Chips is wearing a doll's dress and she drops him suddenly when she sees me and then runs down the garden path.

Jacob waves from the beach and shouts, 'Any slaps?', and he asks me this every day. He is following the tide out now and digging for lugworms as he goes.

When I get inside the house is quiet. There is a smell of cigarette smoke in the hall and in the dining room and if I follow it it will take me to my father who is at his desk in his study now. He would have parked his car and walked into the hall and picked up today's post. Then he would have tapped the weatherglass and walked into the kitchen and lit his first cigarette there. He would have carried it through the first hall and through the second and then through the dining room and into his study. I know this because he does the same thing every day. He works at his desk all evening then, and usually I bring him his dinner on a tray. The door is already closed when I drop my schoolbag and then I hear Rue's footsteps overhead. As soon as I come home the first thing I do is find Rue. Today she is upstairs making their bed.

'Well, hello there,' she says, as if it's a long time since we last met.

'Hello,' I reply.

'And how was school today?'

'My skirt fell off,' and I am blaming her for this.

'Oh, we'll have to do something about that,' she says, and I can hear a little laugh starting down in her throat.

'Here,' she says, and she holds a corner of the sheet out towards me and when we face each other it billows down over their bed. There is a question in my head and I am trying to get the words in order. I want to know if it is all right to ask a boy to kiss you and then I hear myself asking something else.

'Do you remember when you met Dad? I mean, the first time?'

'I do indeed,' she replies, and she is moving quickly around the bed, tucking in the sheet and then pulling the blankets up quickly. She stops for a moment then and looks out their bedroom window.

Their bed is old and there are two hollows in the mattress now.

'What happened?' I ask, and I love hearing about how they met.

'Oh, I just liked the look of him — and he was very charming,' she says.

It was in fact Martha who introduced them in Paris and she has often told me how she wrote out Rue's address for him on a white serviette.

Afterwards he bought Rue pink tulips and they ate fresh bread on a green painted bench. The first present he gave her was the ballerina clock. It is on the shelf over the bed, but it is broken now and the little ballerina doesn't dance on the hour any more. It was a nice present to get though and I like hearing how he surprised her with it and that he was romantic once.

In Paris people eat horses and snails. The poorer people queue for tripe and everyone has money for black coffee and cigarettes. Later he took her to meet his parents and his mother wore a long white apron and there was a red-and-white striped canopy over their door.

They offered her fresh steak and used small pointed knives to cut up the meat. When she blushed and said 'No, thank you,' they laughed and wrapped it in pink paper, and she put it into her bag. There was a little golden horse in the window of their shop and the sign over the door said 'Boucherie Chevaline'.

'Horse meat bleeds bright red,' she says, and she is shaking her head and straightening the eiderdown and I can see how much she must have liked him then. He keeps the little horse on the desk in his study now. It stands between his cigarette case and the pink seashell and the hooves are prancing as if it can't decide if it should stay or run.

Rue keeps her rosary beads under the pillow on her side and on his there is one stubbed cigarette in the ashtray that came with *Time* magazine. She says that romantic men are not very reliable, but I don't want to hear about that. Once when we made their bed we found his pyjamas curled up on her side as if they had gone to sleep over there.

'There's a new boy at school,' I tell her.

'Is there?' she asks, and she sits down for a moment on their bed.

'Leo Adams.'

'Oh, they bought the antiques shop,' she says softly.

'His mother is dead.'

'God help them,' and she is shaking her head.

'Yes,' I tell her, and my voice is low and serious. 'It's just him and his father.'

'The poor creatures,' she replies.

'We should ask them here for Christmas dinner,' and I say this as if it has just occurred to me.

'Well, I don't know about Christmas dinner . . . I don't know what your father would say.'

'But he has no mother,' and all the time I am thinking about asking Leo for my first real kiss.

'I'll talk to your father and we'll see. We should do something for them I suppose.'

'Yes,' I tell her. 'At this Christmas time.'

★ ★ ★

Our crib is on the windowsill in the return of the stairs. Rue got it at half price in Drogheda because there are two figures missing.

'So long as the Virgin and Child are there it's a crib,' she said, and she arranged it on a little bed of straw. We are just missing the donkey and one wise man.

'But how did they get here . . . without the donkey?' Beth asked her.

'They got a taxi,' she said.

★ ★ ★

Martha Penrose is sitting on her bed. She has stayed with us so often that she has her own room now. It is a small room at the end of the

14

house that looks out over the orchard and part of the beach. She is brushing her hair and then twisting it into a ponytail on top of her head. There is a bottle of gin on the bedside table which she drinks to help her sleep and sometimes when she thinks I'm not looking, like now, she also puts it into her tea.

Martha is forty-four and she says she will not get married now.

She knows about things though and sometimes it's easier to ask her something than to ask Rue.

'Martha?'

'Yes, Hélène.'

'Well . . . you know . . . boys.'

'I do.'

'Did you ever ask a boy to kiss you?'

She gives me a grin and lights a cigarette and she is thinking all the time.

'Not exactly . . . are you thinking of asking someone?'

'Yes, but I'm afraid he might say no.'

Behind us there are jackdaws on the beach and they are eating chips from brown paper bags. There are grey crows too and they flip the white shell crabs on to their backs. It is not a romantic beach.

'Just close your eyes — and let him, you know, take you,' and when she speaks there is smoke mixed in with her words.

Later when I am walking through the long grass in our orchard I put my arms around a tree and kiss its wet green bark and then I walk on as if this is normal.

'Take me where?' That is what I want to know.

★ ★ ★

The Virgin Mary stands on an altar at the end of our landing. There is a red-stained-glass window and a cream-coloured statue of the mother and child. We have a vase filled with plastic flowers and sometimes I find a single rose left in a glass. Every morning my father kneels down to say his prayers. The kneeler creaks and he makes the sign of the cross with a quick karate hand.

Rue dusts the altar every morning and I watch as she lifts the Virgin like a toddler in her arms and then rests her on the floor. She tells me that the pope lives in Rome and that more than anything she would like to go there some day. The Virgin is missing one hand. We don't know how this happened, but Rue says it makes no difference and that she can hear our prayers just the same.

★ ★ ★

There is a train station overlooking our village. We go there on the day we get our holidays and when the signal goes down I run with Birdie to the flyover bridge and we wait there for the train. From up here we can see everything we have, the village and the boardwalk and the grey and white sea.

The hotel on the main street is called 'The Horizon' and it smells of dinner all day long. There is a church, a thatched pub and two caravan parks. After that there are black rocks and wet green seaweed and the sand is always wet and grey.

When the Belfast train screams towards us we hold each other and scream back. She says that we are getting older and that we should both have boyfriends by now and I'm worried about this.

Sometimes we spend an afternoon tempting crabs out from under the rocks with bread caught on hooks. When we catch them we take them on to the sand and they walk back to the sea. There isn't much to do here. When the tide comes in it melts our sandcastles and the air smells like fish and chips. The lovers go to the boardwalk and speak together in soft little voices. Afterwards they walk back with their arms linked and they guide and steer each other as if they are both blind.

★ ★ ★

The antiques shop is on the main street next to the church. Sometimes there are bicycles for sale and they are parked with stabilizers on the footpath outside the front door. There are two big windows and we can see the clocks on the walls and the cabinets filled with pistols and jewellery.

We loiter around until Leo comes out.

Birdie says his eyes are too nice for a boy to have and that he will be shaving soon.

'Do you want to come in?' he asks, and we walk across the worn-out green carpet and into the back of the shop where there is an Aladdin's cave. There is a glass case in the back filled with stuffed birds and Leo says this will never sell. One or two have caught mice and there is one in a corner keeping a fish down with its claw. The fish is dried up like cardboard and the bird is looking away as if it has suddenly gone off the whole idea.

Leo opens a desk and shows us where someone has written their name and the date 'March 1923'. He watches my face and is disappointed then because all I can say is 'Wow'.

'Can't you see?' he asks. 'Someone like us, another real person, actually sat there and wrote here. Don't you wonder who did it,

18

what their lives were like?'

The shop door goes 'ding ding' and we leave him inside the window looking out at us. When I look at the birds in the case I see my faint reflection in among them. My hair is cut short with a side parting. Rue's skin is pale but I am darker, like my father. I think about how twelve-year-old girls should look and I see Birdie with her long ponytail and blue jeans and when I see my reflection with my new glasses I think I look like a newsreader.

When we leave the shop Birdie looks at me expectantly.

'You should encourage him,' she says, but I don't know how to do that.

★   ★   ★

Birdie's swimming cap is pulled down near her eyes and she wears her towel like a cloak.

'You first,' I tell her. She takes her swimsuit off with one hand and it rolls down off her legs and stays like a number eight in the sand. Her other hand clutches the towel high up around her neck and she is laughing and shivering at the same time. Around us the sky is grey and spitting rain. I wait patiently and then she throws back her towel and begins to sprint down the beach. When she turns around she gives a shout and I can hear her laugh hysterically as she begins to run back towards me. I catch her towel and hold it up to her and she pulls it around her quickly.

There is a tear on her cheek from laughing and before she has a chance to settle I throw off my towel and begin the same sprint down the beach. When I run my bare feet sound like they are panicking on the sand and I can feel the East wind just about everywhere. Then I turn and see Birdie holding my towel like a flag in the air.

When we walk towards our house I see Rue and Martha standing in the window on the return of the stairs.

'We'll be killed,' Birdie says, and she takes the road up to the village without looking back. When I turn around Rue is laughing so much she has to lean on Martha for support.

★　★　★

The Christmas tree is inside the sitting-room window. We don't have white lights. Ours are all different colours and they flash off and on. When there is no one else around I take Beth and we lie on our backs under the tree and look up through it. It's like being right inside Christmas then. Rue has called Leo's father and invited them for dinner. I heard her on the phone outside in the hall. She sounded really friendly and she just said it out like it would be a really nice thing for everyone to do. She also put extra presents under the tree for them and I ring Birdie to tell her this. Then I whisper that I will ask Leo tomorrow and she is laughing and saying, 'Good luck.'

I know that Rue hasn't mentioned it to Dad yet, but I don't want to think about that. We watch an old film called *White Christmas* and he comes out of his study and sits at the fire with myself and Beth, and if we had snow our Christmas would be perfect now.

★   ★   ★

The shouting wakes me up in the middle of the night. I can't hear most of the words but their voices are loud when they rise and fall. Each sentence seems to begin with 'You . . .' and it goes on and on from there. Beth sleeps soundly in her little bed beside me and as I lie there and listen I am beginning to feel sick and sort of cold inside. I am waiting for the last loud shout and then footsteps and a door to slam as one of them leaves the kitchen, but tonight it is as if it will never stop. I sit up on my elbows and try to hear. I want to block it out and still I want to know what they are saying. When I open the door quietly I find

Martha standing on the landing. She puts her arm loosely around my shoulders and steers me into her room at the far end of the house.

'C'mon,' she says and I can smell alcohol and perfume when she speaks. Her room is warm and her bedside lamp makes a soft peachy glow. There are magazines and books scattered on her bed. She turns on her radio and tells me that the singer is called Nina Simone and we just sit there together and listen. When the song is over, the shouting has stopped and I can hear Rue's footsteps on the stairs.

★　★　★

There is no snow on Christmas Day. Just a soft warm wind and a grey sky that hangs down near the ground. My father, in a new red turtleneck, takes the turkey and leaves it on the kitchen table for Rue. She is quiet today and so is he. Martha has bought me a make-up kit for Christmas and I have put two blue stripes over my eyes.

'Where are your glasses?' Rue asks, and she is in the middle of putting the turkey into the oven.

'I don't need them any more,' I tell her.

'The miracle of Christmas,' she says.

When Leo and his father arrive Rue goes

out to meet them and my father waits in the sitting room. They come in smiling and bring cold air with them and I am suddenly unable to speak. Leo says, 'Happy Christmas' and then looks down at the floor. My father pours drinks and Leo and I have Coke and smile at each other across the room.

There is a fire lit in the dining room and candles and crackers on the table. I make sure to sit beside Leo and Martha pours each of us a half glass of wine.

During dinner they talk about Paris and Mr Adams calls it 'The City of Light' and when my father hears this he begins to smile. Everyone listens when he describes his parents' shop and the buildings and bridges he saw every day on his way to school and then he describes Paris in snow. He has the kind of voice that makes everyone listen and when he uses some French to describe a particular place everyone smiles and I am really proud of him now. After dinner he shows Leo the golden horse.

'It's all I have left of my Paris now,' he says.

★　★　★

When Beth tries to follow us Martha jogs behind her and catches her hand. The adults stay inside and drink coffee and we put on our coats and walk to the boardwalk. There are no cars or people anywhere and we just sit there quietly and look down into the water.

'Do you want to kiss me?' I ask. I just can't wait for him to 'take me' any more. There is a fear and a thrill of doing something wrong and I don't want to and yet I do at the same time.

'OK,' he says, and it is as if I have offered him a cup of tea.

He takes his glasses off and at that moment I am ready to run away. It needed to be quick and without this kind of preparation. I feel sick with fear and instead of looking at him I am looking at the spot where his jumper has lifted up from his jeans. His skin is sallow and it seems soft and sensitive and I would like to touch it, just there in that soft secret place. He leans into my face as if he is trying to see it more clearly and then he kisses me and his lips are warm and dry and I can feel the roughness of his skin against mine. It is awkward and then I feel his arm around me and he kisses me again and this time he puts one hand where my breasts are supposed to be. He kisses me gently and he keeps his hand on my breast as if to hold me still. Then we stop and look down into the water again.

When we get home I stay in my room,

feeling ashamed and worried because I have allowed a man to use me. When I pass the statue of the Virgin Mary I can't meet her eyes.

★   ★   ★

I call Birdie to tell her what happened and she is interested and asking a lot of detailed questions. I am trying to ask her a question and it's difficult to get my words in the right order.

'Have you ever done that? I mean, just let a boy kiss you and then there's nothing. I mean, we're not going out now or anything.'

I didn't know that this could happen and that men and women use each other all the time. I am ashamed because perhaps I am that sort of woman now.

'Have you ever done that?' I ask her again and my voice is timid and full of fear.

'Oh, sure,' she says, and she is laughing. 'Lots of times . . . you just carry on,' and not for the first time Birdie has invited me back into the world.

★   ★   ★

The next morning the house feels quiet and empty.

Their bed is made and the window is wide open so that the curtains are blowing into the room. The upstairs landing is cold and I meet Rue coming up the stairs.

'Where's Daddy?'

'He's gone for a walk on the beach,' she says, and she brushes past me and walks down the back landing to Martha's room. The fire has not been lit in the dining room and so we eat in the kitchen again and at lunchtime he still hasn't come home.

'Should we look for him?' Martha asks, and her words come out very slowly. Rue watches her face across the table and I know they are both being calm because of myself and Beth. I am wondering if I should call down to see Leo later on.

'Did he say how long he would be?' Martha asks then, and she is still speaking slowly and wearing the same little frown.

'He said he needed some air,' Rue says, and as we finish our lunch she is watching the window carefully and then she gets up and telephones Jacob and asks him to meet her on the beach.

★   ★   ★

Rue wears an old cardigan and walks quickly up and down the sand. She finds his coat on a

26

rock then and she begins to run with it in her hand.

'Jacques! . . . Jacques!' she calls, and it is a long time since I have heard her call him by his name. There is a gale blowing now and the waves are dashing up and down.

⋆   ⋆   ⋆

The flashlights move up and down the beach all night. We stay inside and watch as every hour goes by Jacob comes in soaking wet and Martha pours whiskey into his tea. Rue comes inside once and kneels down at the altar and prays. At seven o'clock it is getting bright and the lifeguards begin their search again. When Rue comes inside she is quiet. She sits at the kitchen table and just looks down and then she says there is no hope left.

'Give Beth her breakfast,' she says, and she gets up to go out again. She takes Beth's hand and squeezes it gently around a spoon.

'There you are,' she says to her, and even now her voice is soft and kind.

⋆   ⋆   ⋆

The long green velvet curtains still hang down to the floor in his study. The window looks out over the back lawn and the orchard

27

trees. Their wedding photograph is still on the shelf and they are not looking at the camera because they are looking at each other instead. The mantelpiece is a small marble crescent and there is an old sheepskin rug on the floor. His desk is locked and the key is still in the pink seashell. I am thinking now that by wanting to have Leo here at Christmas I caused the fight.

When I look up I have a strange feeling that something is missing and I see then that the golden horse is gone.

★ ★ ★

Rue steps into the bath and then sits with her forehead on her knees. I can see the ridges on her spine and her skin seems too white and cold. When she breathes out slowly her breath echoes around this cold room. Then Martha appears at the door and she hands me a glass.

'Give this to her,' she says, and Rue is like some blind creature we need to guide and help now. I leave the glass on the windowsill because I know she will not want a drink. Her hair seems too short and weak around her neck and I kneel down beside the bath and just begin to stroke her there. Then Beth comes in and she stands beside me and it is as if Rue is the child and we are the mothers now.

Beth soaks the yellow sponge with water and then holds it up so that a long thin river flows softly over her back.

Martha sits on a chair and she stays completely silent and at any moment now I will find enough courage to speak.

'He isn't dead,' and it is my quiet voice that tells them.

'All we can do is pray,' Martha says, and she sighs loudly when she speaks.

'He isn't dead,' and it is my voice again.

And now Rue turns her face towards me and she just stares and then frowns. I have never seen my mother without clothes on and she looks cold and small.

'The horse is gone from his desk,' and she is looking back at me with strange staring eyes.

'And there are other things,' and now I have to keep going. 'The photograph of me and Beth and his silver cigarette case.'

'Jesus Christ,' Martha whispers, and she puts one hand up to her mouth. There is an awful silence then and for that moment I wish I had kept his secret safe. Then there is another sound and we are all crying together and it seems my father is gone and it was only our small world he wanted to leave behind.

Rue puts on her robe and smokes a cigarette sitting on the side of the bath. She doesn't speak for a long time and then she gets up quietly and begins to go through his things. She says first that she will find him and then she says simply, 'What's the point?' and her face has the same sad staring eyes she had when she was in the bath.

Later she takes everything out of his desk. She folds his clothes and puts them into long black bags. She takes every photograph and we watch as she burns them and this is how she puts my father away. She didn't find the pair of brown shoes under the stairs though and I keep them in my wardrobe now and once I tried them on.

★　★　★

The sun is just beginning to come up when I hear Rue on the stairs. For three weeks now she has slept late and I have made Beth's breakfast and gone to school. Martha brings her tea on a tray and they smoke and talk. This morning she is up early and when I look out my window she is walking in a white robe down the path and on to the sand. There is a part of me that thinks of my father and how he disappeared and I want to run after her and shout her name. Instead I put on a coat

30

and run downstairs and watch her from inside the front door. She takes off her robe and she is wearing her blue-and-white swimsuit underneath. Then I find Martha at my shoulder and she is holding Beth's hand. We stand together then and watch in silence as Rue takes her swimsuit off. She is still slim and there are tiny red freckles on her skin. With a sudden little cry — it is the kind of 'Yip' Birdie gave too — she begins to run. It is a smooth steady jog at first and then she gathers speed and her little fists are punching up and down as she sprints along the beach. Then she stops and turns and runs back, slower now, to her robe on the sand. She catches her breath, breathing deeply in and out, with her hands on her hips. She takes in the wet salty air and lets her head fall back and then she just smiles right up into the sky.

'Let's make some coffee,' Martha says, and she is nodding slowly and smiling, 'and we'll have some nice fresh bread and we'll all have breakfast together.'

'Is Rue OK?' I ask, and I am worried now because my mother might be slightly insane.

'She's just fine,' she says, and when Rue comes she lifts Beth up and holds her on her knee. Her cheeks are fresh and pink and she is smiling at us again.

When we stand on the flyover bridge Birdie tells me she has a secret.

'Sometimes . . . ' and she stops, 'my dad hits my mum.'

She parts with this information and all the time her eyes are still and sad as she looks out across the village. She doesn't look for an answer; it was just something she wanted me to know.

'My dad isn't coming back,' I tell her.

'I know,' she says, and her voice is very soft. 'The woman in Spar told me.' She looks down at her freckled hand, which she is leaning on, and her fingers are spanned out on the wood. We are both tired of being young and pretending.

★ ★ ★

My father's footsteps were slow and easy. He always walked as if he was on a beach. One day he went walking and he didn't come back. My name is Helen Wilton. My secret name is Hélène Fournier and we never talk about my father now.

Leo has gone to a boarding school in Dublin and I don't miss him at all. I miss my father and I miss my silent 'H'.

Last night I had that dream again. My father is wearing the red turtleneck jumper and he is walking on the beach and when I call out to him he can't hear me. 'Daddy' I call, but he keeps walking and it is him because I know how he walks and I call him again. Then he does that thing and it happens in every dream, he keeps walking on and on until he is walking right out into the sea. I am calling him all the time but he keeps walking and walking until he just disappears. And I wonder if he would have stopped if he could hear me.

2

If I could be your girl

November 1986

He puts on a denim jacket and leans into the mirror at the end of my bed. He is tall and he bends forward to catch his reflection inside the frame. There is a white porcelain heart hanging from the mirror and I wonder if he notices it or if he just sees himself.

'You look good,' I tell him.

'Oh yeah?' and beside me he sounds fresh and alive. He has already left me and he is thinking about today's show on Capital Radio. I can see him standing behind the glass with his arms folded, wearing cream-coloured headphones and being important and in charge. He is the Producer and when something unexpected happens his voice takes over and it is efficient and kind.

'Keep talking,' he tells them, 'just keep talking ... describe what you're doing ... keep it going ... keep talking.' Sometimes his words are like sharp barks in his Northern accent.

He's all business as he gets dressed and then he strides into the bathroom and then back out again, taking big steps around my only real room. When he puts on his shoes he pushes each foot in and stamps on the floor to get his heels inside. He is on some kind of mission and it is nothing to do with me now. It is about him preparing to step back into his world while I stay behind in mine.

There are two cups on the table, turquoise blue with matching napkins, and I've even squeezed fresh juice for him. I hardly know this man and I want him to have real oranges today.

'We're live this morning,' he says. 'There's no sound delay — so we can't edit,' and I can see that he is worried about this. I'm thinking there's no delay in real life either but when he tells me what he does he sounds easier, softer and more adult than before.

He sits beside me at the table and we talk like two people who have known each other for years. What was it that Martha Penrose said?

'It's all very well until you see them over a boiled egg in the morning,' but we are easy with each other. He smiles at my little jokes and then pats his pockets for his cigarettes.

When he smokes he runs his finger along my bookshelf.

'I can see you like poetry,' he says.

There is an old clock on the mantelpiece, a present sent by Rue last week for my eighteenth birthday. It reminds me of her now as it calls out the hour with a sweet silvery ding.

'Who are they?' he asks then, and he sounds worried when he looks up at the antique prints over the fireplace. Catherine of Aragon and Anne Boleyn.

'My father and my mother,' I tell him, and we both start laughing.

He stops for a second then and looks at me.

'What?'

'Nothing.'

'What?'

When he stubs out his cigarette there is a half smile on his face and then he looks up at me again.

'You have a great smile — do you know that?' he says. ' . . . A killer smile,' and when he walks past me he touches my head gently with his hand. He does this without thinking and then he is looking around the room for his keys.

Outside the birds are singing, but I am still trapped in Friday night. I close the curtains again and climb back into our still warm bed.

He is probably late for work now, but he comes over and gets in beside me. He is wearing his coat and shoes and he hugs and kisses me as if he has all day — and in my head I am starting to imagine what our life together might be like.

'So listen,' he says, and he is sitting on the side of my bed now looking back at me. I reach up and stroke his cheek and he takes my hand and kisses it.

'I'll give you a call sometime.'

I nod my head really slowly. 'Great.'

And now I am trying to kill him with this smile.

There are some words a girl should never have to hear and one of them is 'Sometime'.

When the front door opens there is a blast of cold air. I want to say something to him, but suddenly we seem to have nothing to say. One minute we were Ozzie and Harriet and now, nothing at all.

'Take care,' he says, and he sounds really cheerful about it and there is a part of me that would like to push him down the steps. When I close the door I get back into bed and just stare at the wall.

I didn't know that a whole night with someone might not mean anything at all. I can still smell him on my sheets and his shape is caught in the duvet and pillows. I thought he would want to see me again. Before daylight, with his arms wrapped around me, it felt like a real possibility.

★   ★   ★

40

Buzz Russell's is a small dark bar at the end of Dawson Street. There are orange globe lights on the counter and a round dance floor in the corner. People come here to drink late and stand close to other people and this is where I met Liam last night.

I was near the bar with Judith and she was telling me how she loved Dave, but that he was going back to New York in a week. She said she always knew that he was leaving and so she kept something back and I wondered how to do that.

When Liam stepped past us she looked at me and smiled. He was taller than me with big dark eyes and black hair that looked like he had cut it himself. I like raggy men. I like their loose untidy edges and Liam was all of that. He told me he was twenty-six and I told him I had just turned eighteen.

He said he was a radio producer and I told him I was studying English in my second year at UCD. I wanted to say that I worked in the Pronto as a waitress as well, but I was afraid to say that.

I didn't know then that he was also the lead singer of the Submarines. Until very recently I didn't know who the Submarines were. Now my friends call him 'The Sub'. It's like he's a footnote on a page in my life and that would be about right.

We talked about a lot of things as we stood there at the bar. I told him about growing up beside the sea and he told me he was from Belfast and I could see how he wore the city in his face. He looked like he had lived through a lot of grey rain and wind and noise. I imagined his family sitting in a kitchen under a yellow light and his mother, a tired woman with untidy hair who could not remember their names.

'You're Catholic?' and I was already sure that he had had that faith stitched into him since the day he was born.

'Well, I was born one,' he said, and he was sulky and annoyed because I had pulled him off the stage and back into his First Communion suit.

His friends hung back and then hovered around him. They never seemed to go away and it was as if there was some sort of current running between them. They watched in the background when we talked and they weren't talking when he wasn't there. They just seemed lost without him.

'Will you be here when I come back?' he asked.

'Yes,' I said, and I could feel my feet growing roots into the ground.

'Cute but dangerous,' Judith said.

Then she told me how Dave had tried to

end it with her the week before. That they had shared a Marks and Spencer's ready meal and then he sat on her sofa and drank two glasses of white wine and watched some TV.

'He ate half my dinner — and then he tried to dump me,' she said, and we said nothing then and looked around the club, feeling quiet and slightly depressed by the kind of behaviour men are capable of.

Then the Submarine sailed past me and said a vague sort of 'Hi', like we had never met at all and then he just kept sailing.

'What's the story?' I asked, and he shrugged.

'What's the problem?' he said, and when he spoke he looked genuinely bewildered.

'Nothing, I just thought we were having a good conversation . . . and . . . I dunno — ' and I was drowning in my own embarrassment already and I had no idea why I was doing this.

'The truth is I'm really shy,' he said, and he threw me that old sprat.

'You weren't very shy at the bar.'

'Well, you know, the old story . . . all talk no trousers.'

'Ha.'

'Can I get your number?'

'Not much point if you're that shy.'

'I'm not that shy,' and I watched as he

wrote my number on a till receipt.

When I turned around Leo Adams was standing at the bar. He looked tall and well dressed beside everyone else and he was watching me like he knew I was walking myself into trouble and couldn't stop. He came over then smiling and when he kissed me on both cheeks I remembered those green eyes well. We were in a dark corner and I asked him if he would like to be introduced. He looked at Liam and over the din of the music he laughed and said, 'No thanks.'

I don't know why, but I guess one look told Leo that he wasn't his kind of guy. He told me that he had been at an auction in Dalkey. He was with a girl who was drunker than I was. She wore a glittery belt and when she danced her arms made snake movements in the air. He looked at me and grinned. 'I'll have to send her home,' he said. They didn't look like they were really together and yet he kept one eye on her when we spoke. I have known Leo all my life, but I wanted him to leave me alone now and I guess he knew that because a minute later he stepped back and sat on the arm of a chair.

Judith says she likes that moment before you kiss someone. It's the pause when both of you stop talking and you're admitting there's nothing else to say and really this is where it was all going anyway and you're tired of waiting and greedy and ready to risk it. It's like sliding down a dark glittering shoot with something new at the end. It doesn't matter how often you do it, there's always something new at the end.

We were talking and drinking and getting closer all the time and when he spoke to me I could feel his breath on my cheek. We were just hovering then, hanging on to each other's words and shutting out everything else.

'Where did you get those eyes?' he asked, and I liked how my eyes sounded in his accent.

'My dad, I think.'

'I hope he knows the trouble they're causing,' and we moved closer.

'Hey, what are you thinking about?'

'Kissing you,' he said.

When he leaned in and kissed me I put my arms around his neck and he pulled me closer to him and kissed me again. I could see a tiny triangular well between his shoulder and collarbone and I could have packed up all my stuff and moved right in. Behind us Leo sipped his beer and looked carefully into the distance.

'C'mon,' Liam said then, and we started walking and his friends followed us and people were looking up at him and asking,

'How's Liam?' He was charming and smiling back, but I was right beside him and he was with me now. He led us down the stairs and then through a narrow hall and finally to a door where he hit the latch with one hand and it swung open.

We walked out into a small courtyard garden with a Japanese theme. There were square concrete blocks to sit on and small trees in urns and the walls around us were painted black. The only light came from the upstairs windows and the music was muffled and low.

He took a joint from his breast pocket and they started to pass it around.

'Ladies first,' Liam said then, and he held it towards me.

I sighed as if I was tired and bored with everything and when he raised his eyebrows I barely nodded as if to say, 'Oh, go on then, I suppose we have to.'

The truth is I wasn't entirely sure what I was doing, but if you offered me a lot of money to leave I would have said 'No'. I wanted to be the dumb girl who just wants to be with the guy. Dumb and happy to be in his general area. But I was cool enough. I knew how to inhale and hold it down low to get a hit and then hand it back and look the other way while I was doing that. I had my hands in my pockets and I got up and walked around and I even kicked a stone or two. There were goldfish in the fountain behind us and they were probably about to start laughing.

All around us there was that sound of muffled music and upstairs I could see shadows of people laughing and working really hard to get to where we already were. Liam handed me the joint again and now my eyes were looking right into his and I was trying to tell him that I had known more dangerous men than him.

It started then and there was just no warning at all. I began to talk and it came out of nowhere. I started off with some sort of question and before the sound had even reached their ears I had moved on to the next thing that I suddenly had to say. I wasn't talking in sentences either, it was a series of paragraphs with a few breaths here and there for punctuation, and it just kept going and going, pages of information about things that they all really needed to know. I was doing this because if I packed every word in there would be no space left for him to show me he might not really care.

And then I took a big breath and started off again.

'Oh, Jaysus,' someone said.

I picked little words too, like the really

47

small Lego pieces, so that there wasn't even a chink of light left between us. Here was the part about my life as a student of English and we had Macbeth and Emily Brontë and Jane Austen lining up to join our fun group. I should never smoke dope. The calm of our Japanese paradise had been torn apart. I was taking another deep breath because there was actually more, and then Liam put his hand on my back to keep me in place and kissed me on the mouth. And I just stood there looking back at him and I was going to say something that was important now because it was about him and us and he just leaned in and kissed me again because it was the only way he could say, 'Will you shut the fuck up?' and the second kiss was just, 'Please.'

* * *

My neighbour, Mrs Matthews, was standing in her doorway when we came in. She does that. She just stands in the hallway looking into nowhere with teary eyes. There were two bicycles chained together against the coat stand and she was standing there watching them as if she didn't know what they were. She is old and sometimes she holds a fistful of her own cardigan in one hand. She was fully dressed because she sleeps in her clothes.

'Poor old smarty had a party and nobody came,' she announced, and Liam stopped and put his hands in his coat pockets and looked at me, but I just kept walking. Sometimes you're better not remarking on things like that.

I live in a bed-sit in Ranelagh. It has flowery carpet and pale-green walls and a big old fireplace that I like to use.

It's straight across from the Pronto restaurant and I have all the neighbours from hell under one roof. The couple next door fight every night. I hear them trudging up the stairs after closing time and as soon as they get inside they lay into each other. Their voices are drunk and they shout meaningless slobbery things. Sometimes I hear him rush at her and then there is silence. She is always alive the next day but I stiffen up in bed when that happens. One night I tapped on their door and asked them really politely if they would mind being quiet. She was breathing alcohol fumes at me and one of her front teeth was missing.

'Look,' she said, 'if I fart in here you're going to hear it in there,' and then she slammed the door and went back to whatever it was they were doing for fun that night. There is an old chintz sofa facing the

49

fireplace in my room and the bed fits between two long Georgian windows.

* * *

When Liam leaned over me in bed I could see his dark hair fall down on either side of his face. He began to kiss me again, but I was feeling strung out and tired and a hug would have been nice.

'You don't have to have sex with me,' he said, as he lay back on his back.

'I know I don't.'

We lay quietly side by side and then he asked me if I would stroke his back and his voice came right out of the blue and it sounded broken down and sad.

'I know . . . I'm such a baby,' he said then, and for the first time that night I knew he wasn't pretending. I also knew that in the morning we would forget about this and he would be cool like before. We would pretend we had made love when all we had done was lie in the dark trying to breathe quietly together.

* * *

There are two messages on my answering machine. The first is from Beth and the

50

second from Judith asking if I got home OK.

I ring Jude first to talk it all through and she listens carefully to everything I say.

'Would you think of maybe calling him?' she asks then. 'At least you would know where you stand.'

'I think I already know that,' and she has no answer for this.

'It's not really me, is it?'

'I dunno,' she says, but she says it slowly as if she's giving it some serious thought.

'I mean, I can't see myself hanging out in the Strand Hotel in Salthill, waiting for his gig, can you?'

'Or Tubbercurry,' she adds helpfully, and in the silence we are both thinking of how pubs feel and smell during winter daylight hours and how hopeless my new life might be.

Then she tells me we should go to his next gig.

'We're not going to any gig.'

'We could wear wigs.'

I had forgotten how crazy she is.

'Look in *Hotpress*,' she says, 'and tell me when the next gig is.'

'I don't buy *Hotpress*.'

'Look,' she says, 'we both know you'll be buying it now and, when you do, check out where the next gig is.'

On Tuesday there is a message from

Antonio at the Pronto asking if I can work a double shift on Saturday and I call him back and tell him I can do as many hours as he needs.

And suddenly anyone I ask has heard about Liam — and when I look at *Hotpress* there are pictures of him performing in Glasgow and Wolverhampton and Bray.

There is one photo where he is finishing his solo under a red light and his face looks angry and dark and full of that song he is singing, and he has one hand pointed upwards like a gun into the sky. There are more taken in the studio where he looks mellow and preoccupied and as if he really didn't know the camera was there. He's wearing a pair of awful striped trousers in one, like pyjamas.

★　★　★

Professor Bob is waiting for me at the entrance to the library. He is a tall elegant man with dark wavy hair, flecked with grey. He wears half-moon glasses and when he sees me he looks over them and smiles.

'What age would you say he is?' I whisper to Judith.

'At least fifty.'

'And he's single?'

'Famous for it,' she replies.

By the time we get to the doorway Judith is already bright red.

'Hello, Professor,' she says, and she sounds a little breathless.

'Judith,' he replies, and he gives a little bow. He is wearing a fresh white shirt with a grey cashmere pullover. He is tanned from sailing and he has a handsome well-proportioned face.

'Aristocratic bones' Judith calls them. The truth is most of us go to his lectures just to look at him — and to hear his voice. It is deep and masculine and almost musical when he recites a poem. He asks questions that really make me think and when I'm answering there is always a little smile floating around his face.

We sit in a quiet part of the library near a window that looks out over the lake. He goes through my essay and then he writes out a list of extra books I need to read.

'OK,' he says then, 'let's see what you make of The Windhover.'

He goes through every line carefully and when he looks up I am staring out the window instead.

'I think the concentration is a little off today,' he says, but his voice is kind. He is wearing silver stud cufflinks and his after-shave reminds me of cinnamon sticks and

53

home. He stretches for a moment and looks out the window with me.

'Anything up?' he asks, and as we watch the sunset together I end up telling him everything about Liam. He listens as if it all really matters and he even gives a little chuckle here and there.

'So you met when?' he asks then.

'Nearly two weeks ago.'

'Ah.' He uncrosses his long legs and taps one foot on the ground.

'What do you think?'

'Well,' he says quietly, 'he's like a chipped plate now, isn't he?'

'Sorry?'

'Probably best to throw it out.'

⋆   ⋆   ⋆

The graffiti on the cubicle door says, 'Beware the limbo dancers.' The lesbian girls write stuff about sex and getting wet under the sheets. You get a free glass of wine when you join the gay society and we have considered this, except we're afraid of meeting one of our friends. I think when women say they will call they generally do, and, if they don't, they think about it a lot and they feel quite bad.

I don't think of Liam during my lectures or waiting on table in the Pronto. He's not

54

there, not now. After two weeks it's like the big cloud we made has started to drop down lower, lower, until the sky is on the ground and I'm just remembering to look left and right when I cross the street. I can't smell him on my sheets and now I know he's not going to call — not ever actually — and I'm beginning to feel the gentle pain of being a fool again.

★ ★ ★

Bob tries to explain the love sonnets to me. I tell him that I don't understand them and that there are too many of them anyway.

'Well, I'm sure Mr Shakespeare would be very concerned to hear that,' he says.

Then he begins to explain a particular line and I'm thinking about something else.

Yesterday Kate Holland, who is Bob's secretary, sent me a note. She told me that Bob would be taking a few weeks off because he's not well and I'm worried about this.

'Have you ever seen that French film?' he asks. 'The one where the guy says he wants to find a girl who makes him 'thump'. What was it called?' and Bob puts one hand on his heart and looks out the window behind me and it makes me smile because I can understand that.

'Well,' he says then, 'Shakespeare found a

girl that made him thump — that's all that's going on here.'

★ ★ ★

It is after midnight when he knocks on my door. I find him standing there in the pouring rain and he is carrying a wet brown parcel in one hand.

' . . . Liam?'

'Hello,' he says quietly, and he looks down at the ground and then at me again. There are little drops running off his cheeks and on to his lips.

'I guess you better come inside.'

When he comes in he drips on my floor and he just stands there for a second looking at me and not saying anything. Then he says, 'This is for you,' and he hands me the wet parcel.

'Sorry if I woke you.'

My fire is still bright and I've been studying on the couch.

He watches me and I just look back.

'You could have just called.'

His hair is dripping rain on to his shoulders and down on to the rug.

'I wanted to see you,' he says, and his voice is low and then he tries to put his hands into his wet pockets. He is searching for a

56

cigarette and his hand shakes a little when he takes one out of the wet Marlboro pack.

'Why?'

And here there is another pause.

'I can't stop thinking about you,' he says, and he seems surprised, annoyed, as if this is my fault. He exhales and glances at my bed. I sit on the couch with the parcel on my lap and look up at him. His hair curls a little when it's wet.

'Why didn't you call me?'

'Helen . . . listen . . . I'm just not great at the relationship thing. I don't have . . . you know . . . real girlfriends . . . and I didn't want to hurt you.'

'I feel like you already have.'

'I know. I'm sorry,' and he sounds upset now.

'I'm just not great at expressing myself,' he says then, and he drags from his cigarette and I tell him to stand near the fire. When he shakes his head his hair makes the fire spit with rain.

Our bed is behind him now. Sitting there. Tidy and well made and without our bodies to mess it up. I would love to touch his wet face, but I can't.

The paper falls away easily. It is a book of poetry and he has turned back the corner of one page.

'I'm not great at this kind of thing,' he says,

and he waves his cigarette gently towards me, all awkward and Northern again. And he stops moving around and watches me as I open the book and I see that the poem he has chosen is called 'Love at First Sight'.

When I look up he gives a big shrug, and then we're both beginning to smile.

With all his awkwardness, he is still something I want to be around. Just because I think life with him will be different. Because I could be different with someone like that.

When I put my arms around him he hugs me so tightly and for so long that he makes my T-shirt wet. We turn the lights off and just stand there in the amber street-lamp glow and look at each other. When it starts to rain again the drops make speckled shadows on my bed and there are dark river shadows all along the floor. His skin is so smooth and white it shines, and there is a part of him, the round caps of his shoulders, that I need to hold on to. Somewhere in my mind is the idea that really there is only me and Liam in this amber world and when we take these T-shirts off it's just skin getting to know new skin. How could we not be together? There is no traffic outside now and my neighbours are all asleep, and really it's just us and here is our first real together word — 'us'.

We get undressed and go to bed because it

just seems like the best place for us to go. He knows I haven't done this before and he doesn't ask me anything about it. He makes love to me and there are no signposts or flags in the air. He just stays quiet and takes care of it all and afterwards he holds me again.

'So,' he says and he is sitting up on one elbow with his hair still wet, 'this boyfriend/girlfriend thing.'

'Yeah?'

'Maybe we should give it a try.'

Afterwards a single drop of blood lands on the bathroom floor and when I see my reflection in the mirror I look at it for a moment and say 'Goodbye'.

★　★　★

In the morning he makes coffee and gives me a cigarette instead of toast. He kisses me high up on my cheekbone and then comes back and kisses me on the lips. He opens the door very quietly and this time I am nearly sure I will see him again. I can hear Mrs Matthews in the hall and she's really close too like she is standing right outside my door.

'Who are you?' she asks him, and the door closes again before I can find out.

★　★　★

59

Paper 1
Poetry
Q1. 'Romanticism is the revolt of passion against the intellect.' Discuss using Blake's 'Songs of Innocence' and Wordsworth's 'Stray Pleasures'.

★ ★ ★

Birdie called me the day she lost her virginity. She told me that they slept together on the floor of his flat and then he cooked pasta and showed her how to flick it on to the wall to see if it was cooked. After that they seemed to cook a lot together and when he went back to Turkey he left her his duvet and a radio cassette player with some tapes.

'Duck down,' she said, and she was sitting there on her bed with it folded on her lap and I couldn't understand why she was so sad. At that stage I really didn't get it. To me he was just some guy who went off and left a duvet behind.

★ ★ ★

Liam is waiting for me outside Theatre L. He stands with his hands deep in his pockets and gives me a grin.

'Hello, you,' he says, and the other students

are watching this and he likes to perform. He lifts his scarf off and drops it around my neck and pulls me gently towards him.

'Let's bunk off,' he says, and we are already walking together into the wet afternoon.

He takes me to see *It's a Wonderful Life* at the Savoy and then we stretch out in front of the fire in my flat. We spend hours like that just smoking and talking about Belfast and about college and home. As it gets dark outside I realize this is the longest he has ever stayed in one place with me and I tell him this.

He sits up and puts his arm around me. 'I feel good when I'm with you,' he says. 'I mean, look at this,' and he circles the room with his open hand. The fire makes soft orange images on the walls and the cars are splashing through puddles outside. There is a real Christmas tree in the corner and milk in the fridge and empty plates around us on the floor.

'I never had any of this,' he says quietly. 'You make me feel safe.'

Later he sits in the middle of the kitchen and asks me to cut his hair.

'You're doing great,' he says, and really in the middle of this I just want to drop the scissors and kiss the top of his head.

'I think I might love you or something,' he

says then, and I am about to say that I love him as well when he tells me he's doing a gig in Derry at the weekend, and just like that I've lost him all over again.

* * *

Judith sits in the waiting room with her arms folded and she looks really tense. I am not at all worried when I take the test.

'Negatory,' the doctor says, and he picks up his pen and begins to write a prescription which I haven't asked for.

'For my next trick,' he says, as he picks up a new white envelope.

Sometimes I try to imagine what sort of baby Liam would give me and in my mind it is a pink dragon that puffs out little fireballs and has wings and a tail.

* * *

When he comes into the Pronto I make him a mug of cappuccino. I walk in behind the counter and make it for him myself. He smiles and tells me my apron is sexy and we're really in our own world now.

'I'm in a Liam-induced coma,' Birdie says.

'He's not good for you,' Judith says.

'He's kind of artistic,' I say, and even now

62

my words sound like an excuse.

'When are you coming home?' Beth asks, and when I mention meeting my mother Liam disappears for a week.

'Are you in love?' Birdie asks.

'I'm in something,' I say.

★ ★ ★

He wears his denim jacket and sings, 'What's the trouble baby?' His voice comes out through a haze of cigarette smoke and guitar riffs and the young guys in black T-shirts stand still under his spell. He says he would like to sing this for 'Helen' and Judith looks at me and smiles.

'Let's get up front,' Birdie says, and I shake my head.

The crowd roared when they came on stage and he just grinned and ran one hand back through his hair.

'Hello, Galway,' he said.

'Hello, Liam,' Judith said, and then she lit a cigarette lighter and waved it slowly over and back. When they thought I wasn't looking they were both cracking up. He tells the crowd that the band is going on tour and that their first stop is Prague and then Amsterdam and Berlin and everyone, except me, cheers and claps when he speaks.

When he finishes his set he runs off stage and holds me for a long time. He is hot from the gig and the sweat on his upper lip is just starting to turn cold. He holds me like he'll never let me go — and I don't know if this is because he loves me now or because he's still high.

*   *   *

Paper 2
Fiction
Q1. The actions of certain characters in the works of Jane Austen are not only self-destructive, but cause the destruction of others. Prove this statement using two of the following works (a) Pride and Prejudice (b) Emma (c) Persuasion.

*   *   *

'So, hey, do you want to go to Prague?'

He asks me this when he is sitting on the arm of my chair. He came over and sat down and just said it right out, and now he is looking around the room like he is tired and fed up with everything. We are in a new place called the Kahuba Bar off Kildare Street and it is late and dark and the furniture is soft and near the floor. He has been kind of ignoring me all night long and I wonder why things like this happen. I saw how he looked at Erica with her cheekbones and her high black ponytail. When you see a guy you like looking at another girl in that way — and she doesn't even realize it — it can make you feel really sad. Even in my head I could only manage one or two words, something like 'Oh' and 'well'. I drank some more and tried to forget about it and later in the dark of the club I told his friend, Kevin, and then I said, 'She's beautiful, you know.'

'Yes,' he said, 'she's a very pretty girl, but, really' — and he pushed his glasses up on his nose — 'what guys want at the end of the day, is a good conversation.'

'That's good to hear.'

'No,' he said, and he seemed more serious now, 'and I don't want to be crude but girls like that — you bag them and run.'

I didn't say anything then so he said it again, 'Bag them and run', and he turned the corners of his mouth down when he spoke.

When Judith asks me if I am in love with Liam I tell her that I'm caught. When we're together — I mean just me and him — it's as if nothing or no one else exists. I keep thinking about the boy who sat at my fire and told me he felt safe. But then he seems to slip away from me and maybe he always will.

'When we're together it feels real,' I tell her.

'After that what happens?' Judith asks.

'After that he leaves . . . for his place . . . for Belfast . . . for Derry . . . for Prague . . . he's always going to leave for somewhere else.'

'Then you should get out of it,' she says.

'I know I should,' I tell her, but my legs stop working when he's around.

'So will you?' he asks again, and his eyes can only settle on me for a second before they look around the room again. It's like he is sitting on a wall looking at some sheep.

'Prague . . . ?' and I heard him really clearly the first time and then, 'Why?'

'I think you'd like it.'

'Look,' I say then, and my voice sounds strained when I speak.

'Is there something here? . . . is there? . . . I mean . . . what is this? . . . this thing? . . . is there something?' and all the time I'm moving my hand over and back in the space between us. I think I am trying to describe the kind of air that lies there and it feels heavy and dark, like an extra person standing in the way, and every time I try to look at him it turns its round shoulders and blocks my view. I think I might be going crazy and maybe imagining this. But we're making it and it doesn't happen with anyone else.

'Is there something?' I ask him again, and really what I'm saying is, 'Please.'

'I think so,' he says, and then he goes, 'Look, Helen, I don't know what it is, but we might find out in Prague. Look, we might go to Prague and get married and we might come back and hate each other.'

'Do you think about me when we're not together?' and this is a good question to ask, especially when he answers, 'All the time.'

And now anything is possible, because I already love this guy and it's only now that I can see it and I'm dead calm, eerie calm. I could scare myself with this kind of calm. I have something now — or at least I know I didn't dream it all up by myself.

There is a group of guys sitting behind him. They are all around forty and wearing black jackets and black shirts and in between everything he says one of them keeps trying to interrupt us.

'Excuse me, excuse me,' and I know they were trying to get me to come over and talk to some guy called Rob.

'Hey, excuse me,' and when I look up one of them starts calling me over with his hand, in the way you would call a cat. They want me to talk to Rob and I don't want to. His breath smells of burnt toast and he looks like he should have been a priest or something and, really, I wish they'd just get lost. I mean, every word I'm hearing from Liam at this point is completely precious, you know.

When we get around a corner he pulls me towards him and kisses me and I feel that I am pulled inside him, in through his clothes, through his cool skin and into him. Then we just walk on like nothing happened except that he holds my hand until we reach his door.

There is a brown metal grid over the glass front door and he has left an orange light on behind it. He lives in a garden flat in a nice old house that has sash windows. Inside the heat is on and he goes straight to a little cupboard and turns a switch.

'Shit,' he says, like he is talking to himself, 'it's hot in here.' There is a tall Egyptian urn standing inside the door and the orange light is coming from a standard lamp in the hall.

Then I'm standing in his kitchen in my socks with my hands on my hips and asking my little question.

'What happens when you bring people back here?'

'I don't bring people back here,' he says.

There is a row of black socks hanging on his chair and ties on the inside of the wardrobe door — and it's funny because I've never seen him wear one. There are three unplayed messages on his machine and there is fresh milk in the fridge.

'My dad's been in,' he says. Then out of the blue, 'Sometimes he calls in and buys milk and shit.' And you think you know someone.

We lie on his bed and I tell him that I like his place and the kind of light that comes through the wooden shutters. They are only half closed and I am only half aware of the furniture around us. The wide marble fireplace and the *Prague Post* on the bedside table. He lies out on the bed. Long and lean. I put my fingers on the tattoo like barbed wire around his upper arm.

'Did it hurt?'

'No, only a little when it started to go inside my arm.'

'Where did you get it done?' and in my head I'm expecting to hear 'Hong Kong' or 'New York' or 'Paris'.

'Just off O'Connell Street,' he says, and I nod my head and look down because I really want to laugh.

Tonight when we lie down to sleep we are side by side and we don't even touch. When I wake up he is still sleeping, but curled in towards me and holding my hand.

When he wakes he asks the same question.

'So are you going to come to Prague?' and he puts his hands behind his head and stretches out on the bed. He is wearing navy-blue shorts and his body looks good. He is also dark and quiet now. Miles away really and trying to figure out what we might be like together in Prague. I sit there cross-legged in his T-shirt and examine my little toe.

'I don't think it's a great idea,' I say, and the truth is I know this is the only answer he wants to hear. I can see us talking and smoking in these little coffee shops in Prague and then dodging rain and laughing and for some reason I'm wearing a red bobble hat and his is navy-blue.

'I have my exams,' I tell him, and I'm looking down because I am too unhappy to meet his eyes.

'That's crap,' he says, but he doesn't sound even slightly mad.

'I need to go — I have to study.'

'Oh, come on, stay, hang out for a while.'

'I can't.'

★   ★   ★

Paper 3
World War Literature
Q1. Compare ways in which writers present the experience of war using

70

Wilfred Owen's 'Arms and the boy' and Robert Graves' 'Goodbye to all that'.

★　★　★

Liam has stopped asking me if I will go to Prague now, and the truth is, if he'd asked me one more time I would have said 'Yes'. Instead I am sitting in the library with a book open in front of me and I might as well be away with him because I can't concentrate now anyway. Instead I am left wandering around his place in my head and seeing the little glass cups sitting over the kitchen sink and the yellow mug that says, 'Fuck work. Fuck bills. Fuck fuck.'

★　★　★

I take a cab home with him from Buzz Russell's and he's quiet. I am thinking about everything that has happened between us and especially the night he came around drenched by the rain. I can't go with him and he won't stay here and I know that the taxi is going to stop any minute now and things will never be the same.
　'Liam?'
　'What?'
　'Do you have to go?' and my voice is

low-down and scared.

And I know his silence can only mean, 'Yes.'

I'm wondering if he has just forgotten everything that happened between us. Like the time he came into my lecture and sat beside me pretending to take notes and the time he held my hand under the table because he didn't want his mates to see.

'I'm just not great at the settling down thing,' he says then.

And here he leans in and kisses my forehead.

He holds me close to him and he says, 'Shhh,' down through my hair.

'If I was that kind of guy, Helen,' he whispers, 'I would want to belong to you.'

'Maybe we should stay in touch then,' I tell him, 'and there are weekends and in a few weeks I'll be finished my exams and then it's summer . . . '

'I think we should be friends,' he says, and when I look up he is looking away.

When the cab stops at his place he tries to give me money, but I won't take it. When we drive around the corner I ask the driver to stop and I get out and lean against the railings and my hands are shaking with cold. Then I get another cab and just go home and at least it's a new cab driver and he doesn't know my new fresh shame of being so suddenly alone. I try to call him, but he doesn't answer the phone.

★ ★ ★

Judith tries to get me to laugh about it and I tell her that I'm fine. She says I should see other guys and forget about him and move on — and I'm agreeing to everything — except the forgetting part.

Nobody else knows the things we sent flying towards each other. The kind of chemicals that flashed in the air. Sometimes I think I can smell his scent on my pillows and sometimes in the dark I pretend he's still here.

★ ★ ★

Professor Bob is standing on his balcony. He is wearing a pink shirt and he directs me into a parking space as if he is writing my name in the sky. I meet him on Monday evenings now for my one on one. Sometimes I bring him brown bread and free-range eggs from home.

'The bread had to be frozen, can I just say that?' I tell him, and I put my hand on his arm when I speak. 'It's just a while since I've been home.'

I feel good then, and I'm glad that I'm doing this. It makes me feel like a better kind of person and when I come here it's as if I'm wearing a gingham dress and carrying a little basket and handing around food to starving people. It's nice to be friends with older people too because they have more experience and they can give me advice about things.

His penthouse is smart, New York-style, and there are proper hallways and alcoves and beautiful windows everywhere and on top of that skylights as if there could never be enough light.

Bob is wearing smart leather shoes and nice aftershave. He looks good and I guess he must be better now. I have never seen him so pleased and I pick up his mood and smile at him and look around his place.

'I'm just going to pretend I live here for the next little while,' I say, and he says, 'You do that,' and he directs me into his sitting room where there are leather couches and books everywhere. I admire everything as I always do.

There is a new abstract painting of a horse and even when I put my head sideways I have a feeling he has hung it the wrong way up.

'I didn't know you had fish,' I say then, and my voice is a little over-excited when I speak and he walks over and puts on a light behind their bowl.

'Maud and Laurence,' he says. 'Now you stay here.'

The TV is huge and there is a rugby match on. He doesn't turn it off for me and when we speak the commentator butts in a little.

'Tell me if there's a score,' and he walks into the kitchen. I sit on the leather couch looking around and my hands are joined between my knees. He comes back almost straight away.

'Wait a second,' and it sounds like he has an idea.

'Here,' he says then and he turns down the volume on the TV and at the same time he turns up James Taylor live.

'Baby James,' he says, and he walks into the kitchen again.

He seems to be gone for a long time and I go through my lecture notes so that they're ready for him and then he appears again and he is carrying coffee mugs on a tray. He moves gracefully for a tall man and he is formal like a butler now.

I clear some books away and he fusses and tells me not to do anything at all, just to sit there and relax.

'Do you know what I forgot?' And he is standing over me taking a pinch of air with one hand.

'Cream,' he says.

'Oh, I don't take it, in fact I don't like it.'

And this is a slight lie.

There is something about Professor Bob that makes me feel good. We meet for two hours every week and it is just our time. It could have been a little weird because he is my professor, but I like being here with him in his home.

We cover off the exam papers quickly like a checklist and then we chat like truant students and drink our coffee without any cream.

When he looks out the window behind me he seems sad.

'The turn of the leaf,' he says. 'I prefer the summer, especially when the mayfly is up.'

Then he goes on and describes fishing on Lough Neagh and the things men talk about when they are out in a boat all day. I turn to face him and I've crossed my legs so I'm Indian style and I'm holding on to my socks when we talk.

'That's an interesting top you have on.'

'Thanks,' and I laugh again.

'What's on the back of it?' And there is a Levi's horse and cowboy in red across my shoulders.

'Ah,' he says, 'a horse and cart affair.'

When Bob talks about Lough Neagh I'm right there with him. They make bacon sandwiches and leave Dublin so early they are dodging the clubbers on Leeson Street. I can hear the water lap against the boat and even feel the gentle rock as if we are sitting inside. All around us the sky is filled with ugly clouds, but it isn't going to rain. Not today.

'I don't fish there any more,' he says, but he doesn't sound sad about it. He tells me he had fished there all his life and he had never given anything back.

'I've taken enough,' and it doesn't even sound like he misses it. The last time he fished he argued with a friend. He caught a pregnant trout and when Bob asked him to put it back he just looked at him and then knocked it on the head with the oarlock.

'Anyway,' he says then, 'what's happening with you and this young man?' And he is talking about the Submarine.

'Oh, nothing.'

'Hmm.'

'He didn't want to be tied down. It doesn't matter.'

He gets up and walks to a cabinet at the other side of the room. When he comes back he drops a napkin on my lap.

'Forgot to give you that,' he says. It has green and blue stripes like a man's handkerchief. I don't want to use it because I can imagine the kind of stain my lipstick will make.

'I'm not sure I believe in the soulmate thing any more,' I tell him.

'You're scaring the fish,' he says.

'What I wanted . . . ' he says, and all the time he is looking right into the painting of the upside-down horse as if it is some kind of 'talking stick' for him.

'You know when people leave a dinner party, I mean when they go home eventually. I wanted to turn around to someone else and go, 'Christ, look how much wine they drank!' — and that person would be staying over, you know, the first real official stayover. When they know they're staying and you know — it's all sorted. And the next morning, you negotiate, one of you has to get the papers and the other one has to get the breakfast going . . . and she's going . . . 'How do you work this stupid grill of yours? With these silly little knobs.' ' And he is twisting and turning imaginary buttons in the air when he talks.

'Anyway,' he says then, and he really just adds this to his last sentence. He just runs right into it like he is heading for a little fence he wants to hop over. 'There's something I want to ask you . . . been meaning to for quite some time,' and he's right up near the wood now, with his hooves just going over and I've leaned forward over my crossed legs so I can hear him really well.

'Can I kiss you?'

There is a place beyond silence and it is a pale cold shade of blue. It goes beyond sound and right past silence to a wide-open space. As soon as he says this I am in freefall, going down the lift shaft, down the rabbit hole, and his words have come out really slowly like toothpaste. When the engines fail something else takes over and it's just a few really short words: 'No,' and then 'Bob,' and it is in a Queen Victoria voice.

'OK, then,' he says, and it is as if the electricity is back on again and the lights give a flash and the TV goes on and the fridge starts to hum in the corner. I'm back and talking to him in one big long never-ending sentence. It takes at least a half an hour for me to finish this sentence and in it I cover all the things we are studying at college and how the weather is better now — and how do people meet at all, it must be fate and isn't friendship really great anyway? This is because I do not want to run out like a child, even though I suddenly feel like one.

I look at my watch and tell him I better go.

'New watch,' he says.

'Yes.'

'Looks like it came in a lucky bag.'

He still talks to me and he even goes into a story about buying new leather watchstraps, but he is different like me, using the voice you use when the power goes out.

When I kiss him on the cheek it feels warm and smooth. He stands still and lets me do it and he doesn't want this at all.

'Well,' he says, 'we sorted that out then.'

'Yes, all sorted.'

'Hey,' he calls after me, 'take the lift.'

But I am already running down the stairs. 'I'm OK,' I call back to him, and my feet are quiet on the new soft carpet.

'You young people,' he says, and he closes his door.

3

The things we did last summer

Chicago

August 1991

Walter is standing on the steps waiting for us and she laughs when she sees him, that's how she greets her husband. They live in a tall white wooden house on a leafy stretch in North Chicago called West Gregory Street. He is a short stocky man and he stands on the steps with his check shirt hanging out over his shorts, watching us park. He walks over and takes my bags and kisses me on both cheeks. I can feel that his hair is still wet from the shower and he smells of verbena. The street is quiet and all around us there is the sound of people, families, sitting down indoors to eat. There is a tricycle turned over on its side in the garden next to theirs.

He kisses Birdie on one cheek and says 'Baby Bird' into her hair.

'Well, look at you, ladies,' he says then in a singsong voice, and he gives a little whistle that makes us laugh, and he doesn't mention our time in New York. When Walter speaks there is an echo in his voice, a light musical warble, it bubbles and curves at the end of sentences and covers up something else. We have just got off the plane and driven through rush hour traffic and that is all he needs to know.

We're coming through the front door when he starts telling her what had been happening during the week she was away. The week we spent in New York together, mostly talking about him — except for the two-hour Broadway show when we sat quietly in the dark.

We walk up a narrow flight of shiny wooden stairs and into their apartment on the top floor. It is bright with white-washed walls and it has the airy feel of a summer-house more than a home. I can see Birdie everywhere now — in the pale-green art deco couch and the prints on the walls and the tiny room with a desk where she writes. There is an old photograph of us on the bookcase. It was taken outside Adams' Antiques when we were very young and wearing the same coloured hairbands and shorts.

She bought the pale-green couch with Walter and she said that it helped their relationship. Later she would discover a 50-inch TV with woofer speakers under a rug in the basement that he had also bought and forgot to tell her.

'Tony Peraza was here, honey,' he says.

'Oh, honey, really? I like Tony, he's a good guy.'

'He brought you the macadamias you like.'

And she picks them up and seems to weigh them in her hand and then puts them back on their fridge again. I can see she is looking around all the time to see if anything has changed while she was away. She can do this very quietly and when she looks around only her eyes move.

I like where they live. It is a long apartment with a small solid porch on the front over their main door and a bigger wooden deck painted green at the back. I like that they can decide where to sit. The front porch is for late on a Sunday evening and the green deck with its chipped paint and pink geraniums and coloured Chinese lanterns is for everyday, for fun. The floors creak when I walk and there are spots of sunlight coming in from different windows. There is a red cat stretched across the back of the couch and piles of fresh laundry on the dining-room chairs. I can hear the neighbour's radio playing, and a long flow of Spanish, a woman's voice rippling up and down, the sound travelling out through their open window and into ours.

Walter has baked all day for us. There are oatmeal cookies and banana bread and he's pouring big mugs of tea and feeding Birdie little pieces of news. I am feeling different and new today. It is as if New York has ironed me out and I feel loose and like letting it all flow.

'Honey, we're meeting Johnny at six,' he says.

'Oh, honey, that's thirty minutes from now,' and her voice is loud and I can see that she's an American now.

There is something about standing there under their voices as they give it over and back to each other that makes me feel like a kid. I am eating banana bread and standing looking out their kitchen window and my head is tilted to one side to avoid the hanging plants overhead.

'Everything is just a little off in this apartment,' she says, and she is saying each word out carefully. I like it when she gets serious about trivial things. I like how she describes them to me.

'The stove is tilted,' she says, and she walks over to it. 'You can only see it when you put some eggs in a pan.'

There is a loud bang then, as the screen door to the apartment downstairs slams shut.

'Those girls . . . ' she says, and she pulls a face at Walter.

'They're still doing it, honey,' he says, smiling and shaking his head. 'They just love to slam that door.'

The guestroom is painted a pretty blue with a pale-blue floral duvet cover and there is an American flag on the wall.

'I can be ready for six thirty,' I tell her.

'Can you? It's Walter, he hates to eat late,' and she hands me a blue glass bowl to put my make-up and jewellery into. When I'm in the shower she passes another mug of tea through the door.

'Mamzelle Fournier,' she says.

'Thanks, Baby Bird.'

★   ★   ★

Walter turns the jeep around and we head down North Broadway. We seem to know each other so well now there's no need to talk. There are red pick-up trucks and billboards with ads for fast-food chains. There are men in baseball caps and girls jogging through the park. Everything seems to have some kind of wholesome star-spangled stripe to it. It's the tip of North Chicago and the thought that wanders around my head is simple and up there with log cabins and patchwork quilts.

'We're in America now.'

When Walter turns the music up I can hear Nancy Wilson singing about what she did last summer and he's tapping out the beat on the steering wheel and Birdie is singing along here and there. Ask me if I was ever happy and I'll think of this song and the soft warm wind coming in over the lake and the promise of two men and two women sitting down together over cocktails and sushi — ask if I was ever happy and I'll tell you — I'm happy now.

When we get to the restaurant Johnny is already there. He is wearing a pale-green khaki T-shirt and there is a small black rucksack on the floor beside him. He is tall and athletic with blond hair that flicks back over his ears.

'What will you have to drink?' he asks, and he turns his head a little awkwardly like a child before he goes to the bar.

'He's nervous,' Birdie says, and her eyebrows are up really high and she is ready to laugh out loud at him. She couldn't care less about most things.

We take a sip from our gin and tonics and then carry them to our table in the corner of the restaurant. Everything is white here except for the small red lamps on the tables and at the bar and they give the room a pale pink glow. We are all looking at the menus and Birdie is smiling at me over hers and then looking down again and I can hear Walter and Johnny ordering all sorts of food and a round of Cosmopolitans. I'm beginning to feel us slide, all four of us together now, and it feels as if Birdie and I are being kidnapped and taken away.

Later in the bathroom she tells me that she hated that Walter and Johnny ordered our food for us.

'Me too,' I reply, and I lean against the washbasin and watch her dry her hands. 'But I liked what they got,' and I add this to keep the record straight.

The truth is I have never had a guy who ordered food for me and it felt nice. It was a little old-fashioned, but that's OK too, I think, and none of us seemed to eat very much anyway.

In the bathroom Birdie is back with me again. She is looking at my reflection in the mirror and waiting for me to speak and there is a low current of laughter coming from somewhere.

'I see it, by the way,' she says then, and she is speaking really quietly and then she's laughing out loud.

'What?' And I stroke my eyebrow once and lean into the mirror.

'You two,' she says, 'sparking at each other,' and then she pulls the door open and walks out into the restaurant again.

It had happened somewhere between our fourth Cosmopolitan and the dessert order. Johnny just looked right at me and I looked right back and I might have known Birdie would spot that.

We get into the Green Mill because Walter knows the guy at the door and when I get back from the bar we stand in a circle looking at each other. When Walter moves, Johnny trips over something because he is in a hurry to stand next to me. When I look over Birdie is laughing like it's the funniest thing ever.

'I can't drink any more,' she says then, and she moves up close to the stage and sits on her own at a table listening to the music. Walter is squeezed into a booth talking to some guy and Johnny stands very close to me and stares straight at the stage.

When we get home we make more gin and tonics and we're making a lot of noise with the bottles and glasses and all those ice cubes.

'I can't drink any more,' Birdie says. 'How can you drink any more?' And she takes out an old battered teapot and points the spout at me like another finger.

'No, thanks,' I tell her. I'm having fun standing at the kitchen counter between Walter and Johnny. I like the idea of being with two men who have grown up in the sun and have always known good jazz and blues. Walter lifts his foot and kicks me gently on the behind. Then he starts doing scat and I have to tell you he is pretty good, but then

Johnny goes, 'Yeah, man . . . dah dah, do do, goo goo goo,' and he's saying every word really slowly to mock him. Birdie puts the Chinese lanterns on and we sit on the back porch. The air is warm and there are crickets chirping and more than anything there is this great buzz and energy moving between us.

Birdie sits on Walter's knee and then he puts his arms around her waist and leans out to talk to Johnny. Later he asks her to move because her ass is too bony.

'So you're, like, at college?' Johnny asks.

'She's doing her Ph.D,' Birdie says proudly.

'What's your thesis about?' Walter asks.

'Contemporary poetry, rhythm, stuff like that.'

'Wow,' Johnny says, and he looks up at the sky.

I lean back and lift my feet up so they're resting on the edge of his chair and then there is a clip-clop sound as my wooden mules fall to the floor. He takes this like he has known me for ever and he keeps talking to Walter over and back and shaking his head and laughing except that he's got one hand on my foot and he's rubbing deep into my instep with his thumb. I lie back and chat to Birdie and in that way we are floating around, feeling light, weightless, like fireflies in the air.

Then the red cat stands inside the screen door and he starts this never-ending meow to be let out.

Then Walter says, 'Stop making that noise, please,' and the red cat stops. By now Johnny has both of my feet resting on his knees and he is working them over, with great care, and we never lose our flow of conversation. It's relaxed and easy, the way people who are easy are. I'm not sure how much I like him yet, but I would like to kiss him and we are both free so there is some kind of possibility. Like everything tonight, it doesn't really matter either way.

When Walter and Birdie go to bed he watches for a second, and then I hear their bedroom door close and without even taking a breath he drops one hand and pulls my chair right up to his. My legs get wrapped around his waist and we kiss and it's a good kiss. He kisses like someone who learned how a long time ago and he's relaxed and easy about it, a real old hand now.

We step into the kitchen and he uses their bathroom and then stands watching me with his hand in his pocket. I'm tired now and I'm starting to feel thirsty and hungover.

'I guess I should go . . . ?' and he looks at me expectantly.

'I guess so.'

'Would you like me to show you around tomorrow, we could go to the Institute?'

'That would be great.'

'See you tomorrow then?'

'See you tomorrow.'

The crickets are still chirping when he cycles away and we are two American high-school sweethearts now.

*   *   *

Walter likes to get up early in the morning. He bakes brioche and buttermilk scones and gingerbread. He leaves three kinds of vitamins on a plate for Birdie.

'Poor little Cat,' he says, and he hands me a glass of water into my room. I am sitting on the edge of the bed with my door opening out into the kitchen. When I woke I could find no air at all. The window is wide open too and the sun makes little speckles on the floor through the screen. It is a good day for the beach and all I can think of is how I might find some air. I slept with the door closed because I was frightened of waking up with the red cat on my bed.

Now I am sitting with the door opening into the kitchen and the window open behind me and still there is no air. Walter moves around the kitchen and cracks eggs into a yellow bowl. His hands are brisk and when he adds some milk he whistles some little tune to himself. He turns his baking out on to a wire tray. He feeds the cats. He gathers laundry from different parts of their home and takes it to the basement and the screen door swings shut behind him. While Birdie sleeps this is his day. He works and creates order and she stretches out across the bed and likes the extra space.

He takes his bike from the basement then and rides to the lake to swim. I am having too much trouble sleeping and my dreams are mixed up and dry. I tiptoe into their room and get under the covers with Birdie. We have a mumbling conversation for a few minutes and then we fall together into a deeper sweeter sleep.

★ ★ ★

There is one message on their answering machine and Birdie and I play it again as we sit in our pyjamas drinking tea. 'Hey, Bird,' and it's a woman's voice, 'I just wanted to say hi. It's so long since I've seen you . . . I miss you guys . . . and, well, you know how it is when you break up with someone . . . Johnny got you guys . . . and I got the cats. Anyway . . . I just wanted to say thanks

. . . for, you know, fixing him up with your friend Helen . . . he's having a hard time moving on . . . and, you know, it's, like, really kind of you . . . and, well, I guess I was . . . a *little* surprised when I heard . . . but, well . . . that's all I wanted to say so . . . ' and here she puts down the phone.

And we are looking at each other in silence. I am too involved in these people's lives to stop now. I have moved into a soap opera in a whole other world.

'Is this the same girl who used to deadhead your geraniums during dinner?' I ask her, and she doesn't answer me right away.

'God . . . she is so weird,' she says.

★   ★   ★

A young Hawaiian man walks across the sand towards us. He is carrying a tube of sun block and he kneels beside Birdie and asks if she will use it to write his girlfriend's name on his arm.

'Well, OK,' she says, and she takes the tube looking at me.

'What's her name?'

'Bernadetta,' he says, and she makes a face at me and starts to write. She asks him to straighten out his arm and she makes the first letter just over his elbow. When she reaches the end of her name she is right down at his thumb.

'I really appreciate this,' he says, and he is not even slightly embarrassed. When he goes away she lies down beside me on the sand.

'God, he must really love her,' she says.

We talk about Johnny then and she tells me everything she knows.

'His ex-girlfriend was weird about sex,' she says, and she turns over on her side to face me.

'He tells Walter everything — apparently she would only give him blowjobs.'

'How long were they together?'

'About six years.'

The waves seem far away now and they are quieter than the waves on our beach at home.

'What is it that keeps two people together, Birdie?'

'God knows,' and her voice is sleepy.

'When I met Walter I was ready to give up . . . you know we had our first date at Thanksgiving?'

'Really?'

'All the good shops were closed. I bought my date clothes in Gap.'

And she is laughing now. There are footsteps moving around us on the sand but we are both too lazy to sit up and open our eyes.

'It's funny, you know,' she says then, 'we used to go dancing all the time and we just stopped after we got married. Isn't it weird?' and her voice sounds genuinely perplexed.

'So what do you think of Johnny?' she asks then.

'We're still at the dancing stage.'

'It'd be nice to have a friend in Chicago,' she says, and somewhere in my imagination there are two couples who meet for dinner on a green deck every Friday night.

*　*　*

At 3 o'clock he takes me to the museum. I'm not sure I want to be there and I'm thinking it would be nice to go to bed with him instead. We have tea on the front porch before we leave and talk in a loose kind of way, over and back through the afternoon's heat. It's one of those days when the heat wraps itself around us and makes us lazy and dead in ourselves — and because of that we are a little too relaxed in each other's company. We lean back in our chairs on the Sunday porch like good old boys and watch the leaves rustling overhead. It's a great porch, high and bright like a treehouse. He thinks he is overdressed for the weather and I tell him he's OK.

We talk about Chicago and he tells me how he moved here without a job or a place to live.

'I was in love,' he explains. 'We kinda helped each other along.'

He says this with a broad bendy smile and he is trying to show me that he has known love. He seems smug about it now in a 'been there and back' kind of way and already I don't believe he knows anything. It's hard to react to what he has just said so I smile and make a soft whispering sound through my nose. We decide we better catch the train and when he gets up I see his sweat has made the back of his chair damp. He tells me we can 'jump the L' at Howard and that is the first thing that he has said that I like.

Outside it is hot and noisy and I feel like there is too much going on inside my head. He has a long loping walk with arms and legs that move in circular slow motion and he is wearing a row of coloured beads around his neck. I find my eyes drawn to these beads and I'm not sure why. I think it's the raspberry colour against his skin and I am thinking about how they would feel between my teeth or folding back over my neck if he were to lean over me. I feel hot and tired and vaguely turned on by everything I see. I can take it all in while my brain plays out other floaty things that are just more interesting to think about.

I nod and listen to some of what he is saying. He points to nondescript houses and tells me how much he likes them. He looks at dormer windows and calls them porches. He doesn't talk much and neither do I. I am busy with the strange sexual signals that my brain keeps posting to me. I don't know what's going on with me today and more than anything I wish I could say this to him. I have a feeling he might understand.

I give him my hand outside the museum and he gives it a little squeeze and then lets it go again and that's how our date at the museum starts. He hurts me and he doesn't even know it.

And I'm still turned on — just not as much as I was and more by the things I see at the museum than by the tall guy I'm with.

There is no form or pattern or shape to anything we see at the exhibition. We start with an enormous pantone book page and I tell him that, of all the colours on the page, one jumps out to me — aubergine. He smiles at this, but he also looks at me as if I have never been to an exhibition before. The images become black and white then and they are mainly of people with 1950s faces. Rows and rows of ghost-like shots. People wearing jackets and ties or cardigans. Pictures of dead people. Everywhere. It reminds me of Auschwitz and all the time I have the feeling that he is imposing this black-and-white depression on me. I find my mind taking off to the beach where I wore a red bikini and talked to my best friend about sex.

We separate off quietly and I find some photographs of naked people in the next room. Depressed ladies with their legs spread for the camera. I stand momentarily in front of one. Looking into her vagina and seeing the golden beach. He is in my peripheral vision and I am conscious that while I stand and obediently contemplate each image he is not watching me at all.

Towards the end I rebel and sneak quietly into an annexe and put on some red lipstick and rest. I sit on a cool wooden bench in my own small museum, glad to be away from the dead people and him. A few minutes later he walks up behind me quietly and blows softly on my neck. We are drawn to each other. Circling and then returning to the same spot again. Not because we are afraid of each other. We both know the biggest fear is that there is nothing between us at all. That we will both try to find a connection and then find nothing and the truth is it's over already but that won't stop us from trying.

We are cool people with colour in our lives

and failure does not exist for us. We just glide now and do our best to look good together.

At 5 o'clock he takes me to the Hancock Center. He tells me he took a friend from New Orleans here too and I know his friend is a butch girl with tattoos and that they slept together. I had heard all about this as I lay with Birdie on the hot sand this morning. I know because he tells Walter everything. I feel mildly insulted and order another drink to smooth me out. He orders a martini and I sit quietly with my head turned towards the view. The tonic is flat and I am thinking of how he let my hand go so easily outside the museum. There is no real conversation between us and I feel tired of trying now.

Behind us there is a fuss going on as a Japanese family leans towards the window. They've spotted a hopper standing outside on the window ledge. We turn to watch and I feel for the little apple-green creature standing stranded on the narrow ledge so high up over the city. I wonder which is worse then — standing on the window ledge of one of the tallest buildings in the world, or being watched by the Japanese family behind the glass. I am embarrassed for it and wonder what will become of it now.

As he watches with me his face softens and he stares sadly at the hopper and doesn't speak for a little while.

'That hopper is very lost,' he says then, and I can see he means all of that.

When we get home we go to bed. He is tall and beautiful in this silent dark room and the nicest feeling is his hands sweeping down over my outer arms. Every now and then I find what I'm looking for — when my forehead leans briefly, flat on his shoulder, or on his chest and when my cheek wipes over the hair on his stomach. There is a strange tension between us. The tension of being attracted to someone you are ultimately not sure you even like. The room is dank in the afternoon heat and we're quiet and almost studious in our attempts to create the kind of sex people like to talk about on the beach. So far our bed is like our date at the museum. We are both in different places looking at two different things.

'There's nothing worse than a bad first date,' Birdie says. I would like to tell her to try bad sex afterwards. Our mutual disappointment and embarrassment are with us like great pieces of bedroom furniture. We are in the dark and just bumping into wood. Meanwhile he's doing everything and nothing for me and I can't begin to tell him because it would take hours.

I start having this conversation in my head

and he's not in on it at all. He is lying on me and I am savouring the new weight of his body on mine. It is a particular kind of feeling. Basic and primitive and it's beginning to cancel out the black-and-white pictures I saw at the museum. He is kissing me and it's just simple and young. Then he lifts himself up with his arms and disappears between my legs and I am thinking about the black-and-white vagina again. In this dark room it speaks to me and gets between this man and me. 'Mono' it says, and then just one small word, 'Me'.

I feel like I have just asked a man the time at a railway station and having glanced quickly at his watch he disappears up under my skirt. The gap between us is that wide. This is the suitcase carrying of lovemaking, the ultimate act of kindness. Eventually he remembers how to make love to me and I am surprised and awake and one of us comes and it isn't me.

I feel roughed up and suddenly grumpy as hell. I am hot and too tense to sleep. We have a conversation about nothing and then he falls asleep. There is a part of this guy I still like. Can you believe that? I know he knows how to make love, but he's doing it the way someone else showed him and he's taking charge all the time. I would have been happy just feeling his warmth next to me. I would have been happy enough just being under him, that's the honest truth. Man and woman. Simple. If he had just held my hand that would have been OK too.

When he snores he gets a sharp elbow in the back. That's for not thinking enough . . . and for not keeping it simple. The romance is already over between us. He snores again and he gets another awful dig in the back, and, I mean, I'm surprising myself with the thump that I give him. That's for not holding my hand on the street.

He sleeps and I can still see the black-and-white men from the museum coming at me, reminding me of death until I turn the corner and a girl in a red dress saves me.

* * *

Birdie has lots of pretty features, but now that we are grown-up women it's her neck that I envy most. Somalian. Like a whole other level. And that wild curly hair, hovering up over the world. I have seen Walter watch her when she doesn't know, and fuss around her and catch her when she walks by and pull her on to his knee. I want them to adopt me, to feed me, to give me some of what they have.

This morning I am hungover and depressed by the bad sex with Johnny. He left closing the door gently behind him. He didn't know I was awake. It was 5 a.m. and when I turned over to forget there was a torn Trojan wrapper on the floor beside my bed.

I sit at the little wooden table under the hanging plants in my pyjamas with one hand resting on my leg and the other on the table. My bare feet are flat on the cold tiles and my eyes are staring down at them. Cool under my skin. My head is bursting with overheating brain cells and Birdie has that smile on her face as if she's one beat away from laughing out loud. And it's as if she's ignoring me as she fills the kettle and gets busy with cups and spoons and slices of toast. She looks so fresh in her denim shorts and her long slim arms are tanned and they just hang when she's not doing something. She puts the kettle on the stove and then bumps a drawer shut with her hip and in between doing these things she glances at me. She asks nothing of me and then she puts a mug of tea down beside me and hands me a slice of toast straight from her hand as if she's posting it to me like a letter.

'I slept with Johnny.'

And here their crooked little kitchen seems to fall apart and all her tidy little moves come undone and her voice comes back to me in a high-pitched whisper.

'Oh my God,' and I'm actually thinking, 'Not you, Birdie, not you, you're not going to judge me.'

And then she says, really seriously, like it's a matter of life or death.

'What was it like?'

'Awful.'

And here she puts her hand toward her beautiful long neck and starts to laugh and we both collapse laughing. She sees my distress. She sees every piece of it. The wreckage is all around us and spilling over off the table and into the cat's feeding bowl.

'When did he leave?'

'Five.'

'Did you say anything?'

'No. And now I feel bad. I thought it might have meant something.'

'Look,' she says, and she puts her hands flat on the kitchen counter.

I can remember the sound he made when he came. I can hear his breath coming out though his lips and the word he said was 'Pooof'. These are the things that you can't even tell a friend. Things like that stay stuck in your head. They can't be diffused over cups of tea and toast. They get stuck there until you forget and sometimes you never do

— and they just pop up when you're standing in line at the supermarket. Those kind of things are left as a form of punishment.

'Tell him you really enjoyed it,' and she is speaking in a quiet lying voice. 'Just say it was great and everything was fine and let's meet for coffee . . . '

'He snores.'

And here we are laughing again and when she opens her mouth she doesn't make any sound because she is laughing so hard.

She says nothing for a moment and gazes over my head and through the window.

'You could have been in bed with him all day,' and she is deadly serious now, and nodding her head all the time when she speaks.

'You need to get more sleep,' she says then, and I curl up on the green velvet couch. The red cat is stretched out on the back and we are growing closer as each hour goes by. The breeze from the porch swirls in around us and I finally feel that it's safe to sleep.

When I wake the sun has gone down and there is a rug pulled up around me. Before I open my eyes I can hear two sounds from the people in the next apartment. A baby gives one short cry and then I hear the ping of a microwave and these are good sounds and they promise me that life goes on. They comfort me. It is good to know that this kind of life exists through these walls. The woman wears sweats and holds the baby high on her shoulder and she checks the temperature of the food in a small plastic bowl.

When I open my eyes the stale drink feeling has gone. I feel human again and when I turn over I feel a moment of sadness when I see her empty chair.

★   ★   ★

The next morning Birdie leaves early for work. She feeds the cats and cleans out the litter tray. She takes her lunch with her in a special chilled bag.

'Sometimes when I get to the office,' she says, 'I just want to keep driving until I get to another state.'

★   ★   ★

Rue answers the phone after two rings and I know she has been waiting for my call.

'Are you having a lovely time?' she asks, and she sounds really pleased to hear from me.

'Umm. I guess so,' and then she talks about the high tide last night and how Martha is coming to stay at the weekend. Jacob has a bad cold and Beth and Tom are fine. When she asks about Chicago I don't say very much. I prefer when she speaks and I like the words she uses, to bring me down to earth again and back to my home.

★   ★   ★

We meet once more after that, for lunch, and I tell him I'm still thinking of the hopper on the ledge.

'That's what you call them?' I ask.

'Hoppers.' He nods. 'Leaf hoppers.'

I love the way he says this. In his soft southern accent with everything dropping down and round on the vowels.

'They don't fly so good,' he says. 'They're like moths.' And then he lifts his hand and lets it flap and float into the air like a big soft moth and he does this very well.

4

Angel

October 1995

Leo Adams stands inside the window of his shop. He leans on one elbow and looks at the wet mist that autumn brings. There are three horses from the hunt standing under the church spire and the clock rings out 'oranges and lemons' through the damp morning air. One of the riders lets her feet hang free from the stirrups and the horses puff warm breath out and nod their heads up and then quickly down. His horn-rimmed glasses are on his forehead and he notices all of these things and the people who just walk by.

With one glance, he can tell who will buy and who will only look. 'Will you knock a bit off that?' they ask, and he tells them that he's not in the discount business. They walk out and say that he is rude. He doesn't care. He matches people with furniture, he says. He tries to explain how good old age smells. He can describe the other life inside an old mahogany desk.

'The secrets it could tell,' he says.

The real buyers are quieter. They ask fewer questions. They stand back and look. When they look at a clock or a wardrobe or a chair they are listening for the life behind it and he treats everyone else with mild contempt. He puts one elbow on a cabinet and listens to them and all the time he is looking over their heads to see what else is going on.

The Dublin bus turns slowly into Main Street and then stops at Molloy's hardware shop. The passengers walk in a quiet troop towards the hotel and when they move they are silent and respectful as if they are going to mass.

When we open the door the bell makes the same sad 'ding ding' sound. He stays where he is, inside the door with his behind against a sideboard and his arms folded.

'I was only talking about you yesterday,' he says. I like that he doesn't get up. I like that he knows us well enough not to bother.

'What a lovely autumnal scene,' Rue says then as the horses begin to move on.

'You're in the right half of Meath here,' and his reply is quick, and it sends a ripple of laughter around the shop.

When he smiles his face lights up and he reminds me of the boy he was when he was twelve. His eyes are still bright and full of mischief now under his dark curly hair and it is hard to believe that we are both nearly twenty-seven. He walks about briskly then, as if he is important and we are not. Rue would like to see the long case clock. She stands in front of it with her handbag over her arm and her hands clasped and she looks up and then down and she says nothing for a little while.

'Is it going?' she asks him then, and he looks back at her and they quickly read each other's faces.

'It's not — but there's a man in the town who fixes them.' They open the door and stand there quietly looking in. There is nothing to see and no gentle ticking sound.

'She'll go,' he says quietly.

'What sort of price?'

'£1000,' and he sends the number out quick and light like a breeze. He hates to talk about money and it always seems to be some kind of embarrassment for him.

A man in loafers is standing at his elbow and he is being ignored. He treats Leo with great respect. He wants to get on his good side. He would like to see the pistols in the glass display case and Leo leans over and with one hand he slides the door back.

'I thought I should ask permission,' the man says, and he looks greedily inside. His hands are joined lightly in front of him and he is unsure of which one to pick up first. He sounds crawly and childish.

'Mmm,' says Leo and he looks over his head and out the window, 'always better', and he mumbles the last two words because he knows he will not see the crawling young man again.

There is a painting on the wall behind the clock. It is a picture of a girl in a red coat and she is standing half turned as if she cannot decide whether she should stay or go. The expression on her face is almost happy and then suddenly it is really deep down sad. She is standing in a garden that looks untidy and overgrown and it reminds me of the orchard behind our house. I keep one hand in my jeans pocket and then point the painting out with the other.

'Can you tell me anything about it?' I ask, and Rue stands beside me and listens for his answer too.

'It's Italian ... about £400 ... it's a painting, you know,' he adds then, and waits for my reaction.

'I know,' I tell him, and he grins at me. We are beyond polite conversation.

'You'll not deny her,' he says across the room to my mother and she smiles proudly. Leo winks at me and no one has ever said I look like Rue before.

He has worked in this shop all his life and the room has never changed. The two big windows overlooking the street and the wobbling glass door and the same worn green carpet on the floor. There is a stuffed owl standing on a plinth inside the front door and it is like a dried-out gatekeeper into another world.

Leo passes all of this through his hands, every item carrying a special kind of shadow that can only come with secondhand goods. Wood made shiny by someone else's hands, another life, everyday use, needed, used and passed on. There are times when I have stood in this shop and felt the ghosts moving around him. The auctions take place on the first Tuesday in every month. The air becomes dense and moves upwards as the crowds pack in and there is a new heat from bodies in warm winter coats pushed tightly together.

'If you're not interested, stand back,' he says, and he can say this without causing any offence. When he asks them to move, they shuffle left and then right again and so don't really move at all.

He watches as Rue looks at the roll-top desk. In a moment she will look around and seek him out with a question. He is talking to the young crawling man and not listening or seeing him. She tugs at the roll-top and leans over to try the other side. She gives a quick nod of her head, understanding that it is broken.

'That's the trouble with these,' she says to no one in particular. She looks closely at the desk surface as if she is observing a child. She is understanding and kind and yet not amused or light in any way. She places her hand flat over an ink stain and makes a circular motion.

'It'll be hard to get rid of that,' she says.

Any moment now she will look for Leo. She picks up a loose piece of wood and fits it into the space where it belongs. She turns suddenly and he's ready and leaving the crawling young man in mid sentence.

'This desk,' she begins, and that is all she says and she is tugging gently at the roll-top.

'It needs a lot of work,' he says.

'What would you think? Five hundred pounds?'

'Less — three hundred . . . four hundred,' and then he tells her she can ring in with her bid if she likes.

'How are things?' he asks me then.

'Oh, fine,' and I have to follow him because he is on the move when he speaks.

'Still studying?'

'Well, finished for a while anyway,' and then I tell him that I've finished my thesis at last and that I'm working at the college now.

'Well done you,' he says, and he stops and looks at me for a moment and I shrug at him and smile.

'And how is Beth?'

'She's great, her baby is due any day now.'

'The first one is always late,' Rue says, and when he looks away, she points to a picture on the wall.

It is a picture of Leo as a boy holding a trophy up and wearing jockey silks.

He's about to say something else and then the shop door opens with another ding sound.

'Why don't you ask him how much the pictures of himself are?' And she walks off laughing quietly to herself.

When we leave we look through the window at the clock and he knows he will see us again. It was in the way Rue looked at it and opened the door and then stood back and looked again, as if it was a person she was not quite sure she liked.

When I reverse the car out of its space he leaves the shop and waits to cross the street. He keeps his jacket flat with one hand and when he crosses the road he runs with his feet lifting high and he looks like a wind-up man.

'There he is now,' Rue says, 'and he's well able to step out smartly in his suit . . . well able to.' She nods her head then to make her point and I imagine driving off and leaving her sitting in her car seat at the side of the road.

Tom and Beth live in a house that has shiny wooden floors. The wallpaper matches the curtains and there is a wine rack filled with wine and sweets that stay in a bowl. Beth is six years younger than me and she married Tom last year. When I come to visit they light candles on the kitchen table and make pasta with chorizo sausage and red wine. They make quiet gobbling noises when they eat and say things like 'nice' and 'good' and their words are like salt and pepper over our food. He calls her 'baby' and she calls him 'Tom'. When they finish they look around and sooner or later one of them will mention the next meal.

'Will we go out for breakfast, Tom?' she will ask, and he will say, 'OK, baby,' and there is silence then as they imagine what it will be like.

'Let's have lunch in the garden, Tom,' and he will think for a moment. 'Yes,' he will say, imagining it, 'a nice selection of open sandwiches. Tuna,' and like a little fish being tossed back, he says, 'Crab.' They spend their time making their good life better. Filling every crack with something tasty, a glossy magazine, a new blue coat, a freshly baked scone.

Their bed has an electronic switch that lifts the mattress up and down.

When I bring her into a sex shop with me she is quiet and interested. There is a pillowcase with the word 'Fuck' embroidered all over it.

'Oh,' she says, and she sounds surprised, but really I think she is wondering if they have curtains to match.

They don't ask me about my life or who I am with and sometimes Beth suggests someone and Tom shakes his head and says, 'He wouldn't suit Helen at all,' and then I am wondering who that someone is, and so far we're getting on just fine.

On summer days they sit in their garden and talk about their hedge, and when a jet flies over it makes a white streak across the blue sky. They drink Moscow Mules and Beth looks up and says, 'Wow, look at that,' and then, 'God, it's hot today.' They give each other some kind of infinite comfort and most of the time I don't think they can see it. In winter they light a log fire and she slides her feet in behind his back to keep them warm. She leaves tea in a china cup with a homemade gingerbread man beside my bed and says, 'Hey, I made that for you.'

★ ★ ★

Martha Penrose is lying on the couch in the conservatory. She puts her feet on one arm and from the back garden I can see her tennis socks and her dark ruffled hair. There are two packs of Rothmans and a small transistor radio on the table beside her. She turns when she sees me, but she doesn't get up. Her face has not changed over the years. She is tanned and girlish and she has the same two dimples under her cheeks when she smiles.

'Hmmm,' she says by way of greeting, and she dimples at me. Her eyes are the same odd mixture of green and brown with tiny flecks of mustard yellow. They are sharp and knowing and they tell me that she has some kind of plan.

She stays with Rue twice a year. Four weeks in summer and then again in November, when it's quiet. They have an old friendship played out over tea and rambling walks on the beach. We wrap up in coats and sit on the garden seat looking out at the sea and we pick up the threads of where we were before. I tell her about my work and she shows me photographs of her niece.

'Wouldn't you like to have a child like this?' she asks me.

And she can see I still don't know the answer to this.

'You're still a chick of a thing,' she says then.

Rue brings tea and rhubarb tart and we sit around the garden table and have a winter picnic. Martha puts her hands on her knees then and sits up straight and looks right at me.

'I have to go,' she says.

'Where are you going?'

'I'm out of cigarettes.'

'I'll take you.'

'I want to pay by Visa,' she says, and there is nothing appreciative in her voice and I like her for that. She is careful to get what she needs. She is honest when she takes from people. Rue rolls her eyes to heaven behind her back when she leaves. Martha carries the radio and her reading glasses and her photo album and I take them from her and we agree to leave these on the hall table until we get back.

When we arrive at the Esso station on the coast road I pull in and turn off the engine.

'I want gin,' she says, and she sounds petulant and a little strained at the same time.

In the supermarket she walks in a very straight line to the off-licence section and it is as if she is moving on tracks. She lifts a bottle of gin and a bottle of tonic and turns to pay. Then she asks for two packs of Rothmans, and a bottle of whiskey that comes in a brown paper bag.

'Can I help carry these?'

'You can carry the booze,' she says, and she sounds intelligent and tired and aware of the kind of trouble she is in.

The sign in the car window says, 'Baby on board', and she reads this out loud. 'I have never understood the point of that,' she says.

We stop at the florist and make a joint decision to buy yellow roses for Rue.

⋆　⋆　⋆

When the telephone rings, Rue runs towards it.

When she says hello she sounds nervous and out of breath. Then she smiles and there are tears in her eyes and she turns to say that Beth has had a baby girl and I am running down the beach to find Jacob to tell him our news. We open a bottle of wine and have a roast beef dinner. We lift our glasses and Jacob says, 'Your health,' and Rue says, 'Here's to Beth and Tom and their new daughter.'

Martha doesn't lift her glass this time, but she smiles at us and says, 'Happy days!'

⋆　⋆　⋆

She's a pretty baby with a Cupid's bow mouth. She is wearing a yellow baby-gro and making that familiar snuffling baby breath. She looks like her daddy. The apple of his eye. Beth is sitting up with her arms around her knees and looking into the cot as if they might begin a conversation. Her blonde hair is cut short now and freshly washed and she has the same pink cheeks she had when she was a little girl. When we step quietly through the swinging door I expect to see a baby up on one elbow, talking back.

'Well, Beth,' whispers Rue, and her eyes are filling up.

'I never would have believed it,' and we stand there, leaning over this wishing well, mesmerized by the small person in the soft yellow suit. Tom reverses through the door then, carrying two cups of tea, and he is all wound up like one big walking smile.

'What do you think of your granddaughter then?'

'Cong-gratulations!' Rue announces and Beth smiles at me and we remember how she has always said this word. I have never thought about Rue as a grandmother until now and she seems small standing there, with her handbag over her arm and her pink lipstick like a flag in the air. We settle in then and I sit on the windowsill and watch as Rue takes the baby and holds her in her arms.

'What are you going to call her?' she asks,

and Tom glances at Beth.

'Angel,' she says, and we say nothing and just smile down at her and all the magical things that she seems to be.

Rue frowns when she holds her and then she adjusts her on her lap and moves further back from her so she can take a better look. A nurse comes in and smiles at us. 'How's the little lady?' she asks. Tom sits on the bed and when I look across the room I like how he grins down at Angel, and then points out something else about her to Beth, like a real family should be.

On the way home Rue is quiet and when I try to talk to her she seems distant and preoccupied. After a while she looks out the window and frowns and her voice is low.

'That baby,' she says, 'that baby,' and she shakes her head slowly.

There is a white wintry sun and a light fog over the hills. Everything we see we admire together. Not the wild green marsh or the sea with the wind underneath it but simpler things like the shape and rise and fall of ordinary green fields. Rue points with all her fingers fanned out and tells me about the different shades and colours she can see. 'I could watch it for hours,' she says, 'this is pure entertainment . . . just life.' And the sun and the clouds begin to roll and the light moves and everything is different again.

'I was down at the bowling club,' she tells me then, and in no part of her mind is she one of them. When she is invited to their Christmas party she laughs out loud.

'They had an Elvis Impersonator,' she says. 'You would want to have seen it. Will you be home next weekend?' And she runs all the words together so there is no space left to feel any disappointment. She says she isn't lonely, but I've heard her talk to the people on TV.

★ ★ ★

When Bob looks into the cardboard box he looks up at me and smiles. He leaves his walking stick against the wall and sits down heavily in the chair. He is thinner now and he has less hair, but apart from that he is the same. His eyes are still bright blue and he has that same slow teasing smile.

'Not a bad view,' he says.

The shelves in my office are bare and behind us the sun is going down behind the science block. There is a West Highland puppy sitting in the corner of the box and when she looks up her eyes are wet and half closed as if the room is too bright.

'What have you called it?' and he folds his

arms and shows me that he is forcing himself to smile.

'Blondie,' I reply.

Bob looks up at the ceiling and then down. 'First lecture?'

'Blank verse.'

'Hmm . . . example?'

'Robert Frost, 'Directive'.'

'Why not *Paradise Lost*?'

'Because I would be there all day.'

He sends his eyebrows into two sharp points, like little devil horns on his smiling face.

'Well, you know what they say about brevity.'

'To tell you the truth I'm really nervous,' and I am waiting for him to say something that will help.

'What are you afraid of?'

'I've never lectured in Theatre L before.'

'Ha,' he says.

The sign on my door says 'Dr H. Wilton' and before we came in he said 'Haw' to it and polished it with his hand.

'We're all afraid, Helen,' he says, and he looks at me over his glasses. 'Every good lecturer has nerves — the trick is to make them your friend.'

He watches when I lift Blondie and hold her close to my face. She makes baby dog noises and she smells like straw and warm hair. She is more than a dog to me. She is a bad girl with bleached-out hair and there are two dark wet lines coming from the corner of her eyes as if her mascara has started to run.

Bob's face is tired and drawn and there are dark circles under his eyes.

'So now you have a dog,' he says. 'And a flat in Sandymount.' And I can see where he is going with this.

'All you need now is a half mink coat,' and he looks at me and grins.

★ ★ ★

Mr Yarimoto sits with the mature students in the front row. They take the same desks every day and make little jokes about how much study they have to do. Their essays are neatly written and their books are all brand new. They are earnest and innocent and they smile at me now as if I am old and they are young. When I ask Mr Yarimoto to read his essay in our tutorials he stands up and then steps out of his place and reads seriously as if he is a little boy. He tells me he is worried about his exams and I tell him there is no need to worry until the cherry blossoms appear.

The chalk makes a smooth dry sound as it writes. The letters are big and looped and the full stops make tapping sounds on the wooden board. When I stand at the podium and face the coliseum crowd my student life is finally over. I am the academic and it is all about them and us now.

'Just remember you're the expert,' Bob said.

'OK . . . Bob?'

'What?'

'I'm terrified.'

'Helen,' and his voice was tired like he needed to sleep, 'we're all terrified.'

The theatre holds five hundred students and standing here looking up at them, with the microphone switched on, I am just one. Some are rummaging in their bags and others are talking to their friends. I wish they would just keep doing that actually, but gradually they stop what they are doing and settle in with bored faces to listen to my words. I wonder what would happen if I just walked out.

'Sorry everyone,' I might say, 'but someone close to me has just died, sorry,' and then just leave the room. I guess it wouldn't really do. Or, 'Apologies, I've just forgotten my notes,' and then leave quietly and not come back.

'Ahem,' I say into the mike. And then I say, "'scuse me,' and it's like I'm up here running off a little conversation with myself. And all the time I'm shuffling my notes and blinking at them and my eyes are making the same sound as a camera taking snaps.

The blackboard reads, 'Rhythm — The Essence of Poetry', and when I speak again the microphone is not working.

The door opens and a young man with red hair runs in. There are no seats left at the back so he is forced to run all the way down the steps to the front seat. His feet are loud in the quiet waiting stadium, dee-dum, dee-dum, dee-dum, dee-dum, and then he is at his seat.

'For God's sake, Lynas,' someone calls and everyone laughs.

'Sorry,' he says, staring up at me, and there is something about his blushing cheeks and red hair that makes me relax and smile.

'Thank you,' and my voice is actually calm, 'that was a good example of iambic pentameter,' and I have their attention again.

I want them to see that there is poetry everywhere, in the simple things like the click clock of a car indicator or the ringing of the college chapel bell. I want them to stop fretting about what every line means and just feel how the poet breathes those words in and out.

I put on the Ink Spots record and we listen to another form of rhythm and now I have what I was hoping for — the silence that shows me their attention, the strange funnelled down stream that takes us all into the same place and suddenly there is nothing to worry about and I remember why I wanted to be here.

When I explain iambic tetrameter they listen carefully and try to write it all down.

'Stop writing,' I tell them. 'All I'm saying is that it rhymes.'

I want them to listen and to carry the sounds and rhythms in through their ears and when I look up the students are smiling and I can see their teeth from way back in the Gods.

★　★　★

Rue takes the red velvet stool from beside my father's old desk. 'Not quite a piano stool,' Martha says, and she waits while it is placed carefully beside the harmonium.

It is Friday evening and we are standing in a half circle in the study. We have not put on any lights yet and it is getting dark outside. I don't like this room. This is where I saw my father before he went away. I stood with both hands on the doorknob and watched him write. I can remember his turned out feet and how he kept the page still with one hand as his pen scratched out letters on the page. My memory goes as high as his elbows and as usual there is no face.

Jacob begins to lift the lid back and a piece of wood drops off on to the floor and we all start to laugh.

When Rue asks Martha if she will play she is smiling and agreeable. 'Well,' she says, 'I'll try.'

She moves easily towards it, like it is no trouble to her, and she pulls out three or four black stops and then begins to pedal with her feet and it is as if she is cycling away.

The bellows begin to breathe a heavy tired breath and its old heart may not be able for it and then she begins to play 'Abide with me'. She moves her hands lightly on the keyboard. She is gentle and knowing and she lets her body circle slowly on the stool when she plays.

'It was on one of these that I found out I could play by ear,' she says then.

'Never hit a wrong note,' Jacob says, and he has one elbow on the harmonium and when he listens he is serious and respectful and he watches a spot on the ground. Then she plays 'Love Letters' and 'Scarlet Ribbons' and Jacob and Rue sing along and every time the bellows sigh I feel like my life is being pulled from me.

When Rue turns around I am sitting on the old sofa bed with my hands on my knees and there are small silver stars moving in front of my eyes. The room smells damp and unloved with its musty secondhand book smell.

When Martha plays 'Bye, Bye, Blackbird' Jacob sings out every line and Rue comes and sits next to me.

'She's a marvellous musician,' she says, and then she plucks something off her skirt that really isn't there.

'Do you remember?' she asks then, and I have to clear my throat to stop myself from crying.

'I remember,' I tell her.

'That was your father's favourite song,' she says, and as always she is matter of fact and she sounds annoyed and I know her well enough to know that this is to cover up some sort of pain. 'He used to sit you on his knee and pedal at the same time and play that song. You loved it — it was the only thing he could play.'

The organ gives a last long sigh and Jacob helps Martha pull the lid down over the keys.

'I need a drink,' she says, and right now I'm ready to join her.

⋆   ⋆   ⋆

Rue is wearing a floral nightgown and her rosary beads are caught between her fingers. The radio on her bedside table is playing softly and the small yellow lamp gives her bedroom a warm comforting glow. The dressing table is at the end of her bed and there is an ivory brush and comb set under the mirror. Her clothes hang in careful rows inside the dark mahogany wardrobe. The wallpaper is a pattern of small yellow and green sprigs. She has surrounded herself with beautiful things like any woman without a man to distract her can. When I open the door she looks up and smiles and I sit on the end of her bed with my feet curled under me. Now that I am here I am wondering why it has taken me so long. There is a silence between us and I am counting to ten to steady myself before I speak.

'Rue?'

'Yes.'

'Do you know where he is?'

She looks at the beads in her hands and then down at the pink satin eiderdown.

'Why do you need to know that?' she asks, and what she is really saying is, 'Helen, don't be ridiculous,' or, 'Helen, let's not go there,' maybe.

'Do you know?'

'For heaven's sake, Helen, at this hour of

the night . . . and where is all of this coming from?'

Her cheeks are red and I am beginning to see that in all my life I have never really questioned her. That I have never refused her protection.

'Aren't we fine?' she says.

'What about us?' I ask then.

'Aren't we fine?'

'I mean me and Beth.'

Silence.

When she speaks her lips move slowly.

'He went to Paris. I know he had a book-shop there. He wrote to me after he left. He sent money. I didn't want anything from him. He sent his new address in case I needed anything. I threw it away years ago. It is years ago now.'

Silence.

Then she speaks again.

'I did write to him once after that, Helen. You were fifteen and Beth was nine. I sent him photographs.'

'Why did you write?'

'I wanted him to see you . . . just how you were then . . . how you are.'

There is nothing to say at all now after all this time, so she says something else to fill the crack and also to break it wide open.

'He was in Paris and after that he went to

New York,' she says, and her voice is tired and dry. It tells me she is beyond caring, that she has worked hard at teaching herself not to care.

And when I look at her she is pulling at her rosary beads and all the old hurt and disappointment is right back with us.

'Aren't we fine?' she asks again, and now when she looks at me she is frightened and lost.

'We are fine, Rue,' I tell her, and I kiss her lightly on the forehead and it is warm and smooth under my lips.

* * *

She stands over my bed with one hand flat across her chest. 'There's something wrong with the baby,' she says. She looks like a little girl standing there in her light floral nightgown. She doesn't use her name and this is because Angel is something new to us now.

* * *

There are four plastic chairs outside the ICU and that's where I find them. Beth is very pale and Tom sits with his arms folded and looks down at the floor. They are waiting quietly outside the glass doors and there is a tall elegant man and woman sitting opposite. He is wearing a long cream-coloured raincoat and when she starts to cry he puts his arm around her. They both have the same dark hair and fine features and sallow skin. There are beeping monitors and doors that swing open and shut. The nurses walk quickly and seem to care more than anyone and yet feel nothing at all.

We are in a secret club now, Beth, Tom and me. Waiting and waiting and still dreading the face behind the glass door that finally beckons us in.

'Everything was fine,' Beth says, and it is always in the same answering voice as though I have asked her if she can tell me again.

'I had a good pregnancy — and she's big.'

'She is,' I agree.

'And then they checked her out after she was born, and everything was still OK, except that they said they heard a funny little 'shh — shh' sound from her heart,' and here she moves her hand like she is turning a doorknob.

'They said it was just that the valves needed to close,' and she says 'valves' like they are car parts because to her they still are.

'But then . . . ' and I can see that she is about to cry again and I sit still and listen and keep my eyes on her.

'And then . . . it seemed worse . . . and they took her away . . . rushed her . . . here,' and she whispers out each word and gives a big gulp at the end.

She puts her chin in her hands and watches the Cupid's bow mouth and we listen to the snuffling little breath.

When Beth speaks her eyes are dull and they are a different kind of blue. She has a new primitive instinct that fixes her eyes on the other smaller face.

Sometimes she just gives up. She puts her head down on the cot and cries into it and when that's done she comes back up again, to more anger and fear and hope.

★   ★   ★

Rue answers the phone after two rings.

'Is that you, Helen?' she asks, and for a second I can't speak. There is real worry in her voice and when I close my eyes I can see them waiting in the kitchen. Jacob and Martha are at the table and Rue is standing at the Aga making fudge. I know how she keeps the phone in the crook of her neck and stirs with a wooden spoon when she speaks. There is usually a red thermometer standing in the pot and a tray of fairy cakes in the oven. She has measured her ingredients carefully. Lifting the old-fashioned weights on and off the scales. Those gentle sounds are like little fences now to keep everyone in check. We are all waiting, new to this limbo zone, not understanding the language or how we feel and so we need Rue to be how she always is, taking all of us in hand, working in her kitchen to distract herself, and so we worry and she churns out fudge.

She speaks quickly. She asks good questions. She nods her head and tells me to take care. She prays. She says we all need to pray. She says that Martha has decided to stay longer and I can see that she is grateful for this.

Jacob goes outside to work and I imagine how he sweeps the leaves into loose bundles and then abandons them quickly, feeling safer inside, with Rue and the phone.

I am the go-between now because Beth cannot speak to Rue. She can't be clear and there are too many sad deep things to deal with when she tries to talk to her mother now. So I make the phone calls and stand near Paddington Bear at the end of the corridor and watch as he raises one paw and a recorded voice says a friendly 'Hello'.

I tell her that Angel needs an operation and how it is about connecting things up and as I speak I try to make shapes with my hands to match my words, and when I look at them now they are like claws.

'God is good,' Rue says, and I can hear how the kneeler will creak when she kneels down to pray. I can see the flowers in the glass and the Virgin with the child in her arms and you would think she would understand some of this.

★　★　★

The door sighs open again and I don't look up as the tall man and woman come in. He is wearing the same long raincoat and his black hair is folded inside the collar. He sits at the next cot and crosses his legs and puts his chin in his hand. He looks puzzled and his face is too straight and I know that he wants to cry but can't.

The sign over the cot says 'Ethan' and the name is written in bright red letters inside a yellow sun.

'Your son?' I ask.

'My nephew,' he says and then, 'I'm Jim, by the way — this is my sister Kate.'

'I'm Helen, this is my niece, Angel,' and they smile sadly and look back at Ethan again.

'The doctors look worried.' She says then,

'We don't even know what the scan shows or how long he'll be in here for, they just said wait and see.'

'How is Angel doing?' he asks then.

'She's having an operation tomorrow morning,' I tell them, and then I try to describe what they need to do.

'They need to connect the pulmonary artery to the left lung,' I tell him and he has forgotten about crying now. 'That way she can breathe on her own.'

He nods slowly and then gets up and looks down at Angel. He leans over and strokes the back of her hand with one finger and I like him for this. I like that he still has time for us, even in the middle of his pain. I like that he wants the facts and then weighs them up before he speaks.

'So there's a 'good-ish' chance,' I tell him . . . 'There's hope.'

'There's always hope,' he says, and he sounds certain about it and I wonder how many hopeless cases have been fed that line. And then Kate talks about Ethan and says he is just one week old. He listens to her and then explains how they must wait and see and that things can be done. And I am wondering about it now. How frightening it all is. How much activity and noise there is around this place. How people like Ethan's mother still

142

manage to drink tea and talk.

'There's always hope,' he says again, and he looks down at the sleeping baby and he touches Ethan gently with his hand.

When Beth and Tom appear they have a picture of Angel's heart. It has been sketched out with a black marker by the surgeon who sat with them and explained what he will do. Beth shows this to me and I can see that she is lower than before.

She opens the piece of paper and tells me about it and she runs her finger along the pulmonary artery.

'It will be joined here,' she says, and there is some impatience in her voice as if I might not be quick enough to keep up.

'If she is getting enough oxygen after the operation we might be able to take her home . . . ' she says, and we both look at the silent sleeping body in a pale pink baby-gro.

'Her tiny heart,' my sister says quietly to herself, and her expression is of someone who doesn't care any more.

★ ★ ★

I don't know where the babies go. They arrive in the night and stay in little cots and sometimes they just disappear. I just want them all to be taken out of here. I would like to catch them in a net and take them with me. When I leave I walk the whole way home, the wind over the canal, blowing the smell of this place of life, place of death, away from me.

'Let her live,' I say inside. 'Let her live. Just let her.'

★ ★ ★

The flat in Sandymount is home now. It is on the ground floor of an old Georgian building and there are four big windows and a real fireplace. The man from the hardware shop takes my order and delivers fuel every two weeks.

'You'll always have company when you have the fire,' he says cheerfully, and I find it hard to agree. There is a big chestnut tree outside the kitchen window and its leaves are changing all the time. There are windows on every side so there is always some kind of sun. When I go to the bakery I buy one slice of chocolate cake.

'Will there be a fight in your house over this tonight?' the owner asks.

'No,' I smile, 'it's just me.'

'Oh, I see,' she laughs. 'You bought it, so it's your cake.'

And inside I'm thinking, 'No, it's just me.'

Bob walks through the campus restaurant with a hardback book in one hand. He walks slower now with a walking stick, but he is smiling as he goes. Big Jo smiles at him and holds an empty cup in mid air and when she moves on her trolley is like a snowplough clearing up used trays and plates.

He sees us then and quickens his step and even now with his stick, he still manages the same slaphappy kind of pace.

'Hello, kids,' he says, and the others break away from their conversation and smile. The English Department is debating something about lecture schedules and now and then I drift away and think a bit more about Angel and the tall man at the hospital. Bob looks down over Professor Dowling's toupee and then looks at me and grins. When his secretary Kate arrives she is wearing a new pair of cream ski-pants and she nods and gives him a tight little smile.

'Nice strides, Kate,' he says and he smiles at me again.

Bob is a relief for all of us and he sprinkles these dry old plants with rain.

'How are we all?' he says, and he bows, regal now in his poor health.

'Hey, how are you?' I ask, and I clear a

place beside me and watch as he sits down heavily on the chair.

'Some days bad, some not so bad,' he says, and he flicks through the pages in his book. He is about to show me something he has been reading, but I bat it off and ask him again.

'I'll have some more results on Friday,' he says, and for a minute he says nothing and looks around the crowded room. There is a long line of students near the self-serve area and around us the tables are filling up.

'I know nothing really,' he says then. 'I ask the doctors what the story is, like how am I doing, you know, and they look at me — ,' and here he breaks away and salutes a student who walks by.

'Eight months of treatment, you know . . . I ask them how I am and they look at me and say, 'You woke up this morning, didn't you, Bob?''

All I can do is listen and try to ask questions in the right places. The boy at the next table takes his girlfriend's hand and then starts to write their names across the black surface in salt.

An envelope slips from between the pages of Bob's book and I get under the table to find it for him.

'Thank you for helping an invalid,' he says,

146

and his voice is only slightly sarcastic when he speaks.

⋆ ⋆ ⋆

At the hospital I sit with Jim outside the ICU. His sister sits away on her own and watches the nurses as they walk up and down.

'It's hard for her,' he says quietly. 'No husband.' And I don't want to ask where he has gone.

'Isn't it strange?' he says quietly then. 'When I came in here last week I just asked for 'Ethan Johnson', and everyone knew him, he's only a week old and here he is, surrounded by people who already know his name.'

'It's a lovely name.'

'Yes, it is,' and he sounds tired now.

'I don't know how to do this,' he says.

⋆ ⋆ ⋆

The phone rings eight times and when Leo answers I can barely hear his voice. The auction room is packed and I can hear the loud rumble of mixed-up voices and some are close to the phone.

'Helen,' he says straight away, and his voice is different. He is in charge of the rabble in the background and this is his auction room.

'It's coming up now,' he says, and I listen and he begins to describe the painting and I can see it in my mind.

'Girl in a Red Dress,' he says.

'Who'll start me off? One hundred pounds . . . ' and there is a gentle hush in the room and I can smell the warm winter coats from different houses pushed together. I can see a cloud of smoke that has risen to the roof and the warm pink faces that look up at Leo's smile. And he is there in his suit, with his black curly hair and his horn-rimmed glasses in his hand, and then on his head and then on his nose and he looks over them and berates them for their lukewarm bids.

The bidding starts then. My limit is five hundred pounds and it's at four-fifty already and then suddenly five hundred and I can feel it falling away and then he's back on the phone.

'Helen, do you want to bid?'

'Five-fifty,' I say.

It goes to six hundred.

'Six-fifty.' I really want it.

Seven hundred.

'Helen?'

Helen?

'Sorry, Leo.'

'All right then,' and his voice is kind before he hangs up.

When Birdie calls me she is whispering down the phone and she is using someone else's voice. It is someone who is cool and doesn't care and she is doing this to stop herself from crying.

'What have you been up to, kiddo?' she asks.

And I tell her about Angel and Beth.

'I can't really talk,' she says, and she draws out every word and leaves a long space as if she is waiting for someone to go. Then she tells me that the red cat is pregnant.

'Who's the father?' I ask, and she just laughs.

'Probably gone to France,' I add.

'God, Helen,' she says, and the words come out slowly in a tired sigh.

'What's up?'

And all I can get is the sound of her taking a slow deep breath.

'Sometimes you can feel too much,' she says. 'There are so many things to feel upset about everywhere and all the time, if you let yourself think for long enough.'

* * *

The nurse lifts Angel and she is like a stiff little doll. Beth takes her and touches her as if

149

she is afraid, not knowing how to feel about this person who is sick and small and there is her warmth and her bright baby smell and I turn away because I can't bear to see it. Her oxygen levels are strong now and we are all going home. It's not that we'll miss it, but for the last few weeks this has been our place, somewhere for all of us to go. There is comfort in the small dark church and there is coffee and time to talk. When I walk away I see Jim standing with his back to the world and staring out the window into the car park.

'Want to get a coffee?' I ask, and I listen as he breathes in, long and slow through his nose and I know that this is to swallow in his crying.

When we walk past the window I see that Ethan is gone. His sister is sitting in the empty room and there is just his name now in the bright shining sun.

★   ★   ★

He tells me that his surname is Madison and that he is worried about his sister, that she will go home now without her baby and without a husband and turn her face to the wall. He says this as he calmly stirs his coffee around and around. Then he puts the spoon on the saucer, and looks into the distance, forgetting to drink. He asks me about myself then, as if he needs me to distract him from his sadness, and I tell him about the college and the scatterbrained students and poets.

'I like how you describe things,' he says and then, 'Thank you . . . by the way . . . thanks for this.'

The babies are gentle as they nudge us together. There is no room for pretension or even politeness and so far what we have in common is fear.

He offers to drive me home and on the way he tells me that he's an artist and that he has designed his own furniture and his home. When he speaks I imagine being inside his life and taking a look around.

When we get to Sandymount we sit in the car for a moment. The wipers making that same-old same-old sound. I would like to say something, to ask him inside, but none of the words I'm finding seem right. One part of me asks, 'Why would I do that?' and another one goes, 'Why not?'

'Thanks again,' he says, and then, 'Good-bye, Helen,' and he has solved the problem for me and it's like a stamp being licked and stuck down.

5

Snow Melting

November 1995

Lynas Monroe runs and then glides in warrior pose. He laughs out loud as he gathers speed and his skin looks pink and fresh. His essay is two days late and was not delivered by hand but pushed under the office door. It was easy to sense his awkwardness, his sheepish demeanour, his urgent need to escape. On this cold evening in November he was captured in the sound of the foolscap pages as they moved across the dusty floor. Now as he slides across the quadrangle it is easy to forgive him and his hair is like a halo in tight red knots around his face.

'Lynas Monroe,' I say, and his name is whispered out into the foggy windowpane.

The first flakes came this morning. Soft and fat at first and then falling lightly like crumbs. They turned into a fine white dust and the students watched and waited, hoping that they would stay. At five o'clock it is almost dark and the campus is strangely quiet as it settles in under the snow.

John Dowling runs with his head low under the amber lights. He moves quickly, lifting his feet high and keeping his coat closed with one hand. He is wearing a green scarf, cast over one shoulder, and hand-knit navy-blue gloves. When he reaches the steps he jogs lightly upwards and then marches the snow from his boots. He turns around then to look back over the campus and the cold air gives him a worried look.

Kate pulls her chair closer to the desk and studies the nib of her pen. Her sandy hair was in rollers last night and her lipstick is a new cerise pink shade. At fifty-six she's 'not doing too badly, thank you', and she likes to talk about the weather and how expensive it is to shop at Spar. From a distance a snowball flies towards Professor Dowling in a neat lob and as he skips inside quickly, the door closes and the snowball makes a pat sound on the wood.

Bob's office is a long narrow room at the end of the third floor and Kate is sitting at his desk now. Her middle-aged breasts are impressive, like zeppelins, and behind her glasses her eyes are questioning and square.

'Narrow escape there,' John Dowling says when he walks into the room and then, 'Well,' as he sees us. The cold air has made red veins stand out underneath his eyes and his toupee, which has a side parting, is slightly askew.

'Ah, Professor,' Kate says, and there is a

long pause for effect as she puts down her pen.

'It's Bob,' she says. 'It's only a matter of time,' and there is another long pause as everyone tries to think of something to say.

'Ah, deary me,' the Professor says and he shakes his head. 'Deary, deary me,' and he stands with his hands joined high under his chin. He is formal and priestly now and it looks as if he might bless this room.

'God bless him, God keep him,' he says, and he stands then for a moment, too formal and lost for words, and then, out of nowhere and in the middle of this snow and sadness, I have a sudden impulse to laugh. I step around the desk and try to avoid Kate's eyes.

'Ah, well, indeed, indeed,' he says, and he begins to walk slowly step by step and really we are all running together from this room.

The walls are lined with books and there are trinkets that show hints of a tourist and a whole other life. An Eiffel Tower, a small brass windmill, and two Hummel students with schoolbags on their backs.

When Kate finishes writing she taps the yellow notes together on the desk. She is wearing a navy and yellow tweed skirt and a tight cream polyester blouse. Her underwear is the serious upholstered variety and the buttons on her blouse are going 'Hold on there, lads' somewhere between her pointed breasts. If Bob was here I know what he'd say.

'Size B52.'

Blondie walks into a corner and gives a fed-up kind of sniff. When she looks up at Kate she seems to go, 'Oh, what now?'

'That dog needs to be taken out,' she says.

Simone Fitzsimons appears at the door. She is wearing a red bobble hat over her straight blonde hair. She lifts an imaginary glass to her lips and says, 'Drink?' and apart from Bob she is my only other work friend.

'Still snowing,' she says happily then, and nods towards the window as if it makes everything OK.

'How is Mrs Doubtfire taking it?' she asks. 'I wonder, would she like to come for a drink?'

I dodge her invitation and tell her I'm visiting a friend.

'You're awfully tied up these days,' she says, and she gives me a little wink and then, 'Did you see the cut of Dowling? It's a pity they didn't clobber him with snowballs.'

★   ★   ★

Simone brings in a mug of tea and puts it beside Kate and we watch as she begins to type. We ask her if there is anything we can do and she shakes her head quickly and doesn't look around.

'They've only given him a few days,' she says quietly.

'I guess the lectures will be cancelled,' Simone replies.

And then Kate turns her head suddenly and watches us over her glasses.

'For heaven's sake,' she says in a fierce whisper. 'Whatever happened to soldiering on?'

★ ★ ★

As we walk towards the car park Simone tells me that she has a new guy. He wears a Yankee T-shirt and so far he is only known as 'Number 9'. He bought her a bar of dark chocolate on their first date and she thinks that he must be sweet. He was also using some string to hold his trousers up and she says his hands are big, like spades.

★ ★ ★

Bob's hallway never changes and it is filled with the usual mundane things. The golf clubs leaning in one corner and the mahogany bookcase that overflows on to the floor. A panama hat hangs on the coat stand and there is the same green tweed cap on the rung below. There is a black-and-white photograph of his parents and near it an old framed advert for Campbell's soup. The door to the kitchen is open and the toaster pops two slices of toast.

The nurse is a small waifish girl with pale skin and dark circles under her eyes. She wears a red cardigan and her uniform dress is belted at the waist. It always seems to be a size too big.

'Hi, Helen,' she calls over her shoulder. She has opened the door after one ring and when she turns to walk down the hall her hand stays for a moment in mid air. She pushes the bedroom door open as she walks past it and I can see that Bob is lying with his face turned away. The curtains have been pulled back and he is watching the small snowdrifts build in hollows around each dark windowpane. She takes short quick steps away from us and, when I see her in that A-line dress and those spindly legs, in my mind I am putting her on top of a Christmas tree.

Bob turns away from the window then and fixes his eyes so that he is looking straight ahead. He is wearing fresh blue Ralph Lauren pyjamas and he breathes carefully, in and then slowly out.

'Well, Florence,' he says, in a bored voice,

and this is his standard greeting. When I pull my chair up close he shuts his eyes and there is nothing to do then except to take his hand. The morphine keeps him at a slight distance from me and the truth is I am frightened by all of this. His hand feels heavy and lifeless, and there is a long silence as he grows used to me and the gentle pressure and warmth from my skin.

'Where are we tonight?' he asks, and he breathes in and out between each word.

'Dobbins,' I tell him, and I wait to see if he will go for this.

'Ah,' he says, and he manages a crooked sort of smile.

We wait together then and let the picture of wooden tables and gingham tablecloths settle down in our minds.

'It's a hot afternoon in July and the butter is beginning to melt in the dish.'

'Hmm,' he says, and this is how he laughs now.

'We're not going back to work and you've just ordered a particularly nice bottle of wine and we're just settling into our booth for a good long chat.'

We walk through the menu together and it becomes an outdoor market for mussels and crab claws and the rack of lamb and brown-bread ice cream I know he likes. We talk about the waiters and the people at the next table and the couple in the corner who we all know are having an affair. Around us the noise level gets higher and higher and then low and conspiratorial as we all play truant together in the late afternoon.

Last night we went to the concert hall and then to Mulligan's for a drink. Sometimes we just walk up to Herbert Park and sit on a green bench in the sun. And this is how we spend our evenings now. Like *The Chronicles of Narnia*. We step through the rows of hanging clothes and leave this sad tired place behind.

The evening dresses belong to Rue, each one with a different story behind it. She found me on my knees at her wardrobe taking out stiletto heels and old dusty handbags and then the dresses one by one. I tried to explain to her that my friend was sick and that I wanted to make the evenings better for him.

'You know, a nice dress, perfume . . . ' and my voice trailed off because it seemed ridiculous then. I sat back on my heels and, for the first time since Bob became really ill, I wanted to cry. Instead I touched the crêpe material in a black cocktail dress and, when I stared into it, it was like a black sky.

'That was a mighty handbag,' Rue said then, and pointed out the kind of bag

Margaret Thatcher would use. Then she looked at me again, waiting for a second or two.

'I don't think that poor man will know the difference,' she said, and her eyes watched me carefully when she spoke.

There was another silence and then she lifted the dress gently from my hands and began moving the others swiftly along the rail.

'Come on then,' she said. 'Try these and see how they fit.'

When I put on the black Chanel dress and tied my hair back she just shook her head and smiled.

'What?' I asked.

'I don't know,' she said. 'I don't know who you remind me of.'

The first night he didn't say much, but as usual he noticed everything. He waited until I was leaving and then cleared his throat.

'Nice threads,' he said, and he opened one eye so it was like a wink.

★   ★   ★

The nurse comes in and leans over so she can see right into his eyes.

When she speaks her voice is light and cheerful.

'Time for some morphine,' she says.

163

It is late when the doorbell rings. I am on the sofa with the fire lit, curled up with a book. I turn on a lamp in the hall and when I open the door I find Jim Madison standing in its glow. He is as I remember him. The same black hair almost to his shoulders and the dark slanted eyes and sallow skin.

'Helen,' he says, and he is smiling as if he is relieved to see me. 'Is this a bad time?' and I tell him that it's fine, that it's good to see him, and I am feeling horrified as I invite him in. He is wearing the long cream raincoat, and he looks calm and in control because he has had time to prepare for this.

There are books stacked high in the narrow hallway and ladybird fairy lights on the wall. It gives the space a blush colour and when he looks at them he smiles. There is also a pair of blue knickers hanging on the radiator and the air smells of toast.

I make tea and offer him chocolate biscuits, and all the time he makes polite conversation. He admires my open fire and ignores the Visa bill on the table and all the time I am distracted and stealing little glances around my room to see what else he can find.

He tells me that he has had flu, but that he didn't forget me, and I can imagine him curled up under a duvet, sweating and in the middle of some raving fever, thinking about me.

He asks me if I would like to have Sunday lunch with him at his flat and I say, 'Yes, that would be nice,' and really I'm thinking, 'Yes, that would be weird.'

'Tomorrow week,' he says. 'About 1 o'clock.' And he draws a beautiful little map for me and I had forgotten how nice his hands are. The lines he draws are perfectly straight and even his little arrows have some kind of soul. He says he will be looking forward to it and I let him out again, relieved that he came looking for me, relieved that it is time for him to go.

He stands for a minute with the East wind whipping around him and he gives me a smile.

The map is folded up in a neat little square, and I keep it in my bag now and look at it every day.

* * *

Judith calls and we talk about Rob. She says it is a relationship now after six weeks. They meet every Friday night and last Saturday morning he got up before her and went back to his own place.

165

'Now that we're in a relationship,' she says, 'why does he suddenly need space?'

⋆ ⋆ ⋆

Jim holds the flowers like a torch in his hand. Irises and delphiniums wrapped in a damp brown paper cone. The stairs to his flat are dark and there are gentle hollows on each stone step. We have left the hospital behind us. Dressed in black, for some sort of mutual sadness, but ready to start again now with flowers that are purple and blue. We are facing the new grey wind together. Not afraid any more because there is just no point, losing Ethan, winning Angel, has taught us that.

He lives on the top floor of an old building on Dame Street. He designs all his own furniture and he drives an old Jag. He tells me he has no TV but likes to look at people going in and out of The Oak. When he puts the key into the door he smiles and bows and in this way takes me into his world.

'Come in, come in,' he says, and for a moment I hesitate. Feeling that I am on the walkway to a new ship, a bright ocean liner about to set sail.

When Jim speaks his voice is strong and clear. He looks away and focuses on

166

something else so that the right pictures come and with them the best choice of words. He runs his hand back through his hair and he listens carefully to everything I say. When he replies each word seems to appear in a perfect line. They are like words written in old-fashioned handwriting with each sentence on a neatly ruled white page. Around us there are colourful shop windows and a few hesitant Sunday cars and people staying inside to keep warm. I saw them through windows when we walked, leaning towards each other, talking about everyday things, and a man who laughed and pulled his girl on to his knee.

When the barman poured our wine he was careful not to see us. He turned the bottle after each glass and looked out over our heads as if he didn't know.

'Now, folks,' he said, as he would say to any couple who knew each other well. And the flowers lay there on the counter, making a line between us that was damp and cold and, still, our new way of showing hope.

There are no walls in his flat, just a dark expanse of polished wooden floor. There is a kitchen area on the left with a low-hanging red lamp and the table is long and painted duck-egg blue. There are three black leather armchairs in a circle near the first window on the right and there is a bed with a red cover, placed at an angle at the far end of the room. When he puts on some music I can hear Peggy Lee's voice and so far all of this is good.

'Let's have some food,' he says, and it is as if he is being spontaneous now, but all around us are the tell-tale signs of a man who has been lying in wait. There are little hints, things that scare me and also turn me on. He kicks off his shoes as he walks towards the kitchen and drops his coat on to a chair.

There are two places set at the table under the light. A bottle of wine waits near the stove and when I see the coffee pot I am seeing a blue flashing light and thinking, 'Go on then, if this is how it is, then OK, go ahead, seduce me.' I have forgotten how the bed moves when the person beside you turns over in their sleep.

He puts on fat cream gloves and takes a blue casserole dish from the oven and his socks sound nice on the floor. He grates some cheese and at that moment is completely absorbed and has forgotten me and I like him for that. He wants me to take him as he is, to see him there in his black turtleneck sweater, with Peggy Lee in the background and his socks sliding a little on the floor. There is a thank-you card on the first windowsill and a red-and-white towel on the oven rail. There are two ripe pears standing together, outside the fruit bowl, as if they are waiting for a bus. The room smells of nothing and yet to me it smells like sex.

I sit in a black-leather armchair and look at him, and all the blacks must have merged because he pays me his first compliment then.

'You look lovely,' he says. 'All in black — and it's like your head is growing out of the chair.'

I guess you could say Jim is a little 'out there'. I can imagine introducing him to Rue and then Jacob and how they would look at me when I tell them that he sells his thoughts. He is so calm and clear when he speaks and then, out of nowhere, this 'jack in the box' jumps out, and it does kind of turn me on. The idea of going to bed with someone who is slightly off his rocker, and I guess you can see now that I'm a little out there too. Sometimes it's hard to concentrate when there is a bed in the corner of the room.

There are two dishes of melon balls on the table.

'*Buon appetito*,' he says, and uses his fork to make a small circle in the air. He has very fine features and high cheekbones. His eyes are dark with very long lashes. When his mouth is closed his lips are perfectly shaped, almost girl-like, and when he smiles his teeth, not a perfect white, are neat and square and functional. His hair is black and cut bluntly in one length over his shoulders and it is turning grey just over his ears.

He asks me all about my college life and the sort of books I like to read. When he looks at me he seems to be taking his time and trying to see what there is behind my face and eyes. I tell him about Rue and Beth and he remembers to ask how Angel is.

Under my clothes I can feel myself starting to sweat like I'm in the middle of an exam and there is a whole other person inside who is thinking, 'There are no melon balls left on the melon ball tree.'

We eat beef casserole then and salad afterwards, because this is how they eat their salad in Italy, and then there is a hot fruit crumble with cream and I have the feeling that I am being fattened up for something.

He has a whole raft of new phrases for me and they are like new modern poetic sounds.

'That's just painting by numbers then,' he says, or 'That's the tail wagging the dog' and later, 'We were trying to paint a rolling ball.' I think about this then and imagine that with the right people involved this could be a lot of fun.

He lights some candles and we sit on the leather chairs and listen to some Cuban soul.

'Would you like to see my studio sometime?' he asks, but I am distracted by a plate of After Eights that he takes from a cupboard in the wall. I don't answer straight away because I am wondering how they got on to the plate and I know now that he must have counted them out earlier and put them there and there is no way to explain to anyone why this is making me feel slightly sick.

'I'm a bit older than you, you know,' he says then.

'Really? . . . What age do you think I am?'

' 'Bout twenty-six, twenty-seven?'

'How old are you?'

' 'Bout thirty-five.'

'That's not much older.'

'I would open another bottle of wine,' he says, 'but it's a school night.' And I'm thinking, 'Oh, you're old all right.'

We put on our coats and walk a little for some air. It is dark now and the air smells like frost and warm pizza. We cross Dame Street and walk down through Temple Bar where there are singers and jugglers and people puffing warm air when they speak. We stroll down a long street and admire the fanlights and he nods and smiles down at me. When we walk back to his flat he takes light springing steps and he is careful to walk on the outside to keep me safe.

When it is time to go he helps me with my coat, as I knew he would, and really I can end it all here. The man who is possibly too old for me and who has nice manners and whose voice is kind.

'This is nice,' I tell him, nodding my head towards a green chalky portrait on the wall. It looks roughly sketched and carelessly coloured in. It is a portrait of an old man with thick grey curling hair. His face is broad and lined like a man who has worked long days in the sun.

'It's my father,' he says. 'It's just an undercoat, you know — it's a colour you use under flesh tones, it's good to use it . . . ' and here he stops and we both look at the portrait in silence.

He laughs then and shrugs his shoulders. 'I liked it — I got that far and I just wanted to leave it the way it was.' And he waits for another thought to express itself and instead his eyes look at mine and then he just says, 'You know,' and I nod because I think I do.

'You never mentioned your dad,' he says.

'Oh, he left when I was twelve,' and my answer is very clear and simple and for once I'm not ashamed of myself and the things I don't have.

He stands over me then and says nothing and just buttons the last button on my coat.

'I'd like to see your studio,' I say then, and he gives just a half smile and nods so that his body bows towards mine. He stops for a moment and then he leans in and kisses me on the lips.

He kisses me as if he is tired of waiting then, even though it is not long since we met. He holds me tightly, pulling me close to him so I can feel his chest rise and fall against mine.

He has made the decision for us and I like him for that. He would like to be my lover and he decided not to ask. He knows me well enough already and he knows I would have said, 'Yes.'

★ ★ ★

Rob buys Judith a brooch for her birthday. She wears it reluctantly and hopes that we won't see.

'What is it about getting a brooch,' she asks then, 'that makes a woman feel one hundred and fifty years old?'

He says it's by a new Irish designer, but she says it reminds her of a tooth.

★ ★ ★

173

Rue sits on my sofa and looks around my room.

'An overmantel,' she says. 'White fairy lights. A carriage clock.' And her eyes take everything in as if she is making a list. 'Two Quaker chairs. A nice Persian rug.' In this way she reassures herself that I am capable of having my own home now. Then she sees a pair of Jim's shoes near the kitchen door.

'A pair of shoes,' she says quietly, and in that way she ticks off the final part of my adult life.

'What's his name?' she asks, and she is still glancing around the room.

There is a green teapot on the table between us now and some chocolate biscuits on a matching plate.

'Jim Madison.'

'Jim,' she says quietly.

'What does he do?'

'He's an artist . . . and he designs furniture.'

'Hmm . . . an arty type.'

'I think he might be different, well, special or something, you know.'

'Well,' she says, 'you're the only one who knows that,' and this seems unhelpful to me.

'When are we going to get a look at him?' and I don't answer her straight away. I have an image of all of them around the kitchen table and poor Jim being carved up on a plate.

'How does anyone know for sure?' I ask suddenly.

'You just do,' she says, and she picks up a biscuit.

'This is a nice painting,' she says then, and in this way she closes the subject down.

★   ★   ★

Two clouds move like silent grey elephants across the sky. They float slowly, easily, with careful direction as if they are being led along.

'Like you and me,' Jim says, and I have to smile. I turn my head to look at the long row of black rocks leading out to the lighthouse and when I turn back he has put one hand under his chin and he's watching me.

'C'mon,' he says, 'it's going to rain,' and as we walk he takes my hand and it feels only a little strange. He lets it go then and runs down to the shore and stands with his hands out a little from his sides. And I stand and watch and I think he is behaving like a dog that wants to jump in for a swim. A wave takes him by surprise and he is suddenly up to his knees in water.

'Bollox,' he shouts, and he has to take off his socks and wear his shoes with bare feet.

'Do you like him?' Bob asks, and the words are dry and slow. These days he is just drifting in and out, but I tell him everything and hope that he can hear. I tell him that Jim sends me flowers and calls me every day. That he has a really interesting job and that he's a great cook. Bob looks away and it is as if he is closing his ears.

'Helen,' he says when I stop speaking, 'does he make you thump?'

★ ★ ★

The flowers on her dress are like marmalade oranges. Giant roses printed across fitted black silk. When she leads us through the National Gallery her black stockings move against each other and they make a shredding noise that's intimate and warm.

She stands at the Caravaggio and waits with her five fingers pointing like a starfish in mid air. She is slightly embarrassed and shy with some sort of secret to tell us, and when she stops pointing she smiles again and puts the starfish to her throat. She is more interesting than any painting now, in that dress and against that coral-painted wall.

The group has been growing steadily and

some tired American tourists rest near us on the wooden benches. They are not looking, but listening with their eyes, blinking down on their white walking shoes. Behind us a woman in a wheelchair moves silently. She glides through the first doorway and into the next empty room. We turn away from her and look at the painting, and she is alone then and more beautiful, with her colouring pencils and her silver wheelchair.

'The Taking of Christ,' the guide says, and she swallows and then says it again. The words are meant to fall with meaning, but what I am hearing is odd and mundane.

Jim nods his head seriously, but when her lips move and the words come out towards me what I'm hearing is 'the buying of the groceries' and 'the driving of the car.' She tells us about the artist and how we know this work is real.

'He made mistakes,' she says with a smile. 'See here,' and her index finger hovers over the canvas like a hook. There is a half circle faded out over one ear and some extra lines around the hand.

'He painted straight on to the canvas,' she says, 'so when he made a mistake he just painted over it.' One or two people in the group look at each other and nod.

'Old paintings age like skin,' she says. 'They

become thin, and blue veins and other things can be seen,' and when she speaks she pinches the skin on the back of her hand.

'I hear you,' an elderly American lady says and everyone laughs, but Caravaggio feels human and near now and he has earned a special place with this secret finger and ear.

Jim puts his arm around me and tugs the end of my hair. We are growing easier around each other and when I look at the old American couples I wonder if we will end up like them. Then the guide invites us to walk around the gallery and then re-group and talk about the paintings we like. It is almost an hour later when I stand up slowly and Jim winks at me and smiles and he is pleased that I'm about a million miles outside my comfort zone.

'I have two paintings,' I tell them, and I begin to open up a tightly folded note. 'Firstly, 'The Heiligewegs Gate'.'

'Oh,' she says, nodding her head slowly, 'by Jan Abrahamsz Beerstraten, an unusual choice.'

I explain to the group that it is a painting of a canal in wintertime in Amsterdam and as usual my words are better when they are inside my head.

'It's very calm,' I tell them. 'Actually for me it's surreal, it's too calm, and the little skating figures are gliding around like they haven't got a clue.'

'Haven't got a clue about what?' she asks, and she sounds slightly amused.

'That something is going to happen . . . it's just too calm and perfect . . . there is a feeling of . . . of . . . anticipation,' and here Jim lifts his eyebrows up really high and he looks as if he is about to laugh. The others in the group are just staring blankly and one woman leans down and checks the lace on her shoe.

'My second choice is 'Woman Reading a Letter'.'

'Ah, yes,' she says, 'Gabriel Metsu,' and she is really happy to be off the ice again. 'And why did you choose this one?'

'I like the way there is a shoe in the middle of the floor . . . everything is forgotten because the letter is so good — and that's the way a good letter should be.'

And here one or two people in the group nod with the corners of their mouths turned down.

'Thank you,' she says, and I know she wants to get rid of me because of her flat pancake smile.

When Jim stands up he speaks for five minutes and the group are with him every step of the way. His words are well planned and everything he says sounds intelligent and clear. Afterwards the guide thanks him and I can see she really means it and part of me would like to kick him on the shin.

'Did I sound a bit loopy?' I ask him as we step outside, and he stops and takes my hand.

'Loopiness has a certain appeal,' he says with a grin.

'I liked what you picked,' he says. 'It was different, and that's always good.'

'How did you like the Caravaggio?' he asks, and I tell him I thought it was great.

He looks at me and then looks away laughing, seeing right through me, like he always does.

I didn't like 'The Taking of Christ' — and I'm thinking now about poor old Jesus being picked on and jostled around. Jim bought me prints of the paintings I liked though, and he kept them so he could get them framed nicely for my wall.

★   ★   ★

On Tuesday night Jim cooks dinner for me. He feeds me fish and vegetables and a dish of home-made ice cream and fruit.

'You need to eat,' he says seriously, 'every day,' like this is a new concept, and then he clears away the plates.

'Now you can do the washing-up,' he says,

and he tosses me a cloth. In the mornings he sets the table and leaves pink grapefruit and coffee in my place. He makes me feel safe and cared for. He fathers me. He doesn't leave.

★　★　★

At 4 a.m. he is still working at his drawing board. He is lost to the dark night world in between the scratches of his pen. He draws neat little arrows and measures carefully and rules. He is like a small bright island and he brings morning into my room.

Over breakfast he tells me he needs to get this commission.

'It's not the kind of work I like,' he says, 'it just means I can pay a better Christmas bonus to the staff.'

'Five hundred quid can make a real difference to somebody,' he says. He showers and puts on a fresh white shirt and he doesn't mention his lack of sleep. He is only focused on where he needs to be. When he kisses me goodbye I am imagining he is my husband going to work.

★　★　★

When we are in bed, Jim tells me when he is going to come. He is tender and sensitive and then when he is inside me he is male and concentrating on getting to another place. I like that he takes us so far together and then leaves us for a moment to ourselves. With every movement he makes I can feel myself falling for him, falling out of myself and into him.

'I'm going to come now,' he says, and it is always in the same intense quiet whisper and he is another Jim then, proud, like a small boy standing on a platform and seeing a train.

★   ★   ★

He sends me Gary Larson cartoons in the post. There is a different bouquet of flowers every week.

'What have we today?' Simone asks, putting her head around my office door, and then, 'Ah, nice peachy coloured roses,' and she walks on then with her chin high and a little smile on her face. Sometimes he writes letters and sends them with pictures of flowers cut out from magazines. Sometimes I imagine how my things would look in his place. He brings me to dinner with his clients and tells me he is proud to show me off. If I drink too much he doesn't say anything, he puts me in his pocket and he takes me home. He makes every day a Sunday.

He is good before his time.

But what is it about good people that makes me want to be bad? And now I am starting to notice other things, like his raincoat, his shoes, and the way he laughs.

★   ★   ★

Lynas Monroe knocks once and puts his head around my office door.

'Hello,' he says, and I am already smiling. My direct line starts to ring then and I leave it. I know that Jim is cooking another one of my favourite dishes and he is wondering when I will be home.

'Sorry this is late,' he says, and he hands the stapled pages to me.

'Not playing postman tonight?'

'Thought I'd walk into the lion's den for a change,' he says, and he grins at me and puts his hands in his pockets.

'Actually, I was just going to have a coffee?'

'Great, thanks,' and I'm beginning to wonder why his essays are always delivered late at night.

He watches as I mix instant coffee in the corner of my office and tap the spoon on the edge of the cup.

He is awkward and a little afraid around me, and yet there is the hardiness of youth, the curiosity and lack of experience that is keeping him here. He studies my face for a moment and then sits down in the chair near my desk.

'So I really liked your lecture today.'

'Thank you,' and here there is an awkward pause as he looks at me and then at his feet.

'What did you like about it?'

'I just like the way you lecture.'

Another awkward pause and I am trying to put him at his ease.

'You know, if you worked a little harder, Lynas, you could get really good grades.'

'What would I need to do?'

'Well, I could help you, maybe give one on one.'

'Great,' and he is suddenly standing up, 'tell me when.'

When he gets to the door he turns and his red curls look warm from here. He is so young I would like to protect him and make sure that he is safe as he walks out into the night.

'I like your hair by the way,' he says then. 'It's nicer down than up.' And I find myself blushing up to my roots and putting my hand to my hair as if I am suddenly confused.

'Goodnight,' he says, and he gives a cheeky grin, and when he leaves me now he is suddenly old and I am very young.

The couple at the next table know each other well. He lights her cigarette without thinking and she sits beautifully with her chin up and it is like watching a ballerina smoke. She keeps the same half smile on her lips and now and then she lifts her eyebrows to punctuate his words. They are Spanish and when he speaks his words come out in a long never-ending flow. When she exhales from her cigarette she gives a little shake of her head. She does that simple thing that only some women are able to do. She humours him. She lets him speak. She listens very well. He passes his food towards her and gently urges her to try. When she shakes her head he doesn't persist and he eats it himself. Under the table his feet are slender and tanned and somewhere during their conversation he has taken off his shoes and it is easy to see that they have shared the same bed for a long time now.

The restaurant has orange banquette seating with matching fabric lampshades that hang low over dark wood. It is a new French bistro and around us there are people drinking wine and glancing sideways as they eat. The walls are whitewashed and have alcoves filled with bottles of wine. There are musical instruments on the wall: some bongo drums, a tambourine, a Spanish guitar without strings.

Outside there is a long row of wine bottles queuing to get upstairs.

When Judith laughs the waitress looks at her for a moment as if she would like to join in. She has the same bright smile, the same brown eyes and now and then she pats the space over her cheeks.

'Look, look, will you,' she says, 'I'm getting laughter lines,' and then she forgets and starts to laugh again.

'It's hopeless,' Simone says, and she looks at me sadly. 'I'm beginning to find the men in Fair City attractive.'

Then Judith tells us that she thinks it's not working out with Rob.

'Maybe he's not so great,' Simone says, and this is meant to be a form of comfort. 'I mean, what does he have to offer really? The fact that he's divorced is not great. The fact that he's so moody all the time is not great . . . '

'The fact that he's an asshole . . . ' adds Judith.

' . . . Is not great,' we reply.

'What happened to Number 9?' Judith asks.

'I've re-named him Number 2,' she says.

The couple at the opposite table are academics. She is overweight and her fringe hangs down over her eyes. She wears a Fred Perry top and she sits with her legs apart.

'I'll just let that one roll,' she is saying, and this is her version of the flirt. She is raising one eyebrow and trying to balance an amused look on her face.

'That's a very sexist remark.'

'Oh no,' he replies, 'that applies to a huge cross-section of society.' They are slow learners and they walk through the date as if they are following a manual. It will take forever for them to get to where they need to be. I would like him to pay the bill and take her out of here and leave us romantics alone.

When we get drunk we talk about Jim.

'The problem is . . . he's great in so many ways. I mean, he's very romantic and generous and he really cares for me.'

'So what is the problem?' Simone says, and her voice is dry.

'It's too intense. It's like he's focused on me all the time.'

'I want your life,' Simone says, and Judith is laughing into her glass.

'He's almost too good . . . and now there are things about him that are really starting to bug me and he's so busy being Mr Wonderful that he can't see any of it.'

'Well, he is wonderful, in lots of ways,' Simone says.

'Yes, I know,' and I'm sighing and shaking my head. 'But there's a bit more to a relationship than flowers and dinners.'

'He is very good to you,' Judith says.

'So what sort of things are bugging you?' Simone asks, and she is not buying my story so far.

'Well, for example, he loves dancing.'

'I would love a guy who loves dancing.'

'He's a terrible dancer, but that doesn't stop him . . . it's kind of embarrassing.'

'Oh.'

'And . . . he has a really funny laugh,' and they are just grinning back at me now.

'Last weekend we were in a restaurant and he just went off — and the baby at the next table got a fright and started to cry.'

'What does it sound like?' and Simone actually treats this as a serious question.

'Like a seal.'

'Oh,' and they look down into their wine.

Simone takes a black Moleskine notebook from her bag and hands it to me with a pen.

'Take a page,' she says, 'and make a list, look at his pros and cons and then see what really matters. He's a good guy, Helen,' and her voice is serious, and I don't need anyone to tell me what a good man he is.

When the Spanish man laughs his girlfriend laughs too. They share the joke and then she takes his hand and whispers into his ear.

'See,' Judith says, 'that's Spanish for 'Shut up you fool'.'

Then we order another bottle of wine and Judith takes the guitar off the wall and pretends to strum it as we write.

★   ★   ★

The Spanish couple leave and the academics hang in there for more. They are beating each other to death and killing everything we believe about love. They are holding on to the dull stuff they're making because they might not find anything else as good.

'It's really hard you know,' Simone says thoughtfully, 'for two people to want each other in the same way, at the same time. You know it's much more like — I want him, he wants someone else. He wants me, I want someone else.'

On a single page of cream paper I hold the man of my dreams.

Jim, it says:
Thoughtful
Kind
Good-looking
Tall
Creative

Solvent

Nice pad

Loves me.

And then the things that are suddenly creeping me out:

Trench coat

Shoes

Dancing

His laugh

Keeps saying, 'Thank you kindly.'

★　★　★

The Spanish man puts his arms loosely around his girl's neat waist. She licks her top lip lightly and smiles up at him.

'I want what they have,' Simone says sadly.

'He didn't stop talking once,' Jude says, shaking her head.

'She didn't stop listening either,' she replies.

I saw it too. In her dark brown eyes. In the freckles on her skin. In her little smile and how each and every word was accepted and loved by her pretty wooden-spoon face.

I ask the taxi driver to drop Judith off first. She is smiling quietly to herself and swaying a little in her seat.

'Call you tomorrow,' I say, and the words are slurred.

'Thank you kindly,' she replies.

Bob doesn't answer and something tells me that this is the end of our game. The last time he spoke it was Tuesday evening, and then out of nowhere his voice was suddenly clear and wide-awake.

'Helen,' he said, and then he just whispered, 'Helen, I'm scared,' and now I don't know where he is. He's not dead and he's not alive and I don't know what to call the 'in-between'.

When I lean over him I let my hair down so that it falls loosely and covers his face. I put my hand gently on his cheek and after that I wet my lips and cover his mouth with mine. There is no life in his lips, but his mouth is warm and moist. I kiss him because I loved him. I kiss him because he is my friend. I kiss him because of all the men, of the boys, this one deserves to be kissed. I kiss him and just hope that he can feel it and somehow know that I have left red lipstick on his face. I kiss him as if we were lovers, in some ways I think we were.

When I look up the doctor is standing at the door. He is a tired grey-haired man and with one glance he takes in the feather bow and the pearls and my hand still resting on his face.

'Unfinished business,' I tell him, and he nods quickly once and as he walks towards the bed he is writing a prescription for me with his eyes.

Later the nurse pours me a glass of whiskey.

'Is that the first time you've seen someone pass away?' she asks, and her voice and all her little movements tell me that she is still happy and now that it's over she is just carrying on.

'First time is hard for everyone,' she says, and she stops for a moment and seems to think, 'After that, you get used to anything,' and as I sit there sipping my whiskey she dries the dishes and folds up the tea towel and puts the glasses back up on the shelf.

* * *

'Hey,' Jim says, and he looks worried when I brush past him without a word. In the kitchen he asks if I will have some tea, or coffee and then in a very hesitant voice, 'A drink?'

There are a lot of pubs between Northumberland Road and Dame Street but because I am wearing Rue's high heels I could only make it to six. When he turns to fill the kettle I wait quietly behind him and I am in another place now. Like a female mosquito my flight

192

is loose and jingling and it is only a matter of time before I zoom in.

When I pull my zipper down it makes a sound like fabric tearing and Jim flicks his head up a little too quickly and he is careful not to look around. Instead he places the kettle on its stand and hits a switch and the red light glows and says 'On'.

I would like to punish him now for my unhappiness, to use my small hard fists. I am tired of his perfection, the way he uses napkins and his excellent door-opening skills. I want to slap him, to tear at his clothes, to drag him down here with me, so we can roll around and sin.

When there is sex in the kitchen it can get crowded and the very idea of it bumps up against all kinds of things.

There is red pepper sliced open on the counter and a sharp silvery knife that has left a deep nick in the chopping board. The red lid on the bread bin is not sitting as it should be and the kettle begins to rattle gently when it boils.

'You're a little drunk,' he says very quietly, and as usual he is extremely polite and his gentlemanly eyes still refuse to look down. Instead he looks up, right up into the ceiling. He is actually beginning to lean backwards then to keep his eyes off me and mine, and in my mind my thumbs and fingers are turning into red arrows and pointing at my breasts and my crotch. He puts his hands on his hips then and finally meets my eyes.

My hand is on the butcher's counter to keep me steady and when my eyes look into his they are sorry now, pleading, filling up with drunken tears and they have two little-girl-voice whispers that say, 'Butcher me.'

He takes two sudden steps across the kitchen and begins to kiss me and with one hand he reaches over and turns off the light. There is a rail on the wall behind us and when I lean into it the soup ladle goes chink-chink against the knife. There is a bottle of Gordon's gin and some red wine that says Crianza 1995 on the counter near the sink. His cleaning lady has forgotten to wipe the dust off the tall pasta jar again.

When we are finished he sinks slowly to the ground. His back is against the fridge and I am slunk low, almost hanging in his arms. The streetlight makes an amber stripe across the floor and the boiler suddenly growls and bumps on.

We are in that post-coital place under a pure white light that only we can see. It flashes on in orgasm and polishes your skin and makes you say things you might not really mean.

I understand the place that he has just visited. I have seen what he has seen. And we are complete now. Joined. Rooted for just those five minutes.

After coming I want to say, 'I love you.' Just because at that moment I really do. But five minutes later we will both be pulled back to our separate places and who knows how much I will really care. So in my mind I say the words I am sure of and they are noisy and unseemly.

'Thank you, Jim, for fucking me. Thanks for helping me to blank out this sad world. Thanks for letting me die briefly and forget. Thank you, Jim.'

Like me he says nothing. Holding on to the precious minutes after sex. The perfection of it. The heat. The damp feeling between my legs. No need to think. No need to stand up. No need to get clean again yet. Like shock treatment it reorganizes our brain waves so they come on again without any clothes. The air is still and even between us. We are just here, and here together, and there is no need to see beyond that.

His voice is sincere when he speaks and I see now that he has waited so he can say what he means.

'I love you,' he says, and the words are dry because they have been waiting patiently on his tongue for such a long time. My mouth feels hard and my lips are stitched neatly together. And different words go around inside me.

'Hold me tighter, Jim,' they say. 'I don't want to die alone.'

So there is silence then and we sink down further and then lie together on his kitchen floor. It is strangely comforting to feel his arms around me and still to trace out the shape of each mosaic tile with my index finger and somehow be alone. The floor is cold and rough underneath us and when I close my eyes it feels like we are lying in snow.

★　★　★

The students gather in a half circle around my desk. They complain about the dark and I tell them that I hate to be in fluorescent light. They take their essays out reluctantly and I tell them to ignore the little white dog.

'Who's the dish?' one of them asks then, and she is looking at Jim's photograph on my desk.

'The dish is called Jim.'

'Do you read poetry to each other?' Lynas asks, and everyone laughs.

'Come on,' I urge them gently, 'Louis MacNeice . . . '

When Lynas reads his voice is gentle in the late evening light and in between each verse he calls out a beautiful rote.

'Is this a love poem?' I ask.

'Not really,' he says and he stifles a little yawn. 'It's about what happens after it's gone.'

★   ★   ★

Jim is waiting on the first green bench inside the gate. The snow has melted and there are small white patches left and there is beauty in this old rubbish now. We pretend not to see it, and look at other things, like the cold grey sky and the wet wood of the trees, as if it is underwear dropped and lost in the grass.

He is wearing his long black coat buttoned against the cold and a maroon scarf and something tells me that we are different now. It is in the sad smile that he gives as I walk towards him. It is in the way he stares at the leaf that lands near his shoe. It is in the circle that he makes on his palm using his thumbnail. There is a smell of decay and autumn is long gone and something tells me I am falling now and landing with the melting snow. It is the Submarine in the taxi. It is being stood up at the Pronto. It is the boy from Carlow who said, 'Look, I don't love you any more' and I said, 'I don't love you either,' even though I think I did.

When Jim kisses my cheek his hair moves and there is a smell of apple shampoo.

'Hi,' he says, and there it is, the new voice your lover finds to pick you up and put you down in a whole other place. He swallows slowly and puts his hand into his pocket and something tells me he is not about to produce a ring.

'I found this,' he says, and he gives me an abstract sort of smile. He is calm as a breeze when he hands me the folded piece of paper and I open it up slowly not knowing what it is.

When I look down I bite on my bottom lip and see Jim's pros and cons list.

'That'll teach me,' he says with a grin, 'never to do a woman's laundry.'

A man walks past with his terrier and he has one white squeaking shoe.

'Helen,' he says then, and his voice is steady and cool, 'I don't think I know you at all.'

The terrier lists to the left and pulls on his lead like he is walking on a sloped roof and I am there with him and understand the sort of bind he is in.

'And I don't think you know me either . . . ' and he gives the page a little biff with his hand. There is a part of me that notices that he has just decided to ignore everything on my little list.

Behind him the beekeeper closes a low grey gate as if he can keep the bees inside. Elegant and mysterious in his long cream costume, what does he say to his wife in the evening? Does he say, 'Honey, I'm home?'

We are in silent orbit around these ordinary lives and so far I am unable to speak.

'Look,' he says and he leans close to me, 'it's not really about this. It just made me think . . . I can't get inside that head of yours, not really, and you're not anywhere near ready for the kind of life I would want us to have.'

'There are good things here as well, Jim,' and I'm looking at the piece of paper, 'and the other stuff, well, it does bother me, Jim,' and here the old man with the long silver hair holds up a sign and it reads, 'You're a bit pathetic, you know.'

'OK, OK,' he says with a big deep sigh, and then he starts to nod his head a little too quickly.

'I think we should give each other a little space,' and he watches me.

'Just for a while, and see how we feel,' and when I nod my head sadly some part of my brain records that he is still wearing those beige deck shoes.

But there it is. Offered up. Some kind of emptiness where there are no other people and it's not what I want. There is space everywhere. All around us, in between us, inside my toes and knees, and there is a really awful thought floating around that goes, 'What is it about the men I know and why do they always leave?'

★ ★ ★

The woman in the bakery hands me one slice of chocolate cake. She is ready with her smile, but she doesn't say a word. I sit at home and eat it in small nibbling bites, feeling ashamed and too embarrassed to think, and really I deserve to be here with this one slice of cake and the greasy stain it leaves on the brown paper bag.

Judith tells me I can get him back, but I just shake my head and say, 'No.'

'How can you make it with a guy when you don't like his laugh?' I ask her, and before she answers, 'How can you make it when he knows?'

Sometimes when I think of the things I wrote about him I have to pull the sheets over my head. I guess I didn't really know him, and until now he didn't really know me either. When I think of him reading that list I could die with embarrassment. With each word I'm sinking lower and lower, in through the mattress and into the carpet and right down into the ground. Even down low, there's no escape, and they're like glow worms in the dark. I think about why he might forgive me and they always surface, 'Solvent — nice pad — loves me.'

6

Alone with everyone

December 1995

The Capuchin monk is young and good-looking. He sits in the front seat and chews steadily on the end of his thumb. He concentrates on something that is distant and beautiful, and it can't be any kind of prayer. The nape of his neck is tanned and the fine hairs behind his ears are bleached white and gold. When the music floats out from the speakers he forgets where he is and plays three or four notes into the air.

We have escaped the Christmas shoppers on Via del Corso and the church is warm on this wet November night. The older priest looks pleased to see him. He breaks into his dream with a wave and the old sallow face lights up with its own smile. They stand near the confessional box then and chat and catch up like any old friends would do.

Rue stands quietly and looks up at the dome. We are stuffed full with stucco and statues and old peeling paint. There are no words left to describe them and so our worn-out eyes just look and look. She sits near the confessional box then with her hands resting on her beige corduroy pants and she is ready to whisper out all her sins. She began the campaign for a good confession on our first morning here, and now as it gets dark and wet I am feeling tired and ready to give in.

'I'm not going to confession,' I tell her, but she just stares straight ahead and I can see she is prepared to sit here all night.

'You will receive great graces,' she says, and these are fierce little words that move through the air. Her eyes are fixed on the tabernacle when she speaks and it is as if she would prefer these words to come from somewhere else.

When the young monk turns on the orange light over the door she gets up with confidence and she seems well-drilled and professional when she marches quickly in. Outside I am supposed to be preparing for my confession, but really I am thinking about the good-looking monk and the sort of life he might have. A woman carrying a Marks and Spencer bag comes through the door and then she stops and points at a statue of the Sacred Heart. Her friend smiles and then laughs, 'Ah, here he is,' she says.

When Rue comes out she is smiling and mischievous.

'Go on!' she says into my ear and she gives a little stamp with her foot. I stumble awkwardly into the wooden box, badly prepared for confession, but interested in the graces that I am going to receive.

'Bless me father for I have sinned, it is fifteen years since my last confession,' and we kneel together then in the strange quiet and there are just the little sounds we both make in the pale amber light. The kneeler creaks when I lift one knee and I can hear him exhale and his breath gives a tiny whistle at the end.

'Go on,' he says eventually.

And then Helen in the maroon school uniform comes to my aid.

'Bless me father for I have sinned. It is fifteen years since my last confession. This week I told two lies, I quarrelled with my sister and I have been disrespectful towards my elders,' and the sins are made up and scampering like mice and the young Helen just herds them in.

'Do you go to mass on Sundays?' he asks suddenly, and I'm taken by surprise as I didn't realize that this was a two-way thing.

'You must make every effort to go to mass on Sundays,' he says then, before I can say anything, 'and to make a good confession once a year.' And there it is again, 'The Good Confession', and I would like to ask for a second attempt.

There is silence then because I am thinking about the cold weather and the hot pizza and red wine we will be having later on.

'Are you in agreement with me?' he asks, and there is another silence.

'Sorry?' and I clear my throat awkwardly.

'That you will attend mass and — '

'Oh, yes, yes, absolutely, yes.'

He absolves me and his annoyance is warm and glowing behind the grille.

'Come around here, please,' he says suddenly, and I step out and walk around to his door and step up as if I am buying tickets at a booth.

'This is the act of contrition,' he says, and he holds the leaflet open for me and continues to watch my face.

'And this is about how to make a good confession,' and the tips of his fingers skim the opposite page. His eyes are turquoise blue and he sees right through me. He is bored and disappointed by my low-impact confession after all these years.

His skin is smooth and young, and when I turn to look again he gives a long gasping yawn into his bible and this is to remind me that he is human too.

Rue waits at the church door with both hands clasped in front. She has become a professional tourist here with a money belt and a camera and a white hat with Madeira written on the side.

'What penance did you get?' I ask her.

'An Our Father, a Hail Mary, and a Glory Be,' she says, and her chin is up good and high.

'I got three of everything,' I tell her, and my voice sounds serious and worried.

'Oh, he must have thought you were a right heathen,' she says, and she dips her fingers in holy water and shakes them at me.

At the Spanish Steps she tries to take a photograph of a gladiator and he sees her and turns and walks away.

'I think you're supposed to pay him,' I tell her, but she sneaks around and tries to catch him with the camera again. He sees her reflection in a nearby shop window and dodges her easily.

'You'd think he knew,' she says, and she goes after him with the camera again.

'What is the purpose of these?' she asks then, looking up at the steps.

And I try to explain that people like to sit on them and just watch other people and she listens carefully, but her eyes don't see it as I do.

'It's just to be in with the crowd then,' she says, and when I ask her if she wants to climb to the top she says, 'No.'

★ ★ ★

Over dinner we talk about Jim. I tell her that once when I was late for a date he went to mass to pass the time.

'Well, he sounds like a very good man,' she says, 'there is no badness in him at all,' and I want to tell her that she has just described our problem.

'He kept saying, thank you kindly,' I tell her, and sometimes he just said, 'thanks kindly', and I really want her to appreciate the trouble I was having with him.

'Do you want me to cut up that pizza for you?' she asks.

Later when we drink our espressos Rue tells me that she can die happy. 'This is the trip of a lifetime for me, you know,' and she looks girlish and shy and happy with everything she sees.

★ ★ ★

We walk for an hour to find the Trevi fountain. We turn the last corner and I just step back and watch her face with a smile.

'What's this?' she asks, and then, 'Oh, yes, I see,' when I tell her. She stands with her back to the water and watches the people staring in. We stand together for the photograph and

210

we would like to put our arms around each other but we can't. She takes a coin from her purse to make a wish.

'That means you'll come back,' I tell her. 'This is my third time here.'

'Time to stop wishing,' she says. Her lack of interest is marked and she climbs the steps quickly to get away.

'Where are we going now?' she asks.

★   ★   ★

We are different people in Rome and she follows me everywhere and sometimes like now she is disappointed with what we find. We sit at a fountain near the Pantheon and she takes her guidebook out to read. She tells me the circumference of the dome and I watch the couples walking by hand in hand. She loves the Pantheon. She leaves me sitting there and she walks towards it to get a closer look. Then she comes back and describes everything she could see through a crack in the door.

We drink wine and pretend that we are not cold sitting outside. She notices everything and remarks on it and I see now that she talks out the thoughts I keep inside. The friendly waiter. The little boy with the accordion — and his mother who waits on the corner with a buggy when he begs. She asks me if I will call Beth and tell her that we are having our dinner in Rome. I call Beth and tell her, 'She made me go to confession,' and she replies, 'Serves you right.'

Rue pushes food towards me. She would like me to eat more. She talks to the people at the next table. She thanks the waiter and tells him that the food is very good. She is friendly and grateful for everything.

★   ★   ★

The house opposite our hotel room has a beautiful balcony. It is red-bricked with a wild yellow creeper beginning to make its way across the floor. Rue sits on the end of her bed and takes off her shoes. When I look at the balcony I think of Romeo and Juliet and I tell her this, but she's not really listening now.

'These shoes,' she says, and she holds one up to me. 'They're the best shoes I ever bought. They're like gloves and there's a good thick sole to keep you up out of the wet.'

She turns on the TV and sits watching it, happy and lost in a place of her own.

★   ★   ★

She wakes me by turning the volume on the TV up. She tells me that it's 7 a.m. and that we are on the back foot today. When I turn over I see that she is fully dressed. 'We're late,' she says and then, 'You'll have plenty of time to sleep when you get home.'

We climb the steep steps at the Coliseum and Rue looks out leaning on the rail.

'So,' she says, 'this is where the animals were kept and all the people sat up here,' and she tries to make it more interesting for herself. After a few minutes she asks if we can leave and I am happy to. We buy a bust of Julius Caesar for Jacob and we take turns at carrying him in a blue plastic bag.

We sit together on a bench high up over the city and from here we can see Il Vittoriano and the Coliseum. I tell her that it is also called the wedding cake and she looks up at it frowning and says, 'Ah, I see,' and we sit there without talking for a while and there is a sudden warmth from the sun.

'They say your life is just a flash in front of you before you die,' she says. 'The nuns in school told us that.'

When we turn and face the traffic we sit on the bench and look at the chariots on top of Il Vittoriano. The traffic spins around the bend and we are quiet and peaceful and high up over this chaotic city, and in my mind I am afraid of what will happen when she dies. Sitting here on this warm bench with my mother beside me, is my favourite time in Rome.

On Sunday morning we visit St Peter's and the guide tells us the height of each letter inside the dome.

'They did this to show us how small we are in relation to God,' he says, and he has broken English and his sentences have a cockney upswing at the end. Then he shows us the statue of St Peter and after years of kissing and stroking the tourists have flattened his feet.

'All this,' Rue says, and I can see that she has been thinking quietly all the time 'all this nonsense' and she dismisses it with her hand. 'They need to come down from the clouds, down to our level and stop all this.' When the procession of priests passes through they lift the red ropes and the crowd rushes forward. It is like the start of the London city marathon and we look at each other and walk slowly behind. 'There is nothing reverential about this,' she says.

The security man stops the American woman as she walks into the small side chapel.

'This is for praying only,' he says firmly, and he is looking at the video camera in her hand. She puts it into her bag and barges ahead. 'I wanna pray,' she says.

At Piazza Navona we order an early lunch to shelter from the rain. We stay under the canopy and then we buy umbrellas and she tries to make me wear her see-through plastic coat. When we walk the rain splashes my legs. We get as far as the end of the square and then we shelter in a damp archway. There is an open courtyard behind us and the rain looks as if it is falling indoors. A statue stands dripping in the middle, looking up to the sky, its white eyes searching for a break in the clouds.

★　★　★

When we get home we are ourselves again. She walks briskly around the house and exclaims at all the things that have happened during our time away. 'Something has eaten all the leaves off the redcurrant bush,' she says. 'And the grass needs to be cut.' She hands Jacob the Julius Caesar bust and he is really pleased with it.

'I like these men,' he says, and he puts it in the middle of the table so he can see it at a distance. I ask him if he knows who it is and he says, 'Cicero, or young Julius Caesar, or Pompey . . . one of those fellas.'

'It's a very quiet house when you're gone,' he says then, and Rue discovers a half-eaten shepherd's pie on the hall table. The eggs have been collected and they are stacked high in the bowl.

★　★　★

The college feels different without Bob. I go to work every day and give my lectures and tutorials and then I meet Simone or Kate for lunch. I stay busy reading and marking essays and I try not to remember what it was like when Bob was here. But when I find myself in a classroom like now, just after the last student has left and taken all sense of life with them, I miss knowing that down the corridor there was the light from his reading lamp and him.

'The loneliness of an empty classroom,' that was what he said, and I know now what he meant. At this time of the day I would walk to his office and wander in for a chat. Now I walk the long way round because I don't like to pass his door. In my office I look out over the campus and whisper, 'No snow today,' into the glass and then I write two names with my finger, 'Bob' and then 'Jim'.

★　★　★

At the end of our first date Joshua summarizes. He puts his hands down like bookends on the table and he begins.

'So . . . I would just like to say I have had a very enjoyable evening. I thought the food was excellent. I know you were not entirely happy with your choice, but I enjoyed it very much. I think you are a very intelligent and very attractive girl — and just for clarity — I would like to see you again.' He drives the last point home with a digger and I can feel my lifeblood begin to drip.

He loves to cook. He tells me that his favourite dish is duck lasagne. I ask him if he's sure two pages of his cookbook aren't stuck together. Drip.

When the bill arrives he looks at it as if it is a disease.

He asks if we can split it and I can feel the words rattle inside.

Then I pay more than my share because I am too embarrassed to think.

I don't know if I should ask him to come home with me or not and the waiter's eyes tell me what I already know.

He gets all formal and says, 'May we go to your bed,' and when he puts his feet up he leaves the track of his boots on my new cream couch. In the morning he tries to make love to me, but I am already hating us both by then.

He brings me toasted cornbread and says, 'Helen is a very different person today.'

★   ★   ★

'What does he do for a crust?' Judith asks.
   'He imports wine,' I tell her.
   'Oh,' she says, 'then what?'
   'Then he drinks it,' I say.

★   ★   ★

Lynas has written a note at the end of his essay.
   'Would you like to go for a drink?' he asks, and he has drawn a smiley face. I write, 'No thanks!' with a sad face beside it, and then I cross it out and write, 'OK'.

★   ★   ★

They live in a red-bricked house with a yellow door and a silver BMW parked in the drive. There is a Christmas tree standing in the front window and the white lights flash on and off and reflect against the polished wooden floor. There are no party sounds and I am wondering if I smell of the beer I drank last night.
   'Here she is,' John announces as he opens

the door, and then Lucy comes running down the hall and puts her arms around me.

'It's so good to see you, Helen,' and there are real tears in her eyes and there is a smell of pine needles and cloves in the hall. There are no party sounds and when I look into the first room there are some men and women sitting and standing near a log fire and there are also a number of babies swimming around the floor. When the conversation stops everyone just stares down at the babies.

'This is all very casual,' John says, and when he speaks he sounds uptight and strange. He is wearing a new V-neck jumper and soft navy walking shoes. 'It's just drop in as you like and then drop out when you need to.'

When I see their idea of a party I am close to saying, 'Drop dead,' but I don't.

I would like to tell them that I spent the previous night with an English tutor called Tom Ryder. That he sat on my sofa and drank tea. That we talked about couples we know, and how I told him I would be going for drinks here tonight.

'Oh, really,' he said, like he was interested.

'They're a great couple,' I told him. 'He's a good guy . . . very generous, and kind and solid, you know . . . He wouldn't cheat on her or anything like that.' Then I wished I hadn't said that because I was hoping that he would cheat on his girlfriend and be with me.

'Here's himself,' Lucy says, and when I look there is another bald baby waving at me from the sofa.

'He likes the ladies,' she says, and she sounds like she is in a dream. 'Oh, he likes the ladies, yes, he does . . . yes, you do, you do . . . you like the ladies,' and I am beginning to think she needs some sort of help. There is a hardback chair now and I am put sitting on it and I can feel myself moving into the centre of the room.

'This is Paul,' her husband announces.

'Helen, Paul, Paul, Helen,' and we smile weakly at each other as people who are being set up do. Paul is wearing the kind of bobcats I wore in school. He selects a baby and begins to give him what looks like an Indian head massage and this is to show me how good with children he is.

'I have a five-year-old,' he says to the mother beside him, and they get into a detailed discussion about changing nappies. 'A boy,' he says, and they move their chairs a little closer and laugh knowingly.

And the woman says, 'So you've had the fountains?'

And he says, 'Oh, yes, the fountains.'

And I'm thinking, 'Oh, goodnight.'

When I look up I see Raymond and Claire coming through the door with Judith, and I excuse myself and step over the babies and across the floor.

'Hey,' I whisper to her, and her eyes are scanning the room.

'OK,' she says calmly, 'this is some kind of hell.'

Raymond is a small man with a round mop of blond curly hair and a striped scarf tied in a knot under his chin. He looks tired and he is talking a lot.

Claire is taller than him with long black hair and sleepy blue eyes. She is wearing blue cowboy boots and a black trilby and she stands on one foot and then the other. When she starts to speak, Raymond looks up at her as if every word is a new invention. He looks really pleased to be with her and a little scared as well.

'Did Raymond tell you about my birthday?' she asks.

When she speaks she moves her mouth and the rest of her face is perfectly still. She begins to tell us all about it. I still haven't been introduced to her and it's just like she's reading the news.

'We stayed in the Shelbourne,' she says, and Raymond gives a sudden grin. 'In the best suite,' and Raymond gives another big grin, and this time it is so big it makes his head shake a little.

'Aren't you bold?' Judith says to him, and she even shakes her finger. We are starting to get very drunk. Judith is leaning too far forward and Claire, by the way, is still reading the news.

'First of all we had a special breakfast,' and I realize now that this is going to take a little while.

'Oh,' we say, and we are both nodding and swaying.

'Real porridge . . . and strawberries . . . and . . . flowers were delivered to the room.'

'Ah!!' we say, and at this point Raymond does a little dance. It is as if he has scored a point or a bell has rung, and he is just so pleased that he makes four little steps in a square on the floor.

'There were helium balloons tied to the bedpost.'

'Wow.'

'Then we went to my favourite movie, *Breakfast at Tiffany's*.'

'Did you have your breakfast at Tiffany's?' Judith asks, and she is speaking really loudly.

'Then we went shopping and we went into this shop — Travanterino — do you know it? They have all these designer bags and I tried one — it was very expensive, five hundred pounds, so I put it back.'

Raymond is warming up for another dance.

'Did you have your breakfast at Tiffany's?' Judith asks again, and I can tell she doesn't care about anything at all now, and Claire is just ignoring her. Instead she turns to me.

'My feet are killing me,' she says. 'I put on my sister's boots by mistake when I was coming out.'

'Oh, really,' I reply, and we still haven't been introduced.

'We went back to the hotel.' She is still going and each word was being pushed out really carefully like it matters.

'There were lilies on the bed . . . and under them . . . the bag.'

'No!' we all say together, and Raymond is doing his little dance again.

She opens her bag so we can read the label inside.

Judith leans forward again and she might fall into it.

'Wow,' we say, and then Judith says, 'I can't read that, it's too small.'

The baby who likes the ladies is crying now, and I can see that Paul is delving into the finger snacks.

'These are great,' he says and he offers me the bowl.

'Thanks, what are they?'

'Some kind of nutty things,' he says, and he sucks each finger noisily in turn. He rolls his eyes up and down my body when he thinks I don't see.

Later Lucy tells us that she wants to get drunk. We stand in the cold at her gate and I really want to get into the cab, but she's not letting me.

'I just want one of those nights when we start with cocktails and then have wine and then more cocktails — I want to be scraped up off that garden path,' she says, hugging herself against the cold.

'Leave it to me,' I say, 'I'll organize it,' and I won't because single people don't drink all the time in spite of what couples think.

On the way home I talk to Judith about Raymond and Claire.

'He's actually an OK guy,' I tell her, and, 'She's fine too, a bit dim but fine, you know . . . but put them together and you have some kind of nightmare.'

Judith says nothing because she is thinking, and then she leans over and talks right into my ear.

'The trouble with him is . . . he's got no balls,' she says, and then she looks around the cab like she has said nothing at all.

★ ★ ★

The English students are talking about love. They are breathless and excited now and for once they have something real to say. We move happily off the beaten track and I pull them back and then I let them go again.

'There's no such thing as love,' one student says. 'It's a chemical imbalance that occurs in the brain.'

'Mr Yarimoto? Have you any thoughts?'

And he shuffles his notes and stands up and then steps out of his place.

I like this little Japanese man with his neat dark suit and his tidy smile. I like to ruffle his perfect feathers and pluck one or two from his tail.

'I'm not so sure about this,' he says.

'Mr Yari-mo-to . . . have you ever been in love?'

'Oh!' he says, and there is silence, and he thinks a little and then he goes, 'Haw, haw, haw,' and gives the very best answer he can.

★   ★   ★

Lynas lives in a yellow Georgian house on Mount Pleasant Avenue. The garden is overgrown and there are two rusty bicycles chained together against the wall. We walk in through the hall and he puts the lights on. It is a long narrow house painted cream inside with brown carpet on the floor.

'Anyone home?' he calls. He drops our coats over the banister and we walk down three steps into the kitchen. There is a small butch girl sitting there in the dark and she waves at us as we come in and says, 'Hey.'

'This is Tara,' he says. 'One of my flatmates.'

'Hey,' she says again, and she gets up and stirs a saucepan on the stove.

'What are you making?' he asks.

'Mushroom soup,' and they glance quickly at each other and Lynas turns bright red and gives a little laugh.

'Where did you get them?'

'Golf course in Howth.'

'Jesus,' he says, and then he turns to me.

I have been pouring my heart out to him all night about Jim.

'Just what the doctor ordered,' he says.

The soup has a fusty taste and I drink it and feel nothing and then we light candles and sit in the sitting room. It is raining outside and we just sit there side by side and look into the fire. There are cars going up and down outside and every sound becomes louder and more musical then.

'The last time I had mushrooms,' he says, 'I went into a pub and I thought everyone was on crutches.'

'These things never have any effect on me,' I tell him, and I look back into the fire again.

When he asks me if I would like to go upstairs I say nothing and I haven't spoken for a long time now. I follow him then and he leads me into the bathroom at the top of the stairs and closes the door.

It is an old house and the tub is big and old-fashioned and I watch as he turns both taps on. They make a squeaky sound and then gurgle and splash down into the old white tub. The mirror steams up and outside there are drunks shouting and singing Christmas carols. He lights five candles and I am just watching, dumb to this young man who is smiling wickedly at me and taking off his clothes. We have both stopped talking now and when he steps into the water his shadow crouches down over us on the wall. His skin is white and shiny against the pale green tiles and there are drops coming from the taps making a plink-plink sound. I get undressed too and then step in and we face each other. He bends his knees and pulls me towards him and taking my arms he begins to wash them carefully one at a time, and then he circles my shoulders with soap and curls his fingers around my back.

He lifts my feet and massages them slowly with soap and then puts them back down into the water again. He lifts a jug and when I turn around he pours it down over my head and begins to shampoo my hair. He leans in and in the middle of the steam and splashing water, he caresses and then kisses my cheek. I stay there in his arms until the water begins to grow cold and when there is no more hot water left I step out and he follows me and we share the same rough white towel. We get dressed quietly and he lets the water out. I put on my hat over my still wet hair and he walks me to the door and waits until my taxi comes.

'You should call him,' he says then.

'Jim?'

'Yes,' and he gives a little laugh, 'Jim,' and he waves as I get into the taxi and go home.

★   ★   ★

'You did what?' Simone asks and Judith is leaning in so she can hear.

'I had a bath with one of my students.'

'Oh my God,' and Simone's voice is low.

'It wasn't sexual.'

'What was it?'

'I don't know. We had some mushrooms . . . have you ever had mushrooms?'

'I don't need to hear any more,' Simone says, and Judith is laughing behind her hands.

'Lynas Monroe is nineteen,' she says. 'Oh, Helen, you'll be arrested.'

'It was really nice. It was innocent. He helped me with Jim.'

And Simone is shaking her head and looking away.

I wait a few minutes before I ask my question.

'Did you know . . . ?'

'Know what . . . ?'

'That when a man takes a bath . . . it . . . his . . . '

'Yes, I know,' Simone says, and she is trying not to laugh now. 'It floats.'

★ ★ ★

Jim writes to me and says that he is sorry to hear about Bob. He has made the card himself, as he always does, and it's navy and cream. His writing is beautiful, like I remember it, and he signs with the 'X' in front of his name as if the kiss is more important than him.

★ ★ ★

'I love my girlfriend,' he says, and an hour later we're kissing.

There is a long hotel corridor and every

door is the same and we have stolen away and left the world behind. It is quiet here away from the noise of the Christmas party and there is only us now. The man is dressed in an astronaut suit and I am Groucho Marx. He is worried because he is sweating under his suit.

'I smell like I ran the marathon,' he says.

When we get into the lift I stand behind him and adjust the aerial on his radio pack up and down.

'Is this off your TV?' I ask.

'Yes,' he says, and his voice is deep and serious. 'I sacrificed my portable to the cause.' The lift stops and two girls get in and they are wearing the same tight, striped polo necks. One of them has her hands in her pockets and she is crying quietly and looking down into the floor.

'She's just had her bag stolen,' her friend says, as if we have asked what the trouble is, but we are already too caught up with ourselves.

She puts her arms around her friend and hugs her for a long time.

'She had her life in that bag,' she says, and over her friend's shoulders her eyes are calm and insincere.

When the doors open the astronaut stands back and counts us out one by one. He is well mannered and he makes a point of showing me how polite he can be.

He has been paying me compliments all night and everything he says sounds like it is being read from a card.

He has painted his Wellingtons white and his helmet is made from a flip-top kitchen bin.

'You're a very attractive woman,' he says, and I still have my moustache on.

His shirt is all wet and stuck to his skin and I watch how he bends his back when he pulls it off over his head. He showers and wears one of my T-shirts and we talk and talk until we are both nearly dead. When he kisses me again it's no good, like wood, and I am worried that rigor mortis may have set in.

'It's no good if you talk too much,' Judith says.

And I tell her, 'I know,' and in my head I'm kissing a tree.

⋆　⋆　⋆

When the man comes to fix my heating he is red-faced and out of breath and sorry because he is so late. He tells me that I need to replace a switch and then he opens it out on the table to show how the wires don't connect. His eyes are dark and round and then I look right into them, just to see what

231

will happen and I can see that I nearly scare him half to death.

★ ★ ★

Last night I had that dream. The same white beach, the same grey sea and my father's slow easy step. Now that Jim is gone I feel cold and lonely inside. I am afraid to go out in case we meet, because I can't bear the stale feelings we will have, the dead faces, the need to be overly polite. I have never understood the need to end. Real time spent together, doing small things, like a crossword, or how he called me from his office to make sure I was up or the time he gave me his white handkerchief, and then suddenly nothing at all. Jim built a fence around me. He opened his long coat and locked me inside. I don't love him on a grand scale, but I need him, and maybe that's a better fighter than love.

★ ★ ★

Lynas comes in and sits at my desk. He is wearing a new brown leather jacket and a red scarf tied in a loose knot across his chest. He watches me for a moment and he doesn't say anything.

'There's something I want to tell you,' he

says, and he is blushing now.

'OK,' I say, and I wait as he tries to find his words. Then he tears a corner from his foolscap pad and scribbles something and makes a tiny folded note.

He pushes it across the desk and then he gets up to leave.

'I'm gay,' the note says.

'OK,' I tell him again, and then he tells me I am the first person he has ever told.

'The thing is . . . ' he says slowly, 'it's really hard for me to meet someone. I mean, the chances are just slimmer you know . . . and you . . . well . . . you've found someone really special. Why would you let him slip away?'

★　★　★

The Shelbourne bar is a place to drink and swim in. We are all bobbing around the old ship and not fully sure when we will start to go down. The men are older and sleeker here and someone else has had the job of whipping them into shape. Their eyes are always watching, always looking, always hoping, because every old wreck deserves chemistry and love.

'It beats meeting people at the laundrette,' Noël tells us, and he is older than all of us together.

'I'm sure the people are more discerning here . . . ' begins Simone.

And he interrupts her right away.

'It's all about chemistry,' he says, and this is announced to us as if he has discovered something that we don't already know.

'One look and you know . . . chemistry,' he says.

'Do you find me attractive?' he asks then, and we pretend not to hear.

'That was quite direct,' Simone tells him, 'and also quite likely to make you less attractive.'

When we talk I can feel his eyes on us and when he breathes his breath has a stale Guinness smell.

Later he walks through the bar carrying a small round leather stool. He has found someone who has not objected to him and he's all business now and he moves quickly and is careful not to bump the stool against anyone as he goes.

'Do I look that old?' I ask her, and I need a good answer.

'No,' she says, 'you're just fresh meat.'

In the toilets there are girls in black dresses and clunky sandals. They have short old-fashioned haircuts and earrings that jangle from their ears. There is a bank function going on in the ballroom and they are out now and fluttering around the mirrors and checking their hair.

'What are those for?' one of them asks me, and she points to the stack of hand towels beside the sink.

'For drying your hands,' I tell her, and I'm careful not to express anything at all with my eyes. There is a woman arguing with her boyfriend on the phone in the hallway. She sits on an armchair in the corner and speaks loudly, feeling that she is safe with the other women here.

'I'm disappointed in you, Jeremy,' she says, 'there is no reason why you can't leave . . . why can't you just say, 'Folks, I've had enough,' and then just leave . . . just leave, Jeremy, just move yourself and leave . . . I am so disappointed in you, Jeremy.'

She keeps it going on and on, and I can tell he's not listening or moving anywhere.

At the bar there is a man wearing a long dark coat and Simone tells me that he's just her type.

'I think he might be married,' I tell her.

'Maybe he's not,' she says, 'he might like wearing a ring.'

She has decided not to go for good-looking men again and she says it is all about personality now.

'Don't mess with the baldies,' I tell her as

two bald men walk in.

'They're a right pair of tadpoles,' she says, and she looks away.

Noel is taking a sad tired woman across the room by the hand. I can see it all now, in her neat court shoes and brown trouser suit, the children tucked up in bed, the husband who left, the tired, fed-up need for someone else's warmth at night.

'He's making her wait,' Judith says then, and I see that he has left her standing behind him as he talks to two women at the bar. They are in their fifties with white blonde hair and hot pink tops with low necks to show off their flat hanging boobs. He leans in close so he can talk and he is practically balancing on one foot to get his face right in. They are the honey-pots of the bar tonight. And all the time the lady in brown hangs back and watches the floor, and we feel for her, and I would like to draw her into our group, and tell her it's OK to be on her own. Outside the rain is bouncing off the tarmac and I would do anything to run out into it and take her with me.

Noel turns and shrugs and pulls a face and then turns back and talks some more. In one look he has told her that he is a man with options and that she is lucky to be standing there.

The door opens and first I see the sleeve of a trench coat and then I see Jim.

'Just play it cool,' Judith says, but I've never been any good at that.

'Do whatever you feel is right,' says Simone, but I'm not really listening. I'm drinking faster than before and looking at Noel and the two whores at the bar. It is like walking across the playground then and just when he sees me one of my students shouts my name and taps me on the shoulder. Jim is standing near the bar with his sister Kate.

'Hey, hey,' the voice says, and when I turn I see Lynas, and there is something about this boy that always means good luck.

I smile at him and listen to him and all the time my eyes are trying to watch Jim at the bar.

'Go for it, Helen,' Lynas says, and then he glances at Jim. 'I would.'

Jim is leaning on one elbow talking and when he sees me he stops in mid-sentence and then gives me a sad sort of grin.

'Hi.'

'Hello,' he says, and it is said in a voice that means, 'I know you too well.' 'How's it going?'

'Fine . . . fine . . . and you?'

'Oh, fine, you know . . . fine.' And then he says, 'You remember Kate?' and she smiles warmly at me.

There is a silence and he keeps this leaning thing going and he's not really doing a thing to help. Kate glances at me and him and she excuses herself and walks to the ladies.

' . . . Jim . . . '

And he just raises his eyebrows.

'I know we're taking a break, but . . . ' and I'm swallowing hard and trying not to plead.

'I know I've been a bit, well, you know . . . but . . . ' and that's as far as I can get.

But he just frowns at me and there's that look again.

It says, 'I know you. I remember you. You're a little insane.'

Then he looks right at me and asks me what I mean, and there is a heavy sort of silence as I try to pick the right words.

'Try saying it, Helen,' he says, and it's as if he is coaxing the words out.

'I miss you, Jim,' and he answers with a soft grown-up smile.

In the mirror I can see Noel is ready to go home now and he leads the woman in brown through the door.

'How about we get a coffee somewhere?' Jim asks, and then he looks around for Kate, but she had taken her bag and gone home.

* * *

The window bangs shut in the middle of the night. The sound of the traffic is dulled and there is just silence and the warmth of Jim. When I look at the clock it says 4.46 a.m. I lie still without moving, because I don't want to disturb his sleep. Blondie gets up and walks from the kitchen area. She sits looking at me because day and night don't really mean a thing for dogs. At 6 a.m. the radio comes on and I listen to the news and the weather forecast. 'Rain and wind,' he says, 'and by Wednesday, there will be gales.'

'Here's a blast from the past,' the DJ says, and he tells us that the Submarines have released a song, and there it is, that voice that can still snap me back in time.

Lately I have been thinking about how it was between us. How he held me against the fridge in his kitchen late on an autumn afternoon. How he had made me say what I was thinking and how I was laughing out loud.

'OK,' I said then, 'I was thinking . . . I kind of love you.'

And his dark eyes looked into mine and they had already seen too much for a young kind of guy. 'I was thinking I kind of love you too.'

His voice is beside me now in this red bed and Jim is turning over in his sleep.

7

Amsterdam

April 1997

Vlad Popinov sits on the steps outside his front door. It is a warm evening in April and the light over the water seems green and grey. The barges drift by slowly, each one on a secret journey, moving easily on silent creeping feet. He opens an orange between his thumbs and then stops, looking first at the canal and then at his dog. As we cross the first bridge on Herengracht, Pop is a beacon for us. With his blue shirt and the orange and the black glossy spaniel, they look so good waiting there.

He stands then and smiles and smooths down his shirt and walks towards us.

'Well, hello,' he says, and hugs me to him and he kisses my hand.

'Nice ring,' he says with a big bright smile, and he holds my hand high to see if it will sparkle in the air.

Pop smells like fresh splashing water and oranges and ice knocking off the edges of the glass and we take a moment to look around then, as there is suddenly too much to say. There is a worn-out houseboat shored near us with a plastic doll and a broken red bicycle lying on the deck. They have all been abandoned and, like the rest of us, could use some love and some paint.

They have brought me to Amsterdam to say their goodbyes. I found them at the airport standing sheepishly in a row: Birdie, Judith and Simone.

'Surprise . . . ' said Judith doubtfully.

'It's a wedding not a funeral,' I said, and I was laughing out loud, but even I could hear the slow drum begin to beat. 'Red Rover Red Rover Send Helen Wilton over,' and they are like little girls now — holding hands together, stopping me, turning me, loving me — and still hurrying me away and up the aisle.

The stairs in Pop's house are steep like a ladder and we follow his flip-flops upwards until we reach the top.

'This is our kitchen,' he says, and it is a comfortable room with old-fashioned white painted cabinets and red-and-white napkins and pictures of Pop baking bread on the wall.

Our room is at the top of a narrow spiral stairs. The door is only four feet high so we must bend down and then come back up again when we are inside. There is a short narrow corridor that runs from the bedroom to the sitting room and the tongue and groove roof is painted cream and stretches into a low narrow point. There are two big windows that open out over the street and already we can see the people who live on the other side. They have two orange couches and the wooden floorboards are painted grey.

It is a small room and we are already apologizing and standing back to let each other by.

Pop stands there quietly with us, watching as we settle in and his turned-out feet say three o'clock to the floor.

'Now,' he says, and his hands open slowly like a flower.

'This is your own little kitchen,' and he points out the fridge and the microwave and the Typhoo tea. Then he closes the windows and turns on the fan.

'You will need to watch out for mosquitoes,' he says. 'The canals bring them in.'

There are no edges to Pop. His skin is tanned and shiny and his eyes are clear and very blue. He has a fresh new health about him, a bounce, a vitality, and still he's quieter than I remember and someone must love him here in Amsterdam.

There are footsteps on the stairs then and a young man with icecream blond hair comes in with our bags. He is breathing heavily through his nose and he is red-faced when he drops them on the floor.

'This is Peter,' Pop says, offering him to us

and then standing back in silence when we shake his hand. His skin is moist and I can feel the hot curl of my suitcase handle still locked in his fingers. He is reluctant and almost polite and his face is disgusted from running up and down the spiral stairs.

★ ★ ★

We ask if we can have more towels and the Icecream hands one to Birdie and she looks at him, waiting with a smile.

'Listen, sweetie,' he says, 'this one's big enough to dry you and your girlfriend as well.'

Pop stands in the background where he doesn't belong. His hair is silver at the temples now and his dark framed glasses give him a groovy professor look. He was so smart in college and I'm wondering when the Icecream managed to get the upper hand.

We come down the spiral stairs like four old ladies and he is waiting for us. His white hair shiny and flipped up into a little cone. He stands with a cheeky smile on his face.

'Clip-clop clip-clop,' he says. 'In a few days you'll be skipping down these stairs like lambs.'

★ ★ ★

After dinner we take a walk through the neighbourhood and then Birdie opens the door of a coffee house and we quietly file in.

Smoky Joe's Rastafarian hair is pulled back into a fat ponytail and he watches us with a half smile on his face. He says nothing as we look at the menu, and really we are just looking for words that seem human and nice.

'You smoke before?' he asks, and he is trying to hurry us along.

'Sure,' says Judith, 'it's just been a while.'

'We'll have two of those and two of those,' she says, and she points them out just like she's picking fruit from a stall. Then she spoils it when she asks, 'Would you recommend these?'

'Sure,' he says politely, and when he smiles he has nice crinkled eyes and he is missing some teeth. He takes a white plastic lunchbox from under the counter and shows us some soft green curls.

'Smoke it myself,' he says.

The room is dark and small and it smells like warm ponies. There are people sitting in a circle in the inside room. Just sitting and smoking, sometimes talking, sometimes just staring at nothing on the wall.

We take the high stools at the bar and order four cups of English tea. When we inhale it is like pulling an old car out of the garage and then driving away in too low a gear. So we move slowly and watch each other smoke.

'We have one hundred and fifty different varieties of tea here,' the girl behind the counter says, and then waits, but we are just looking and then looking away.

When Birdie inhales, she gets off the stool and puts her hand lightly to her neck and then sits on a low bench near the wall. When we leave, the grass is half smoked and we walk outside to get some air. 'Jesus,' says Birdie after a little while, 'I thought I was going to get sick in there.'

⋆ ⋆ ⋆

In the red-light district we see a woman standing in a window. She wears a G-string and behind her there is a pale-pink light. She looks like a vampire, and her skin is dull and grey. She stands with one hand on the glass and someone must be tempted inside so that she can escape. We drink it in, but can feel nothing from it. Our eyes are big and dark and they allow every kind of image inside. The woman turns her head so that her hair falls forward and then turns right around so they can see some more. The men gather in twos and threes, watching and goading each other along. Mostly they laugh and still they keep looking and anyone can see that they are really just scared.

A man on his own drops down the three small steps to the basement door, and after one knock it opens, and he steps inside as if he is home.

★   ★   ★

We ask for beer and peanuts and sit outside a bar and laugh. We start sentences and talk for a long time and then someone goes, 'Hang on . . . what are we talking about here?'

Birdie tells stories about Chicago. They are long and rambling, and it is only when she reaches the end that we realize that it makes no sense at all.

'Oh, well,' she says, and she eats more nuts and then wipes her hands on her jeans. 'That was another one from the archives.'

I would like the world to stop here. With my girlfriends, near a calm, still canal, and stoned. How slowly everything moves around us. How gentle the world is now and with our worries locked safely away. There are three girls at the next table and they gather their coins together. They buy one drink between them and take turns drinking it when they play cards.

We buy Cola bottles and Rolos and Twix and Bounty.

'Did we eat all of those?' Judith asks the next morning, and no one can really remember. When she stands up she bumps her head on the ceiling and she says, 'It's all a bit Alice in Wonderland in here.'

★ ★ ★

Pop gets up at 5 a.m. He lifts the cheese plant and leaves it in another corner and then stands back and looks at it from the other side of the room. He bakes bread and he mends the elbows on the Icecream's cardigan and when I look at him I see someone who is motherly and content.

He hands me a cup of coffee with the handle turned towards me and tells me he is happy with his life.

'This is home now,' he says, and he shrugs at the room around him. His apron is freshly washed and ironed and he rubs the butter and flour together as if he is sowing seeds. The coffee smells good around us, and there are four ripe plums waiting in a bowl. Behind us there is a row of jam pots and I can see how Pop wrote out the labels and then fitted each little cloth cap.

'How did you meet Peter?'

'At a club,' he says simply, and it is quiet then, with everyone still in bed around us and the tall wooden house creaking in its sleep.

He lowers the dough into a baking tin, and then nicks it with a knife. He winks at me when he sees how I watch him and then folds over a tea towel and opens the oven door. He lifts his glasses on to his forehead and looks at the timer and he says, 'Let's see,' under his breath. Then he pours some more coffee and hangs his apron behind the door.

'He has improved,' he says then, and he smiles at me. 'His clothes were dreadful,' and he pulls up a chair.

'Every time we met it was a new theme — as if he was performing in a show,' and he moves his hands like wipers and we are both laughing as he speaks.

'I shouldn't laugh,' he says, and then he becomes serious and he takes my hand.

'It's a lot of work,' he says then, 'but . . . I don't know . . . when I see him . . . first thing in the morning and last thing at night, it reminds me that I'm alive.'

'What if it doesn't work out?' I ask slowly.

'Then I'll find someone else,' and I am too scared to tell him I was talking about myself.

When Peter comes in he looks sleepy and cross.

'I'm going to yoga,' he says, and he pecks Pop on the cheek. He is wearing a navy sailor hat and matching shorts.

When he leaves the room Pop rolls his eyes.

'Seaside Barbie,' he says calmly. 'I need to work on that.'

In the evenings he takes his dog and sits on the steps to eat his dessert. He enjoys the silence and doesn't have to worry about being alone. In the evenings they visit their neighbours who run an Indian restaurant on their street. They drink black coffee and smoke and use the owner's everyday delph. They sit side-by-side facing the street and now and then you can catch them looking at each other and starting to laugh, like any other couple facing out on to the world.

★　★　★

On our second night we go to the Exotine. It is a dark club near the red-light district and Birdie says she has been here before. It is painted black and shaped like a cave and inside the black domed roof is covered in silver stars. There are women dancing to live bands on the stage and pockets of pot here and there in the air.

We stand at the bar and order drinks and I tell Birdie about the Icecream and Pop. 'Really, in a club?' she says, and I say, 'Yes. In a club,' and everything is fine and then the Submarines walk out on to the stage.

Someone says, 'Oh my God,' and I feel as if all eyes in the club are turned on me. I have always hated bumping into ex-boyfriends, but most of them have the decency never to appear on a stage. They usually come creeping out from a corner in Doheny and Nesbitts or the Shelbourne and smile in a way that makes me feel sick.

They start with one of their old songs and I'm just standing there staring, not moving at all and just looking straight ahead.

They are a little faded out now and slightly battered and torn, like men who should be at home talking to their wives or watching the news on TV. Liam is wearing a maroon-coloured shirt and black jeans and when he speaks into the microphone it is the same Northern accent that I heard so often in my room. He sings out the melody and swings the microphone stand around him. He points his index fingers over his head and I can see that he is the same black devil he was before. The audience love it all and he loves them loving him still. He sings a ballad in a tired voice and the guitarists stop playing and we listen to a single beating drum. And when the crowd shouts and claps he jumps off the stage — and moves towards us — with the same defiant face, the same impatient walk and that old familiar grin.

'What are you so mad about?' I want to ask him, my voice miles away and drowned out by the crowd. When he walks towards the bar there are people patting and touching him and I know he would hate that. Then there are those awful hanger-on fans of his. Still the same faceless pointless people caught like cobwebs on his clothes.

He leans on one elbow and asks for a drink and as he waits he looks around. I can feel his eyes begin to buzz around me and suddenly they settle and get quiet like bees. I can feel them before I move, before I turn, and in my head there is a voice that says, 'Get out of here and run and run.'

'Howaya,' he says — not exactly the magic I have dreamt about — and his hands are in his pockets and he's keeping them there. This guy — and everything I remember about him — and now I just say his name. 'Liam.'

And I'm walking right over now and nothing will stop me and I know I'm about to do something very wrong. He's grinning and it's evil and it's as if we're joined together through the pupils of our eyes. The neon sign inside me says 'Go, cat, go' and I just want him all around me now. The way it was between us. Falling softly together into a deep secret sleep.

★ ★ ★

The naked girl in the window eats a sandwich. She eats and reads magazines when she's on a break. She wipes food from the corner of her mouth and turns the page slowly. She licks one finger before she does this and then looks up as someone opens the door. She nods her head and folds her sandwich up in the paper napkin and we are walking and still watching when two hands pull the curtains closed.

★ ★ ★

He stands at the window in this grey hotel room and when I sit up he gives me the only smile he has. We have built this place together now and we have worried each other right through the night. It is a room with no name, dull with pictures of nothing, and dumb things like sewing kits and shoe buffers and small squares of soap near the sink.

He lifts the tulle curtain like he is lifting hair back from his face. He wears his black

255

trousers and his chest is bare, and I like his mannish underarm hair and I like that he is oblivious to it. He is thinner now. His stomach hollows in and his shoulders are still the same pale smooth rounds and even now I would like to touch him there. There are men who are at their most beautiful when they stop noticing, like this one, who daydreams and forgets.

'How do you like this place?' he asks, and he comes and sits on the bed, and I can feel it move somewhere near my feet. He still has his hair, all of it, which is good because it would have killed him to go bald.

It is a room with a high ceiling and I feel tired now and sink back into bed. The stiff white hotel sheet feels tight under my arms and I lie there feeling slightly dizzy and weak. He walks to the dressing table and picks up a pen and taps it on the wood. The wallpaper has thick green flowers all over it and there is a standard lamp with a wide magnolia shade. Somewhere there is a service lift that goes 'ping' and when a toilet flushes nearby it sounds like water running down the walls.

He is trying to say something and I would like him to stop.

He hums a song when he looks in the mirror and now and then half a word comes through. He looks out at the canals again and the hooped bridges and the people floating past on high black bicycles and I can see he can't get his head around Amsterdam.

'I like that song,' I tell him, and he smiles and walks slowly towards me again.

It was easier in the dark.

'I thought about you when I wrote it,' and then he looks down at the grey carpet.

'Do you know it's spelt sub-marins by the way?'

'Yeah, I knew that . . . so, why are you breaking up?'

'Because we're not able to spell.'

He tells me they are touring the UK the following week.

'What about the States?'

'Certainly, send money, please.'

And I miss all of this you know.

The unexplained meaning of 'Us' — just how we are together — and then there is Jim who leaves none of our feelings to chance. With me and Liam that's all there ever was, a chance, a risk — flying through the air without a net.

There is a new sadness between us now and I think it's just us feeling slightly older. Knowing that it's too late to start over, knowing that we missed the chance.

'I could never find the right words for you, Helen.'

And he looks at me frowning while his left hand finds his pack of cigarettes.

'I'd like to try,' he says quietly.

'I think I've found a new line for that song,' I tell him, and he leans in and starts to kiss me on the mouth.

And in my head I'm thinking, 'No, you wouldn't, baby, and I don't like you when you try.'

★   ★   ★

I am nearly grown up at twenty-eight and when I look in the mirror of this hotel bathroom I write out my name in steam.

'Helen Wilton.' Engaged to Jim.

'Hélène Fournier.' Wanderer and unclean.

So Jim loves me more than I love him. I love Liam, but I know, especially now, that he will never settle down. And there it is. The kind of thing that makes you look up through the sky and say, 'Thanks a bunch, God.'

I know that it's OK to take a piece of someone else. I know that's it's OK for no one else to know. And so I carry my Submarine with me. My hidden weapon against down and dull dead love. He gives me life because he is just a boy who still knows nothing about the world. When I sit up I wrap my arms around my knees and he curls his index finger and runs the curl softly down my back. We have love. The bad kind. The kind that makes you feel so charged up and full of fire, so alive, alive, alive. We have always had that for each other and today is my last chance to live.

When we make love we sit in the middle of our double bed, and my legs are wrapped around his waist. The bed moves in silence, and there is just us, only us, and the sounds we make when we try to swallow each other's breath and in a little while it becomes blurred again, who we are and what we are doing and we can forget about the light. Sex is all there is between us now and really for me it's enough. It makes me remember who I am, it makes me forget what I have. There are so many reasons to do it, to have it, and so few of them have anything to do with love.

★   ★   ★

The pale-pink light is turned off now and the naked girls are at home. The cleaning ladies come in, talking briskly to each other and running their hoovers over and back across the floor. They lift the lamps off the bedside tables and polish in one circle with their cloths. It's just another room really and it's normal too, now that they've cleaned up a bit, and opened up the windows for some air.

⋆   ⋆   ⋆

We are lying side by side now. I know if I cry the tears will run back off my face, wetting my hair and filling my ears. I know this because the last time I cried in this position I was back with him. He has always worked me over in this way and there is no point in crying even though I know I will never see him again. So we talk. As if we are two normal people and it all feels like we're trapped inside a Leonard Cohen song. Even now I can feel he has taken some lifeblood from me. Even now I know he is thinking about being somewhere else.

'What's with all the anger?' I ask him, and he knows straight away what I mean. He puts his hands behind his head and talks easily to me like I'm his best friend.

'Oh, you know, us Northern men, living under siege.'

'You don't mean that,' and my voice is quiet.

'Nah, well, when we have peace no one knows what to do. Belfast in peace . . . is a right old hole.'

He says nothing for a while and then sighs

long and loud out through his nose.

'The Troubles make us something. In a strange way they lift us up. People are interested when they hear you're from Belfast, when there's peace there's nothing to say.'

He gets up on one elbow and flips open his cigarette pack. He can do this and put the cigarette between his lips all with one hand. The lighter wheel is reluctant. Small metal wheels scraping and then suddenly a spark. I wish I smoked now. I can see all the things it gives him to do. He picks up an ashtray and turns it over in his hand and then pretends to look at a picture on the wall. When he lies flat again he holds the cigarette up high in one hand. There is something about him, about us, that leaves me feeling like I have lived all my life in one night. I watch as his eyes follow the smoke and he is thinking about the Troubles and I have never loved him as much as I love him now.

'Ah, yes,' he says quietly, as if he is talking to himself, and then he turns around to face me. 'Give me back my lovely war.'

★   ★   ★

Birdie finds me on a bench near Anne Frank's house. We talk and smile sadly at each other and I tell her about the kind of trouble I am in. She listens like she is tired and when I stop she looks out over the canal. There is a middle-aged couple kissing at the next table. His beard is grey and when they kiss she keeps her dark glasses on.

'When I look at you now,' she says, and she shakes her head slowly, 'I see it. The kind of night you had. The sex. The love you made.' She stops speaking and tries to find the right words.

'You're not in trouble, Helen. You're alive.' And then she tells me she knew that they were playing in that club on this weekend in Amsterdam.

'I don't want you to end up like me,' she says, and we stare straight ahead at the cool grey water and we are deaf to the traffic and the bicycle bells.

We can see the dark blacked-out windows of Anne Frank's life and as we sit here we are thinking about how awful it is to be locked inside on a hot summer's day.

'Poor little girl,' she says, and when she smiles over at me there are tears in her eyes.

Birdie has always done her best to set us both free.

★   ★   ★

On the flight home Judith says it's important to stay calm. She listens carefully to the details and then looks out the window before she speaks. She looks worried and frightened like we are flying a bomber into war and when I look at Birdie she winks at me and gives a gentle smile.

'You had to do it,' she whispers softly, 'I would have,' and I know that her life is still very different to mine.

'There is something about him,' she says then which is less helpful and Judith sighs heavily to herself and turns around.

'Jesus Christ . . . ' she whispers, and her voice is furious, 'it's not like he's Elvis Presley,' she says.

I am feeling as guilty as hell now, so I tell her she's showing her age.

8

Making Strange

July 1997

I want to know the woman sitting alone in the Indian restaurant. She is dressed in an old sweater, sipping water and candle gazing. I want to know who she is and why she is here alone. She eats slowly and carefully and sadly pays her bill and I want to know where she is going. I imagine she drives a small red car and has a cat named Gwenivere who came secretly pregnant to her home. When she leaves I would like to follow her and ask her why she is alone, as I too am alone, except that I am with people.

Beth is pregnant again and she moves now like she is on wheels. She rolls silently across the carpet towards me. She is quick and smooth and healthy. Her blonde ponytail is tied high on her head and beside her I feel like I am made of wood.

I'm getting married next week, and I don't think I can do it, and so far nobody knows this except me.

Beth is younger and shorter than me, and looks at me the way I look at the old man sitting in the park. I see him every day sitting in the leaves, smoking and rocking from side to side. She gently shuffles the menu in her hands, adjusts her chair, skims her surroundings and all the time she makes little gasps and comments about the restaurant. She is pointing out what she calls 'nice touches'. The glasses, the tapestry on the wall, the candles in the centre. She does not delay to discuss anything, but pats her adjectives about like soft foam balls.

I am trying to tell her that I no longer want to sleep with Jim and I am marrying him next week. I am trying to tell her that when I came home he had my black cocktail dress out of the wardrobe, just looking at it on the hanger, and I am wondering if I came home earlier would he have been wearing it. I am wondering why we don't sleep in a warm circle in the middle of our bed and when I knock against him in my sleep I say 'Sorry' and he says 'Not at all'.

'I think the chemistry is gone between us,' I tell her.

My sister is looking at me the way I look at the old man in the park. Sometimes when he stands up he leaves a curling lake of urine behind him.

'I just feel weird about him now,' I tell her. 'I feel like I need to get away. I actually can't bear to see him.'

'Oh,' Beth says, and I can see she's

beginning to get the picture.

She picks up the menu and a minute later asks, 'Can you imagine life without him? How do you feel when you think of him?'

'I feel sick,' I tell her.

'I see,' and she says this quietly and then suddenly from nowhere we both start laughing and it's not funny at all really. My irresponsibility is mind-blowing. I ask her if I can stay with her for a few days and she says, OK,' and I know she doesn't want this.

'I do love him,' I tell her. 'Just recently . . . not so much . . . maybe I don't love him enough . . . how much do you need to love someone to marry them? . . . How do you know the chemistry will stretch far enough?'

Beth loves Tom. Tom loves Beth. Their mutual admiration runs between them like a skipping rope. He holds one end and she holds the other, and you can almost see them make the smug thing skip.

And in my head I'm thinking about it all now. The kind of men who deal in chemistry and I know what it is all right. It's the way they smile and . . . kind of bubble at you . . . sending out chemicals — and I bet they would show up in the dark.

'What's the trouble, baby?' I want her to ask, and then put her arms around me and rock me back to sleep.

The next day I call Jim and we meet for breakfast . . . eventually.

At first I am so late that he leaves.

When I get there I take a corner seat and actually hope that he has stood me up. I really do. When he appears I would rather look away. If he were on TV, I would turn over. It's pretty bad between us, I can tell you. But first he calls the restaurant and there is this big fuss.

'For God's sake, where were you?' he asks.

He sounds really mad — and I know straight away that he has been there and has probably sat for an hour and eventually left thinking I had stood him up. The difference between us right at this point is that he is praying I am there — and I am praying he is not. Then I annoy the hell out of him and say, 'I'm here. Where are you?'

I know he is at home, calling me. He has been to the restaurant and has walked the whole way home and called me. He called me as soon as he got in. He didn't even take his raincoat off. He barely closed the front door when he went walking with hands out-stretched for the phone. Then he began to explain the whole thing and of course I knew all about it. He went to the restaurant and he was waiting and waiting, and then he bought a newspaper and he was wondering if I had got his message and, of course, 'You're always late anyway,' and so on and so on.

And I'm going, 'Oh, I see, I seeeeeee. OK, OK. No, no, I'm here. Yes, yes, that's a good idea. See you in a little while then.'

And I hung up and imagined him setting off again. Still in his raincoat and walking the same walk he had already done twice that morning.

Boy, I'm making a real mug out of him now.

I am ashamed to say it — but it did occur to me to leave then. Yes it did. And the thought didn't go away immediately either. I let it ramble around for a while and imagined the consequences. They were grim enough, but I was willing to risk it. But even I couldn't do that. Eventually he arrives windswept and grinning. I give a nice enough laugh — a flat little 'ha ha ha' to break our tension.

By now I guess the guy is a bit confused, but relieved because I have returned his grin and he doesn't notice I am holding on to my seat to keep me there.

He starts by giving me the look now — and I have to say it is one of my favourites. He has walked all the way across the restaurant to hang up that damn raincoat. Then he's sitting down opposite me and throwing me the look

— and this guy has great eyes, I have to tell you. This is the raised-eyebrow-leaning-back-in-his-chair look and it says you're making a total mug of me and I hate you. I know I have him and he knows it too. I'm like a cat fooling around with a mouse, and I just can't quite decide when to kill it. Usually he doesn't need an explanation. Usually he doesn't go there. Today he wants to be killed.

'What's going on?' he asks.

'Nothing,' I reply.

'What's going on?' He says it again — in exactly the same voice except that he then goes, 'Himp? . . . Himp?'

He sounds a bit mental actually.

He looks at the entrées and then up again at me . . . 'Himp.' He adds this little sound at the end. Himp? He is trying to be sort of casual. He is the most un-casual guy I know. He is wearing a thick denim shirt buttoned up to the neck with a tie. Even if I was in the mood and, as you might have guessed, I'm not, I can't imagine trying to get him out of that shirt. It would be like unzipping a tent and trying to crawl in. He is holding the menu very tightly like a steering wheel in his hands. I have a sudden image of our table starting to move, suddenly taking a low circling swing and then we are off. Jim driving with the menu and me sitting beside him. All

272

the tables are turning into dodgems and off we all go, swirling and swinging around the restaurant. My mind is blanking with panic because he's cornering me. And all the time I feel like bursting out laughing.

Then he does what he does best. He lets it go. There is no reason in the world why he should do that. But I guess it's that thing where you see you're on really thin ice and instead of treading carefully you just get the hell off it. Not only do you get off it, but you walk well away from it, crunching in the frosty grass until it's well behind you.

As I watch him eat breakfast there is a thought circulating around my head. There is someone for everyone, I am thinking. Over and over — there is someone for everyone. I am telling myself this in the same way that you might stroke a cat. There is someone for everyone.

There is someone for everyone.
From the head down to the tailbone.
There is someone for everyone.
I'm really scared now.
There is someone for everyone.
Shorter strokes.
Fewer words.
I am alone.
Just pats on the head.
Alone. Alone. Alone ... and now I'm

tapping on the small wooden heads that cats have.

He puts his hand in his pocket and takes out my engagement ring. 'You forgot this,' he says, and I am genuinely impressed by his casual approach. He pushes it across the table towards me as if he is giving me car keys. I keep my eyes fixed on the menu and tell him I feel like something sweet. He picks up the ring and holds it towards me, pinching it between his finger and thumb.

I don't look up for a while.

When I slide it over my knuckle it feels new again and cold against my skin.

9

I, Hélène Fournier . . .

August 1997

'It's a long time since we shared the same bed,' she says.

Birdie puts her suitcase on the floor and tosses her hat to one side. It lands on a chair and is forgotten as she walks to the window and looks out at the sea. She puts on a pair of small gold-framed glasses and stays there watching with her chin in one hand. The tide is in and there are choppy grey waves that seem to flatten and just give up when they reach the shore. The sky is what you would expect in August. The light is silver and cool. The sun goes down in a faint lemon colour and there is a long thin strip of cloud like a single white stocking left in the sky.

Walter stands on the beach with Jacob and his white shirt billows in the wind. When he looks at the tugboat, he seems to salute it with one hand shading his eyes.

'Pilot,' he reads, and they stand together watching the tug as it jogs its way through the waves. A man walks his dog near the water and he holds a stick in his hand. The dog is wet and he stops to shake himself and then he runs sideways out of the shake. The tug goes out further and it seems brave and small then as it guides the last trawler out to sea.

'Ahoy, there!' Walter calls, and Jacob just looks up at him and then looks away.

She has brought a new scent with her. She's an American now, a well-seasoned traveller, unfazed by all of this, but when she turns, her eyes rest themselves on their double bed as if it is some island she doesn't know.

When Birdie speaks her voice is quieter than before. There is still that smile and the sudden merry laugh, but her words are more carefully measured out. She has learned how to speak in a whole other language, and it's all about waiting and being more careful and knowing when not to speak.

'My God,' she says as she watches her husband, 'we both need glasses now.'

She seems older, wiser, and like she has seen more than she needed to see.

'Now . . . ' she says, and she lowers her suitcase on to the floor and begins to tug at the straps. She is always generous and will use any excuse to give a gift. She hands me a book of poetry and then a pair of silver earrings and some antique Christmas decorations she found in a thrift store.

'These are sweet,' she says, and after I open them she takes them back and looks at them again.

It is an old cast-iron bed and we sit side-by-side with our bare feet hanging down over the striped rug. There is a picture of Jesus in a silver suit hanging over the dressing table and there are shafts of light coming from his ankles and wrists. I have been in and out all day, moving things around, leaving carefully placed books and Rue has left fresh roses by their bed.

'You should read this,' I tell her, and she takes the book in her slender hands and turns it over and reads the back cover. Her eyes wander away from the text and she seems to be distracted again. Downstairs the telephone is ringing and I can hear Angel cheering loudly in the hall. On the night before my wedding we are clinging to each other, Birdie and I, both understanding this feeling of borrowed time. We're not interested in Christmas decorations or books of poetry, we are both wondering if things can stay the same.

When she speaks again her voice is light and dreamy as if she is thinking out loud.

'We're like roommates now, you know, and when we talk it's just about everyday things, like our neighbours and who will pay the cable bill. When Walter moved into the spare room that was really the end . . . '

She says she will leave him, and when I ask

279

her when, she always says, 'Not yet.'

'Helen!' Rue calls, and she is at the turn of the stairs. 'Jim is on the phone.'

'OK,' I call out to her, but I stay where I am, giving Birdie some more time.

'What will I wear this evening?' she asks, as if to change the subject, and I'm just watching her, and then looking at the other suitcase and wondering why she brought so many things.

'Will this be OK?' she asks, and she holds up a lilac sundress.

'Will it make me look pregnant? It'll make me look pregnant.' She folds it up and takes out something else.

'I'm not pregnant by the way,' she says, and during all of this I haven't said a word.

Walter walks up the stone steps and leaves Jacob watching the sea. His hair is shorter now, greased back with a quiff. He is unaware of us, upstairs looking down, like a regular 1950s man.

'I am fond of him,' she says. 'It's just not enough.'

Rue puts her head around the door then.

'Are you coming down? Don't keep that man waiting,' and she smiles at us, and marches off down the landing again.

*   *   *

Birdie has grown up, and into an interesting woman. She has that slightly sorrowful look, the beauty of faint distress. Somewhere inside she enjoys the sadness, enjoys the disappointment, is bored by the notion that nothing else can go wrong. When I show her my wedding dress she sits perfectly still and with her face turned sideways and her curls loose down over one shoulder, she has a Pre-Raphaelite look. There is a doll called Susan on my dressing-table and she is wearing a pink jumpsuit. Beside her there is a collection of blue hardbacked books called *Stories for Girls*. They are shades of childhood, belonging to another person, sitting perfectly still now, lonely and left behind.

'It is perfect,' she says, ' . . . perfect,' and she can make this word smooth like white icing on a cake. When she shakes her head her auburn curls move like little holly branches and she is smiling and pretending to be perplexed.

'You're gonna be beautiful . . . just perfect,' she says.

She produces two bottles of champagne that she took from the flight then and suddenly she is happy and full of mischief again.

'Come on, we'll have these by the neck,' and that is how I remember her. Feeling the kind of sadness that doesn't seem to last, casting it off like a light shadow and drinking happily to get drunk.

'So you're really going to do it,' she says, and there is some disbelief in her voice, but she is watching me really closely and there isn't anything I would want to hide.

'I guess I am . . . for once in my life, Birdie, I'm going to do the sensible thing.'

She drinks more champagne and the sudden bubbles make her blink.

'Helen and sensible don't belong in the same sentence,' she replies, and we are both looking at the photo of Jim beside my bed. 'Your husband to be,' she says quietly.

'I know,' and I smile, and take the photograph in my hand. I'm always proud to show him off. To tell people that this man is really mine.

When I stand up she suddenly catches my hand.

'I really do wish you, with all my heart, Helen, the very best of luck,' and she is so serious we both start to laugh.

'Because . . . you will need it,' and she is laughing deep down in her chest now, and then she gets serious again. 'People say you know for sure. Helen, take it from me, when you walk down that aisle, you've got no clue.'

'Did you love Walter, Birdie?'

'I did love him, Helen. I still do. And sometimes even that's not enough to make it work.

'You've got no clue,' she says again.

★　★　★

Rue takes Walter through the stone archway to the vegetable garden and she is describing everything as she goes. The sun has only just gone down and it leaves a bright yellow sheen. The back lawn is freshly mowed and the gooseberry bushes are weighed down with fruit. There is a scarecrow over the onion drills with his arms out, like Jesus on the cross, except he is wooden and wearing a sailor hat.

'American Beauty,' she says, as they pass a small apple tree, and he answers her saying that she has a beautiful home. She has pulled a long white net over the rhubarb patch to protect it from birds and it looks like a wedding veil.

When she stops she plucks a weed from the corner of the lawn. The old tennis court has been mowed short and Jacob has used whitewash to mark out the lines. I can hear her point out the glasshouse then and the sound of the door opening and I'm sure he'll find the right words to admire her tomato crop. As they walk through the garden gate he steps back and bows low.

'Walter,' Birdie says, laughing softly, and she is smiling and shaking her head and I can see why she's still not able to leave.

★   ★   ★

When Martha Penrose crosses the lawn she is wearing a straw hat and a light floral dress. She walks slowly, finding her way as if someone has turned out the light.

'Is she drunk?' Walter whispers, and when I don't answer he turns to Jim. 'Is that lady a little drunk?' he asks, and his eyes are delighted and schoolboyish behind his new glasses.

We are sitting under the sycamore tree on the front lawn having our tea. The tide is going out, and in; between talking and eating we watch it. And now and then Rue waves to someone walking on the beach. Beth holds Angel in her arms and gives her a bottle while holding her fork in the other hand. There are crab sandwiches and homemade sausage rolls and the only thing we're missing are a few teddy bears walking through some woods. We're all talking loudly, making little jokes, and there is a strange tension in the air. Jim leans back looking relaxed and knows when to join in. They offer him tea and feed him, and tease him like a new child they're going to adopt.

'The trouble and strife,' Tom says, and everyone laughs.

They ask if I am going to promise to 'obey' him and I tell them that I already do.

Rue watches us, and, now and then, reminds someone of something that still needs to be done. She tells Beth that she must call me at eight and make sure I have breakfast, and then she tells us she will pick the peonies herself. She will make the bouquet and keep some petals fresh to scatter over the wedding cake.

'You might forget to get married otherwise,' Beth says, and they are all there now laughing like hyenas. Like old horses who have already run and won this race. They slyly watch to see how Jim and I are around each other, seeing what fresh love is like. They want to remember what it is like — when one person offers another her life. I am talking a lot, babbling, and then I look at the teapot and ask Rue is there no wine?

'There will be no drinking tonight,' she says, and that is when Martha begins to wander across the lawn.

'Sorry we're late,' she says.

'We?' Rue asks, and she is looking worried

and then another person appears.

'This is James,' Martha says, and he is a pale-faced man with round glasses and a straw boater. He is Martha's age and he walks unsteadily, lifting his feet too high as if he is riding a bicycle across the lawn.

'Sweet sacred heart,' Rue says, staring at the table.

'James Joyce,' Birdie whispers, and then we are all trying not to laugh. Jacob gets up and offers her his chair.

'Good evening,' she says, and I can tell she is working on her sober voice.

'This is the groom,' he says, holding one hand towards Jim, and Martha leans back and studies him and then she takes his hand and doesn't let it go. Jim sits beside her smiling faintly, patient, polite, waiting for her to release her grip. There is silence and some muffled laughter and I'm just glad they came. I like the smell of whiskey on her breath. I like that she is seeing all of this with blurred-out eyes, and right now I think we are feeling the same.

The stars are coming out now and the sky is still not fully dark. Beth and Tom begin to clear off the table, and Rue takes Martha and James inside to show them their room.

'I'm putting you in the pink room,' she says firmly, and I can hear Martha giggling to herself. All of this time James Joyce has not spoken. He is sitting in a deck chair smoking silently and watching the grass.

I stay at the table with Jim and when everyone is gone we look at each other and smile and then we sit there talking and holding hands.

'I'm looking forward to having you to myself,' he says, and he puts his arm around me and I smile up at him.

We have all grown quiet now, one by one, alone and together, each one preparing for a different kind of day. There is nothing left to say now, just to let it all start to happen and watch how families merge and then separate. There are so many things to think about now and sometimes it's easier to look at the ordinary things in between, like the breeze that lifts the tablecloth and the bee that circles the jam.

★   ★   ★

It is late when Leo calls. He knocks softly on the kitchen door and then quietly lets himself in. He curls his head around the door and smiles when he sees me sitting there.

Rue is talking about Martha and her shoes.

'God help her,' she says, 'her sister bought them for her and they're like two boats.'

She is making soup so we can have it before we leave for the church tomorrow. She slices vegetables and slides them from the chopping board into a red saucepan.

'It might be a very long time before you get to eat again,' she says, and I'm sitting there in pyjamas watching her, and I feel like a four-year-old with my gingersnaps and milk. She tosses some salt and pepper in, and then stops for a moment and looks up at the clock.

'You should try and sleep,' she says. 'Even if you are just lying down with your eyes closed, you're resting. It'll do you some good.' But we both know that's not really true.

She is wearing the dressing gown I gave her last Christmas, and her shoulders seem thinner now.

There is a freshly baked loaf of brown bread standing on its side at the Aga and upstairs there are footsteps and the hushed sounds of the others getting ready for bed.

'I was hoping to catch you,' Leo says, and then he apologizes for calling so late, but we know him well and he's another good reason not to go to bed. He is carrying a big parcel under his arm, which he lays flat on the kitchen table.

'I wanted to give you this,' he says. 'To wish you luck.'

When I open it I recognize the painting straight away.

'Girl in a Red Dress,' I say, and then, 'Leo.'

'It didn't reach its reserve,' he says, and he stands awkwardly and looks down at his feet. When I look up, Rue is not looking at the painting, instead she is watching me. She kisses me goodnight, and Leo stays on at the kitchen table and we make hot whiskeys and talk.

'So tomorrow is the big day,' he says, and this is the sort of thing everyone seems to say, like I didn't know it or something, but with him it's different because there is a gentle tease in his voice.

'Sure is.'

'Any doubts?' And when I look up I see that his face is waiting for an answer.

'Honestly, yes,' and he lifts one eyebrow and nods.

'Hard to know anyone for sure,' he says quietly.

'I know him well enough to know that he'll be a great husband . . . ' and here he just looks at me.

'You know what I'm like, Leo, always flitting around. I'm tired, I've worn myself out.'

'I know,' he says. 'It's just that . . . oh, I don't know.'

'What?'

And then Rue comes back into the room. She has her hair in pin curlers and she walks on tiptoe.

'I need to take more bread out of the freezer,' she says, and goes out into the scullery and then back through the kitchen again.

'How is she?' Leo asks kindly.

'Better now,' I tell him, and then I add, 'Getting older, you know. I want her to have a check-up after the wedding, but you know how she is, she never complains.'

'She probably just needs a holiday,' he says, and then, 'You know Rue, she just keeps going on and on,' and we sit together thinking about this and stretching out our time.

'I should be going,' Leo says, and I'm feeling lonely now and wondering if that's how a bride is supposed to feel.

It's strange how everyone keeps their distance from me when what I really want is for them to gather around.

Leo sighs and looks at me smiling.

'Good luck, kid,' he says.

'Thanks. I've never had so many people wish me luck.'

'Helen,' he says, and then, 'Helen,' again, and he puts both hands on my shoulders. 'I guess they want you to be happy.'

'And what do you want, Leo?' And I'm not

sure why I've asked this.

'Me?' And he puts his hands in his pockets and looks at the ground. 'Just to know you're not, I don't know . . . giving up.'

He kisses me on the cheek and then he hugs me close to him.

'See you tomorrow, Leo.'

'Goodnight, Helen, sleep well.'

★ ★ ★

Upstairs Martha's voice comes out and it sounds spooky in the dark.

'There is a bat in our bedroom,' she announces, and then I hear the first words from James Joyce.

'Do you have a tennis racquet?' he asks.

They are both so loose and jangly now, and I don't want to think about what happens when they get into bed.

★ ★ ★

Rue is almost asleep when I kiss her good-night. When I go to sleep the same thought goes around my head and I'm thinking about Rue and the day my father went away. What was it she said? 'You just know,' and I guess I am supposed to understand what this means by now. We are too sad to talk about

291

my wedding tomorrow. The church is empty and waiting. The flowers are in the fridge. The mother and daughter are quiet now. It is as if it is already done.

★   ★   ★

It is 4 a.m. when Birdie lifts the covers quietly and gets in beside me. Her feet are cold and she can't sleep. She says she wakes up every time Walter moves and I'm just glad that she's awake too. I saw how they walked on the sand together when it grew dark. Not seeing the sea or the stars or tasting the wind. Just walking together with serious faces, as if they were walking to get to another place.

'I would like to have children,' she says, and her words ring out with hope in the dark. 'But I don't have that much time left.'

She smells like warm bath water and soap. Her hair covers one pillow and is mixed in with mine. Then we talk the way we always do. About nothing really. Sending out thoughts and seeing if they will fly.

'What is it that makes one person sexy and another one not at all?' she asks, and we lie there thinking about it. She is thinking about Walter, and I am thinking about Jim, and then I'm thinking about Liam.

'I think some men are really wizards,' I tell

her. 'They just look at you and put you under a spell, and it's the worst kind of joke because they're always the ones you can't really have.'

She sits up on her elbows and the room is beginning to get a little brighter. The floral pattern on the curtains seems to be pushing itself out towards us and it makes dull flowers in this half-light, black and grey.

'Do you still think about Liam?'

'Sure, you know how it is with us, he has always kind of lived inside me.'

'Would you have married him if he asked?'

'He didn't ask.'

'You could have spent your entire life waiting for him.'

'He didn't ask me to wait either.'

We say nothing then and we turn on our sides and face each other and she laughs. 'Some men are not for turning,' she whispers.

'Do you think he was in love with someone else?' she asks a moment later.

'Yes,' I answer, 'himself.'

She is quieter than usual and I'm glad she is here, and when we drift off to sleep her arm falls loosely across my waist. I am used to Jim and how he breathes and moves. How he likes me to turn over so he can put both of his arms around me and cradle me when I sleep. It is like that with Birdie only more comforting. Her smell is different too, female, like roses, and her arm is lighter, like one of my own.

At 6 a.m. the house is still quiet and we creep out wearing swimsuits and carrying our towels.

'For old times' sake,' she whispers, and she is laughing like it's the middle of the afternoon, and then we are quietly opening the front door and walking in bare feet towards the steps. When we turn around the house is still quiet and all the curtains are closed. It is cool outside and still not completely bright. When we step down on to the sand it is a familiar feeling. The sand is cold and wet under our bare feet. There are hard little ridges where the sand has been whipped up into little waves. Tiny sand-storms, snow drifts across this beach we know well. The tide is a long way out and there is no one else around. Our feet sound like they did when we were children, slapping, hurrying with cold. Now and then keeping time.

When Birdie stands up her towel flows out behind her. It billows and she holds on with both hands. We leave our swimsuits curled up together on the sand and then with one glance, and I think my life just flashed past me, we release our towels and sprint across the shingles and out towards the sea. We gallop through the shallow pools and up on to flat sand again, and then down into the water, and finally there are waves and we are splashing, laughing and panting when we run. The cold makes us gasp and laugh at the same time.

'We'll be doing this in our eighties!' Birdie shouts, and then she dives in head first. When she comes back up she pulls her wet hair back and wipes the salt water from her mouth.

'Forever young, Helen,' she says.

★ ★ ★

Rue stands in the front garden and snips off a single pink rose. She is wearing a small neat hat and a powder-blue suit. Behind her Jacob is wearing a new white shirt and his good grey suit and he is walking in slow circles on the lawn.

'The car should be here any minute now,' he says, and he takes out a pocket watch that I haven't seen him use before. Rue is calm and peaceful, as if her work is done. They wait then in their new clothes, well prepared like two soldiers going to war.

She turns and looks out on to our beach. Just facing the fresh breeze for a moment, and then she turns and fixes the rose into Jacob's buttonhole. She says something to him and he replies and they both laugh, and then they see me there inside the window and they smile and wave.

* * *

'The new curate will have us there all day,' Jacob says.

'He's very dramatic,' Rue replies, 'I think he spent some time in America,' and then she turns as if she suddenly remembers me.

'We'll see you at the church,' she says, and she kisses her fingers and turns them to me and I do the same for her.

* * *

Jacob has hired an old Bentley and it's like riding in a living room. When we get to the coast road the driver turns the radio on and Bob Dylan sits with us in our moving room. He sings out with honesty and a jangling country and western rhythm and he tells us that he wants his honey. I'm sitting there in my white dress and thinking, 'Actually, honey, maybe I don't,' and I'm trying to keep my breath even and steady. I'm telling myself that everything is OK, but it's all beginning to feel a little crazy now.

'What if we just kept driving on and on?' I

ask Birdie and Jacob.

'You'd end up in Drogheda,' he says seriously, and he is starting to look worried.

'All them people,' he says then. 'All them people.'

We take the longer route down through Laytown and Mrs Ford is at the door of Centra, smiling and giving us a wave. I look at Birdie, and we are both looking petrified when we wave back. We are like the circus coming to town, some kind of joke, an accident on wheels. There is a mustard-painted building called Rosie's Takeaway, and it has a red-and-white sign that says 'Chips Pizzas Burgers'. There are flower boxes filled with spiky geraniums that look like they need a drink. When we turn into Main Street a black-and-white dog puts his head out an upstairs window and he is barking at us as we go by. Then he stops, and like everyone else he's just taking a look. 'Mick the Butchers' sells Prime Beef and Lamb and he is at his door in a bloody apron. When he sees the fluttering white ribbons he waves his knife.

When we pass the new Chinese takeaway Birdie reads the name out loud.

'Good Will,' she says.

Jacob directs the car under the arched bridge where Birdie and I have stood and watched for trains. Adams' Antiques is closed and the green blinds are down, and this is because Leo is at a friend's wedding today — and I think it only really dawns on me then. We drive out past the green swamp to a thatched pub called Sweeney's, and it is famous because it is sinking down into the bog. The driver pulls over and there are two men in tweed jackets leaning on the windowsill with their arms folded and they stop talking when we arrive. Birdie helps me with my dress and we all have to bend low as we walk through the door.

The floor and roof slope to the right so that when we turn left we must climb a little hill. We line up on benches and there is a jukebox and two faint posters — one says 'Irish Writers' and the other 'Boulevard of Broken Dreams'.

When the pint of Guinness appears, Jacob seems to relax.

'This is where people pour out their hearts,' he says, and he folds his arms and stares down at his black pint.

He lifts it to his lips in one quick swooping movement, and swallows three times. He turns his lips in then and shakes his head laughing.

'My brother,' he says, 'God rest him. He died sitting on that very stool,' and he holds

298

one finger towards it.

He looks down, and he is sad for a moment, and then he lifts his pint and drinks again. There is a smell of urine coming from the gents' toilet behind us, and a man at the counter talks loudly to the barman. 'Oh, Jaysus, oh, Jaysus, yes,' he says. We drink gin and tonics and they feel dirty and cold. We have one and then one for the step.

'Time to face the music,' Jacob says, and he winks at me, but I am thinking about his brother and wondering when you stop missing someone after they go. Then there is that half-crazy feeling again, and no matter what we drink we are still sad and stiff like three statues in a park. We are lined up on the wooden bench, a bride and her two good friends, and right now any one of us might start to run.

'Are you the posh ones?' the man at the counter asks, and no one knows what to say to that.

'What are you so sad for?' he asks, and then, 'C'mon, be happy ... you're in the bog.'

Outside there is a single magpie balancing on the top of a cypress tree. When the wind blows he is bounced gently up and down as if he is riding the waves.

A bird flew into my room this morning and I don't know what it means. My skin aches and my eyes hurt and every noise is too loud. The air smells of rose petals and it tastes like old cake. Everything feels different and still it looks the same.

We leave our drinks behind and there is no more time left. We climb into the car and Jacob tells the driver to go straight to the church.

★　★　★

Yesterday I sat in my bedroom and watched Beth cut Tom's hair in the back yard. They carried out a kitchen chair and she put a towel over his shoulders. He held a small mirror in his hands, but he didn't look into it until the end, and now and then it flashed at me in the sun.

They were talking at first and then they stopped and there it was — the easy acceptance of just being around each other with just the sound of the scissors left. She stood close to him and I don't think she noticed how his knee rested between her legs and how the small tufts of hair rolled off into the wind.

There is an old man lighting candles at the back of the church. He stands solemnly with his hands joined and his face brighter from the flames. He takes another candle and lights it from the first and when it is fixed in place he stands back and offers up another prayer. His dog waits at the door with her lead resting on the ground. Her ears are flattened and she looks up at us, longing for something, apologizing for being there. When the old man unties her it is as if he still doesn't see us at all.

'Ah, Poppy,' he says then, 'you were waitin' for me. Waitin' here for me. You were waitin', Poppy,' and he speaks to her like she is the centre of his world.

He walks out of the porch and he doesn't wish me luck. Inside the organ is playing some sort of elevator music and in my mind I am following the man and his dog. I am wandering after them like a ghost, back to their cottage, putting on the kettle, finding a seat, asking them to adopt me. 'Is this my room?' I am saying to him, and he is opening a door and then turning down the bed.

This feeling I have is like a fear of flying. If I don't think about it everything will be OK. We are almost airborne. I will concentrate on the words of a poem I know and try not to look down. When the organ begins to play everyone stands up and they also turn around. I don't know any of these faces and they are like rows of flowers with their heads turned towards the sun.

Then I see Leo and he looks so formal and strange to me now. And John Dowling and Kate, and I'm thinking, 'Who invited them?' And Martha Penrose, who stands up and then quickly sits down.

Jacob stares straight ahead and he puts one foot carefully in front of the other, and now we are starting to move. I do believe it is only just dawning on me. Not that I am getting married, but just how afraid of it I am. So he wheels me up the aisle and the bridesmaid is behind me. We are the last two vestal virgins and we are all going to be buried alive. Jim looks good with his dark hair shorter now and combed back. He is freshly shaved and smells like pine needles and sunshine on a forest floor. There is an odd smile frozen on his face and he is breathing quickly in his black suit and I'm thinking he is a Reservoir Dog asking to get out.

And all this time there is a smell of candles, and different people who are looking forward to their big day, and a bird is flying up around the roof of the church. I am looking everywhere now and panicking because I need to see her face — Rue — who would never allow me to go wrong. I need to see that she is smiling, relaxed, happy to release me into the wind. Her little smile and her eyes telling me, 'Go on, Helen, it's OK. He's a good man, Helen. Go on, Helen, go on.'

★   ★   ★

When Birdie took off her wedding band she said her hand felt strange.

'Undressed' was the word she used. We sat on the beach with our towels around us, looking out to sea and waiting to feel cold.

'I bought our wedding rings for thirty-five pounds each on Camden Street,' she said. 'I remember buying them well.' It is a light band of gold, light as if it could break.

'Walter lost his, you know,' and when she spoke she traced a line in the sand. 'He got another one. It's awful. He insists on wearing it though. It's like something out of the barm brack.'

I watched her when she spoke, wondering if she was really making a move. Making some final decision. Setting herself free. Beautiful bird — and I wanted to take her hand and turn her around and push her out into the sky.

'I took mine off for a while,' she said then, 'just to see how it would feel.'

'How did it feel?'

'Oh, the same, really. Walter didn't notice at all.'

I was wondering what was going through her mind, and if she would take the ring off, and gently push it into the sand, and what she would think then and perhaps the prayers she might say, or if she would just leave it in its fresh little grave. It is a strange thing to watch someone change their life. To watch them take another direction in one easy move.

When Birdie stood up, she was tall, almost Amazonian. She walked a few steps ahead and she took the ring and flung it forward. It was one strong movement that sent her body with it, but only for a moment. She pitched it like a baseball into the sea. When she turned the sun was coming out, and she gave me the kind of a sad smile that told me that she would be fine eventually, but for now she was wrecked inside.

★   ★   ★

The priest speaks very slowly. He lifts his hands up high and waves them at the congregation.

'Praise God,' he says, and then as if nobody

had heard it he says it again. He is a missionary priest who speaks to us as if we don't understand English. He explains everything very carefully and then he wishes everyone good luck in Croke Park later on. Rue says he is a football fanatic. When he comes out on the altar on a Sunday, she rolls her eyes and says, 'We're in for it now.'

Jim and I stand side by side and light a candle together, the first of many things we will share. When Judith reads she takes her time and directs every word to us. She tells us that love is never angry. That love is patient and kind, and in my mind the response is, 'Ha, ha, ha. Hee, hee, hee.' And I want to tell her that I know all there is to know. It becomes smaller then and Jim and I are in our own little place. Two little clowns, dressed to the nines, about to tie the knot.

Father Matthews rocks gently on his feet and tells us we are about to take our vows. There is a hush behind us as if everyone is whispering, 'OK, this is it.'

When Jim speaks, he turns towards me, and with every word he directs his jet of love right into my eyes. I would like to look down or put on dark glasses, but I just stand there and let it all in.

'I, James, take you, Helen, to be my wedded wife. To have and to hold from this day forward, for better, for worse, for richer, for poorer, in sickness or in health, to love and to cherish till death do us part. And hereto I pledge you my faithfulness.'

'Now, Helen . . . '

★ ★ ★

The minute I met Jim I stopped feeling like I was alone. He filled all those extra spaces other people don't seem to have.

★ ★ ★

Someone coughs and it is low down and deep from their chest.

'Ah, haw, ah, haw,' it goes, and it is a damp earthy sound like a sheep coughing in a field. There are echoes in the church and the sound of people rustling leaflets. They are thinking about what we will all have for dinner later on. Some are smiling across at each other. Some of them are possibly wiggling their toes inside their shoes. And there's that deep cough again, and I'm seeing an image of a sheep in a hat and a powder-blue suit coughing politely behind her hoof.

'Helen . . . ?'

Father Matthews gives a weak smile, and my eyes move to the left and they meet Jim's,

306

and by the way he is scarily calm and that little smile tells me that he is quietly freaking out.

The priest leans forward, and lifts his eyebrows up.

'Helen? Is everything all right?' he whispers, and he glances at Jim as if he is wondering what medication I am on and we're all in slow motion. I trace my tongue over my lips, tasting lipstick and salt. Jim takes my hand and squeezes it just a little too hard, and then there is that coughing sheep again. I turn around looking, looking . . . all them people . . . all them people, and in the crowd everyone gets mixed in together and they all look the same. I thought you were my friends, I want to say, so why are you all just sitting there staring? Why can't someone help me say these words? Then there is Rue looking as if she might cry and she is suddenly so small and pale.

'Helen?' Father Matthews says, and now he is looking worried and glancing at Jim and me. There is nothing for it. Nothing else to do now. I have waited and kept everyone waiting for long enough. 'Don't you know me, baby? Don't you know me since I went away?'

★ ★ ★

'Men are so weird,' Birdie said, and she was buttoning up my dress and then she tells me how Walter would never allow her to cut her hair.

'Men are so weird,' she said again, and I said nothing and I didn't want to tell her that Jim likes to blindfold me with a pink silk scarf. I say OK, because it doesn't seem to matter, and because the bedroom is usually a pretty dark place.

★   ★   ★

There is a little bleating sound then and it is actually my voice, and Jim nods and draws each one out of me like little carriages pulled behind a train.

'I . . . Helen, take you . . . ' and my first step is taken, my right foot going over the edge and it is in mid air, not on solid ground, not yet reaching the water, it is somewhere in between. Sometimes when I drink too much I need to sleep with the light on. Sometimes slipping into all that blackness is more than I can bear.

★   ★   ★

A bird flew into my room this morning; I didn't know what to do.

I am on the edge of the swimming pool and with one deep breath I will send myself forward, gasping, splashing, crying, drowning and going down.

★ ★ ★

When Rue falls, her forehead makes a light slapping sound as it reaches the seat in front. She must have fallen gracefully, because it is the same sound a domino makes as it falls. Someone gives a little cry, and I know then that it's Beth, and when I turn around I see they have gathered in a huddle and someone is saying, 'Stand back, stand back, please,' and there are worried faces all around the church.

Tom is leaning over Rue. He loosens her collar and speaks calmly to her and then he asks someone to get his bag from their car. Jacob is beside him and down on one knee. I stand rooted to the spot, Jim and I frozen together, and just slightly turned to one side.

'Is everything all right?' the priest asks, and even I know that this is a dumb thing to say. Priests can behave as if they're above everything, even common sense, and sometimes they remind me of a light smell of dinner floating upstairs.

A bird flew into my room this morning and

I put it out before anyone came.

When I run towards them there is no room for me, and I send in one hand and touch her cheek.

Then Jim comes over and lifts me up and makes me step back. The guests are looking flustered and worried and asking each other what they should do.

Father Matthews reaches for a small black bible and puts a purple cloth around his neck and I'm watching this and shaking my head and inside are the words, 'Oh, no, why did you have to do that?' and then he is down on his knees.

And all this time Jim stands behind me holding me tightly, not wanting me to see what is happening and also not wanting me to escape. The guests stand awkwardly and then one by one they sit and look at each other, holding toddlers on their laps and shaking their heads.

'Helen,' Tom says, 'you better come here,' and I walk slowly over, and as I walk the peony bouquet rolls over the floor.

'Jesus Christ,' Jim whispers, and he is behind me trying to take my hand. Jacob moves back and I creep in to her on my knees. Beth is on the other side and she is crying into Angel's hair. There is no music and I think the organist should play Bach again. Rue would like that. I already know before they say anything. I had felt it all around me since I stepped into the church like air being sucked out of a room.

A bird came into my room this morning, but I didn't let anyone see.

I will stay perfectly still. If I move my skin will shatter and break. I am holding on to her hand and holding on to her and it is her hand that begins to let go first. The warm glow of life pulling backwards and then off, away, to another new space.

'No, Rue,' I tell her, but she is already gone, flying gently upwards to the dome and the sky.

And my heart is breaking when I say her name. I can feel it fall into real pieces inside my chest. A part of me already understands what has happened and my next thought is that I won't be able to talk to her ever again. There is a silence then, just as I expected, like the end of a piece of music, the end of her life, the end of sound.

★   ★   ★

'I'm sorry,' Jim says to the guests, 'we're going to have to postpone everything,' and Father Matthews says, 'Of course, of course,' and then Jim bends down and picks up my bouquet and takes it out of the church.

'Will I come with you?' he asks, and I can't even begin to answer him. He sounds about a million miles outside this family now.

'No,' I tell him, and then I turn to Tom and my face feels dead and expressionless when I ask if they can bring my mother home.

★　★　★

Beth stands in the kitchen buttering slices of bread. Tom saws the loaf and she butters with tears running down her face. They are together as they always are and this is how they cope. Jacob sits on the steps looking out over the beach and now and then I see him run his hands back through his hair and then put his face in his hands. Martha sits alone on the porch. She smokes until the ashtray is overflowing. There is whiskey in a glass beside her. She doesn't drink. I move past them without speaking and then walk upstairs and stand outside the door to her room. I feel I should knock now, although I never had to before. I don't want to disturb her. I think she might want to be alone. I open the door slowly not knowing how to feel. I feel something and nothing, I only know that there is someone here.

Rue is lying on her bed. She might just be

sleeping after all. But she never slept like that, so well turned out and organized. Her ankles neatly touching. Her hands clasped around her rosary beads. She is wearing her good blue suit and she is so still and her chest is not moving. She looks a little surprised, her arched eyebrows have always given her that look but she is surprised, there was so much energy left, so much more living to be done and now that she has gone, a great pocket of power is taken from this house.

Here are her hands and here is her brow. Here is her sweet face and I put my palms around her cheeks. Here are her fingers. Here are her lips, her eyes, her ears, her nose. Everything I need to make a person, and the truth is I am frightened of her as she is now. I am crying and can see that I have known and loved every part of her. The dark freckle on her forehead. The slender beautiful hands. The hands that made bread and stroked my cheek and embraced me when I was too old for it.

'Helen, if you want to live, to be really alive . . . ' I can still hear her voice.

'Rue . . . what if I just want to die?'

I put one hand over hers and try to say her name but I can't make the sound.

And then I try again and this time it is a whisper, 'Rue?' and I want to ask her where she has gone and why she has left me. With her warmth and humour and her eagerness to find something new every day, and everything we talked about, where is it now?

I put my face in my hands and think about my question and all the things I would like to ask her and all the things that can never be said. And it occurs to me then, as simply as this, that I will never hear her voice again.

Our words were like a long flowing sentence that should always have run between us and all the things she said — I never once told her, that she, this pale cold figure, was the very beat of my heart and now that she is gone I don't know how to live. I have loved her too much, even for a mother, and without her the pain is too great, and it can split me down the centre so that from now on I will have half a life.

With one hand over Rue's, I put my head down on the bedspread and breathe into it. She is still here with me because I can see her and some part of me thinks that this is good. And yet this corpse is all I can cling to and who wants to cling to that? I stay there though holding on and crying into her bed, because anything is better than no Rue at all.

Then there are hands on my shoulders pulling me back and then roughly lifting me to my feet and I have just reached a numb grey place where there are no more feelings to knock me about.

'I never told her,' and I say it over and over.

'Helen,' Jim says, and in here his voice seems too loud and hard. 'Don't put yourself through this,' and he begins to half carry me, half drag me from the room.

Then there is Leo, and we stand around on the landing just like we're on a street corner waiting for something to happen, and I walk back towards her room.

'Helen.'

'Leave her be, Jim,' Leo says.

'I never told her, Leo,' I tell him.

'Helen,' he says, 'she knew.'

Outside it is quiet and there is that pale warm sun from an August afternoon. The birds seem to have stopped singing and three have gathered quietly on the window ledge. As we watch another one lands, and then another, and they line up, paying their respects, just quietly waiting there.

★   ★   ★

I find Leo's arms around me then and he turns me gently and tightly faces me into his chest. He will not let me go, or turn me towards her again, but he doesn't try to take me from her, instead he lets me cry into his chest with his chin resting on my head.

'Everyone must lose a mother, Helen,' he is saying.

'I can't let her go, Leo.'

'You will,' he says, and his voice is soft and low.

I would like to open these windows up. To bring new air into every part of the house but it's autumn now and without her, the house will fill up with leaves.

We sit in a chair together and we are surrounded by all her lovely things. We stay there quietly keeping her company and when I turn my face towards her I whisper her name like a mantra, over and over 'Rue — Rue — Rue.'

★   ★   ★

Tom tells me that she was dead long before the ambulance arrived, but he is not telling me anything I don't already know.

He tells me that when he listened to her heart it was like an orchestra without a conductor and I tell him I have inherited that gene.

★   ★   ★

316

'She doesn't like that hymn,' I tell them, and my voice sounds snappy and rude. Her favourite hymn was 'Amazing Grace' and after that 'Sleepers Awake', and when I see them huddled around her kitchen table I would like to ask them to leave. Beth is wondering what to do with all her things and I wonder, 'What things?' She is everywhere, in everything, she is everything we have. Jacob folds the sack neatly and then kneels on it as he works. He makes small hollows in the damp clay like a dog looking for a bone. All of his movements are concentrated and his eyes tell me that he is far away.

'Snowdrops for January,' he tells me. 'Freesia for spring. Roses — Albertine for summer time. Red hot pokers for autumn,' and then he plants yellow 'Creeping Jenny' all around the edge. As he plants each seed and bulb I see that he is determined that Rue's grave will bloom all year round.

The next day he brings tomato plants and Tom says this is going too far.

'I don't think so,' Jacob says, and his voice is firm. 'I think she would like it. I think it would make her laugh.'

He takes care of things as he always does. Coming into the kitchen in the usual way, except now he puts the kettle on himself. He winds the clocks, he sweeps out the hall.

He shows me in his own simple way that, even without her, life can go on.

Later when I see him walk along the beach and then stop and pick up seaweed with his fork, I know that he feels it. He takes care of everything, because she would want it, and then retreats to grieve in his own wild space.

★   ★   ★

After the funeral Leo takes me to his house. He lights a fire in his sitting room even though it is warm, and we sit next to its comfort surrounded by chiming clocks. Blondie stretches out and sleeps and now and then whimpers in her dream.

Leo takes us in and understands that we really have nowhere else to go. He shows me he understands by not speaking. By making tea and putting a hot water bottle in my bed. I told Jim that I needed some space. I used his words and he said he understood, but he looked sad and worried at the same time.

Leo lives over the shop in a warren of narrow corridors and rooms with slanted ceilings. There are footprints from the sixties like the old Bush radio, the scrubbed pine table in the kitchen, the orange chairs inside the front door. He tells me that he had lost both of his parents by the time he was fifteen.

He has kept these things to remind him of them and he has added himself in then, in between. The art-deco coffee table, the books, the different chiming clocks. We wait for the electric kettle to boil in the kitchen and I watch life move on in Main Street. There are people shopping in the hardware store across the road. The window is all cluttered up with brushes, rolls of wallpaper and paint. Some late tourists eat ice cream and their legs look cold and white underneath their shorts.

There is a strange cool comfort here as we sit surrounded by ordinary things. The red light on the kettle. Milk poured from the carton. Toast crumbs in the butter. The sliced bread left in a crunched-up yellow pack. I think we can live on tea and toast for days and I see how it is for us now, why we meet and re-connect. Two small children left, as they are now, home alone. He leaves me curled up on the single bed in a small bedroom at the back. He pulls a rug over me when he thinks I'm asleep. He goes downstairs and begins some repairs in the workshop and I am dead here really. Staring in silence at some old faded wallpaper in a room I have never seen. I am dead to the world, isn't that what people say? Except I am wide awake. Then I feel alive again, only because I am remembering what has happened, or remembering some small detail I would prefer to forget.

They come at me like hard grey rocks out of the sky, each one a perfect hit. Just remembering her. Just how she was around me and then some small thing, that is also momentous, like the small hollow on the pillow, when they lifted her head.

★   ★   ★

Jim calls every day and then he asks Leo how I am. There are no hints in my voice. I have already learned to contain it, and Leo tells him I'm doing fine. Then he draws a bath and leaves it for me with the bathroom door open.

Tom and Beth call in to see us. She tells me that they are going back too and taking Martha with them. It seems now that, apart from Jacob, we are not able to bear being inside our own house. I sit up all night and can't sleep and the bath water goes cold again.

Leo expects nothing from me. He takes me in like a piece of old furniture, understanding that I have been somehow abandoned, orphaned. He tells me he was just old enough to begin to realize that his parents were real people. That their sole purpose on this earth was not just to take care of him. He doesn't make me eat. He doesn't tell me to sleep. He doesn't ask any questions. He does little things to make me feel safe, like the cup of tea, the fresh cotton sheets, the books of poetry. He lets me be.

When I wake up he is sitting in the armchair reading. He looks at me and smiles sadly. He knows that in the first seconds after waking, I am not fully sure what exactly is wrong. He waits. He holds me. He never asks me to speak.

At night we sit together under a rug and watch the worst kind of television. Sometimes I get up and leave the room to cry. Sometimes I don't come back. Sometimes I go to bed and stay there all of the next day. Sometimes the same single thought goes around and around my head.

'She was all good,' it goes, and, 'I am all bad.'

★   ★   ★

Leo opens up the chest of drawers and looks inside. He slides each drawer open and shut to see if they are smooth. A knob comes off in his hand and he places it neatly in his pocket, without any comment or surprise.

'Victorian,' he murmurs quietly. Then he

mixes his polish and begins to work. He has measured out linseed oil and warm beeswax and he tells me this is the best way to bring up the grain and the colour of the wood. I sit watching him on an old armchair in the corner of the shop and after a week of 'Yes' and 'No' I discover I have something that I need to get out.

'We don't want it to shine,' he says, and he moves his hand carefully along the wood. 'We just want to bring the colour up.'

I have learned to hold tears in my eyes. If I don't blink they won't fall out. It's just like swimming around with your eyes open under water. It's like the wreck of the *Titanic* with floating tables and chairs.

'What's the matter, Hel?' he asks, and his voice is very gentle. Leo is kind in a way that doesn't leave me feeling small. There are so many things inside of me. I would like to let them out, but I'm scared that they will be like mice and rats running around.

'Come on,' he says, 'I think you better tell me,' and we sit together on the old mustard couch with the daylight fading around us and time slowing down. We sit there looking out on to the street, me bolt upright and Leo with his hands behind his head and it's just like we're watching TV. If I could only say this one thing to him it would help. It would be like releasing an airlock, apologizing, asking for forgiveness, being frightened and then well received.

A tractor turns the corner and there is a farmer standing on the buck rake at the back. He is bounced gently along and he waves and then gives Leo the thumbs up. Around us is the smell of damp fabric and dust and camphor and it's like a great old stew, not as comfortable as we would like, but still doing us some kind of good.

'I keep thinking,' and my voice is slow and faltering. 'I keep thinking . . . what if she wakes up? You know, just opens her eyes down there and finds that she's alone.' And the words come out more quickly and I'm feeling everything I think she might feel.

'She would want someone . . . she'll be on her own . . . she would want me.' And he stays with his hands behind his head, but has turned his chin slightly so that his eyes are steady and meeting mine.

'I mean . . . I feel bad about that. It's not like she's left me at all. Even though everyone keeps saying they're sorry for me. I really don't know why. At least I had her for all this time . . . ' And during all of this Leo's eyes stay where they are, in mine.

'I'm afraid for her, she would want someone, maybe me . . . ' And then the tears that I've learned to hold in my eyes start to fall out.

'She's not down there,' Leo says, and he takes my hand.

'She's not down there,' he says again, and his voice is level.

'But where is she?' and my own voice is angry now.

'Where would you like her to be?' he asks.

Leo puts his arm around me and it's getting dark outside. 'She's not down there, OK . . . so where would you like her to be?' And he lets it go as I think about it.

She's in the garden. She's in the orchard, under the first apple tree. She's in my room. She's calling me for school and, when I stop, I think about how she must somehow be all around me, filling up every space and sound. When two warm hands rest themselves on dough, she is in the flour, against the palms, and in the space in between. That's where she is. Rue. Mum.

'Leo.'

'Yes?'

And my voice is down to a slow whisper now. 'I just really miss her,' and I realize that after everything, that was all I needed to say.

★ ★ ★

Sometimes when I begin my walk to Mornington I forget to stop before I see our house. And once I sat down on a rock and just said, 'Fuck you,' to the sand.

* * *

Leo hands me a little cloth and some polish.

'C'mon,' he says, 'you can help me. Sometimes it's good to just work.'

We work on together quietly and the wood feels strong and steady under my hand. He gets up and examines my polishing.

'Not bad, not bad,' he says, running his fingers lightly against the wood. 'Now,' he says, and he folds the cloth over, 'try not to go against the grain.'

* * *

He tells me he remembers me at school and how I played Joseph in the Nativity play. He laughs quietly over my aviator glasses and my red and yellow kilt. He works slowly in the same way he polishes. He works carefully and gently pulls me back out. Eventually through all of this he makes me laugh and becomes my closest friend.

* * *

Birdie stands on the platform with her suitcases at her feet. She tells me she has sent Walter on ahead to Chicago and then she tells me that she is not going with him, that she is going home to her mother in Dublin. She says there is pink flowered wallpaper in her bedroom and that she hasn't seen it for five years.

'I want to put my hand against it,' she says, 'and sit there on my little single bed and remember how it is to be a girl again . . . before all this.'

She is going home to her mother who will take her in and not say too much and give her time to straighten herself out.

'It's the beginning of an era,' she says, and she is making her voice strong and bright. 'The beginning and the end.'

We sit there on a bench with chipped green paint. There is no one else waiting and the station guard comes out and lifts a sign and brings it inside. Somewhere down below, at the end of the long winding hill to the station, there is the sea, and it is down low and far away. We could not walk on the beach. It seemed unfriendly as if we had both let it down. When I stand up I can see grey waves in the distance and rows of mobile homes and caravans.

'I just took the wrong road,' Birdie says

then, and she simplifies things for all of us, me, the station guard and the family in the mobile home.

When she asks me about Jim, I tell her that everything feels different now, that I need more time. Once I thought I couldn't live without him. Now, after all of this, I find I'm still alive.

The train moves around the bend and she stands up bravely and lifts her case.

'Helen,' she says then, 'you don't need more time.' She hugs me and holds me close to her. 'Don't stay here,' she says, and she is like an Olympian with the flame. 'If you stay here, you'll die.' I see it, that thing about Birdie that I never had. A tiny light inside, still there in spite of everything, making her bright and glowing, flashing her off and on. We are perfect tourists now and I watch as she stands and waves back through the door of the train. We say goodbye when we need to. We always leave smiling. We hardly ever cry.

I climb up on to the bridge and wait for the next train to fly through. It comes at me, roaring, making a deafening noise, and shooting under the bridge, and even now until that moment I think it will take me and the bridge with it. It lifts my hair and sends a hot blast of air up to my cheeks and even now it makes me gasp and laugh.

★   ★   ★

We meet in a sad hotel on the sea front and I'm wearing a pink angora scarf to remind him of who I am.

'I am the woman you almost married,' it says. It is a perfect place to meet. The sea, cold and black on that late September night, and all around us, battered green chairs, and velvet wallpaper and standard lamps that make our space too bright. It is the perfect place to end. To finally call a halt and to say goodbye. He gets up and kisses my cheek and his hands feel cold and his cheeks are fresh against mine. Funny, but I almost pull him close to me to get him warm and then I stop because I remember I am not supposed to do that now.

The thing that I will remember most about Jim is that he loved me just as I am. He was the only guy who I really knew loved me. He just did and no matter what I did he would still be there. It was like settling into a warm corner. There was nothing to fall out of. Nothing to harm me. Only myself in the end, as it happens.

There is a new formality about him; he is tidier and more polite in his dealings with me now. I try to lighten things and look around the hotel dining room and smile.

'This is the kind of hotel where you expect a murder to take place,' I tell him, and he laughs in spite of himself.

'I better get out of here so,' he says, and I am a little taken aback. It is as if he thinks I am capable of just about anything now.

The waitress comes over and I order tea, even though she looks at him first and has to drag her eyes off him and roll them towards my voice.

He says, 'And for me,' and she says, 'Two teas, then,' and I think we are all relieved she doesn't say, 'Two for tea.'

He doesn't look well and I am wondering if I have also managed to make him sick. He has dark brown circles around his eyes. He is wearing good clothes as always, a long wax coat and a good tweed jacket with a black turtleneck underneath. He has cut his hair short now and it looks dry and he runs his hand back through it when he speaks.

We sit there for a long time, and we make eye contact for all of that, and, do you know, I'm not sure if he is really looking at me at all. Where does it end? I want to know. The circle of infinity that you think you have with someone else. The connection, the communion, the reason to get up every day. We have slept together and when we didn't make love we were wrapped around each other. What had happened to those two people and what is the point of it all now?

'Jim — we need to talk. About us I mean,' but he carries on as if he can't hear me.

He says he is pleased with a new commission he is working on. He is excited and looking forward to it he says. And yet he is like a bad actor, reading lines carefully but without any real feeling at all.

I don't see his fire, his energy and I think I have actually killed him now. He is shattered and broken into pieces and he is just barely here now, nodding and listening, and letting me know that I should go.

When he talks about his work he is more like himself, and then he tells me that he has started to paint again.

'Some part of me needs to be seen,' he says. 'Something inside me wants to be alive, to live outside — lately I have had an awful feeling that some part of me will never be seen.'

He asks me then if I would like to leave my things in the flat so that I will have a place to stay. He is not being kind, just hoping that I can give something, but from now on I want to play fair.

'Jim,' and my voice is level, and then I just say it in the easiest way I can. 'I'm sorry, Jim.'

'Why are you doing this, Helen?'

'Everything feels different since Rue died ... and to be honest, Jim ... I'm not sure things were right between us anyway.'

'Why did you say you'd marry me?'

'Because I loved you. I still do ... but I can't marry you, Jim.'

Then I tell him that I'm leaving for Paris, and I say it quietly, and we listen together as my words trail off.

He starts to say something and I know it's about us, the first word is silent and then he stops and looks at me and then looks away again. His eyes look far away, and they take him with them and I don't know him now. He sips his tea and says nothing. I will never know what it was that he might have said, and I think what I saw was him giving up on me right in front of my eyes.

I still have the ring in my pocket and I wonder if I should give it to him. So I do and he just looks at it in my hand and shakes his head. He is really in control from here. I don't have a prayer. He is punishing me by not saying a word.

I can't find the waitress when it is time to pay, and I make a big deal of going back and tipping her so that he can see that I am not completely bad.

Then I walk into a wall because I think it's a door.

'It could happen to anyone,' he says politely.

When we walk on the gravel there is a need to find more pointless words. They are sickening words, useless, dead in themselves, like any words between two people, fresh out of love.

I tell him that there is an apartment in the college in Paris. I tell him that I hate noise and the smell of other people's food. I can come out with some awful rubbish when I can't think of anything to say.

I wrap the pink fuzzy scarf around me and we walk to our cars, like brother and sister. I look at him then and I want to say it, 'We were together, Jim, and now, look, it's just gone.'

It is the kind of hotel where you would go for sex on a wet Sunday afternoon. Vaguely turned on by the springy carpets and the smell of dinner. If he had wanted to sleep with me I would have let him. How about that? But Jim is above me now and apart from our little pecks on the cheek he doesn't want to touch me at all.

10

City of Light

December 1997

The fountain on Rue Soufflot has not frozen yet, but Audrey has promised me that it will. She told me about it, with her red gloves pointing upwards.

'Slower . . . slower,' she said to describe the water that will gradually freeze over, and then 'Shhhh' and it made me smile because I could see this thing of beauty she described so well.

'Paris in winter!' she exclaimed, and her voice had some impatience in it and then her words trailed off and she looked out on to the street and shook her head sadly. We both know that it is a city with a mind of its own and Paris in December is in a whole new mood.

Audrey is a woman in her early forties. When she says her name it is 'Oohdray', and it is like the beginning of a song. Her words are simple and clear and always full of meaning. She is beautiful and she gives me hope.

The first night we met I told her that my mother had died suddenly and that I came to Paris because I felt I had nowhere else to go.

Then I told her about my father and how I was almost married — and she nodded her head sadly and looked out on to the street again.

'You have an interesting life,' she said.

'It's kind of lonely,' I told her.

'Everyone is kind of lonely,' she answered.

We met awkwardly at first, pushed together by Simone who could not have known that we were both there to feel the loneliness she was trying to prevent. I like the feeling of being cast free, out through the city, like sheets of coloured paper, and then finding Audrey, like some pretty island, a woman on her own.

Every Friday night we sit side by side on the terrace of Café du Trésor and talk like this. We are afraid to like each other too much though. We are afraid of overstepping the mark and then the other wild bird might need to escape.

The café is painted a deep green colour and it wraps around a wide corner between Rue Soufflot and Boulevard Saint Michel. There are chairs on the terrace and tiny round tables like thumb tacks stuck into the ground. The waiters move things around reluctantly when three people come to sit down.

The chairs are parked in twos facing out on

to the streets and this in their opinion is how people should sit. The best kind of conversation takes place between two women who talk and then fall silent and look away. This is how secrets are exchanged, over and back, the most daring pieces handed out without any facial expression at all.

There is a loose colonial theme inside, with polished herringbone wooden floors and tall green plants. We will begin our evening on the terrace and then move inside reluctantly because of the cold. The waiter will not acknowledge me. Four weeks now and I have never missed a Friday and still I will say, '*Bonsoir, monsieur*,' and he will rebuke me with a syrupy '*Bonsoir*,' the kind he uses for every old tourist, and I will sit feeling a little humiliated and wishing then that he would leave me alone.

I take a table at the back of the terrace and order tea. The city is friendlier in the cold and there is comfort in the muffled coats that brush against me as the Parisians move in and out.

Tonight Paris is like a snow globe that sits smugly knowing full well how beautiful it will be when given its first shake. It has the attraction of a woman who eats without thinking and whose skin is warm and smooth and likes to be touched.

When I lean my head back I think of home. Only because I know it is under this sky too.

I wonder how it is for it now that it's locked up and empty and cold. When I close my eyes I can see every piece of furniture. The overstuffed yellow cushions. The music lying silently inside the piano stool. I can smell all of it and see every tiny detail, right down to the dusty white button left on the windowsill. Sometimes I walk myself from room to room, placing my hands flat against each cold wall.

'I'm here,' I whisper into it, 'I won't forget you,' but after three months I am still here because when I say home now, I don't know what I mean.

Audrey is late and arrives breathless, her long black coat floating out behind her and her black silk dress making an umbrella shape just below her knees. She wears black wool stockings and flat shoes with a strap across her foot. There is an orange silk scarf around her neck and it belongs here, with us, as we sit in the frosty night air. She is like a special winter doll and she kisses me on both cheeks and then sits down with a bump.

'Oh my God,' she says, sitting squarely in her chair. She has been rushing and is still a little distracted by whatever has tried to push past her in the street. She carries Paris with her in her clothes and hair, which is full of soft loose curls and is never untidy. Her eyes fall for a second on the small silver teapot and then looking into the menu she says, 'Well, I'm not having one of those.'

She picks up the wine list and the waiter arrives from nowhere with his head to one side and says, '*Ah, madame.*' His voice is warm and welcoming and he seems to say, 'Ah you came back, we are so glad.'

*   *   *

I came to Paris in September in the middle of a heatwave and as I stood at the end of Rue du Trésor, which is a tight winding street that leads to the college, the city said its first 'Hello'. I told Audrey about this on our first Friday together and described that hot day in September and how I had stood in a yellow alleyway with my suitcase watching an old man paint. There was no need to look over his shoulder because it was easy to see what he wanted to re-create. The jasmine that hung over the wall of the local school with just a shaving from the Panthéon, barely in view. He worked on quietly, ignoring the rattling truck and then the roller blades and finally the nun who peeped over his shoulder. He would not be deterred or distracted and, in his long grey beard and wide-brimmed straw hat, he was as beautiful as the city itself.

'Have you ever stood and watched someone paint?' I asked her, and I realized then that she was a woman who listened very well. Whatever I said seemed important now and she could keep her eyes on me and her body was very still.

'Ah,' she replied quietly, nodding, and then she turned away quickly and then looked back at me again. 'This place,' and she opened her hands towards me. 'You think you're having a bad day, and then you walk around a corner and see something,' and here she gave a big shrug that made me laugh, 'and nothing matters then, and you just look at it beside whatever is troubling you, and you say, 'Oh, all right then.''

She is part of Paris and she wears it in her orange scarf and her flat shoes and in the way she looks up at the waiter over her tortoiseshell reading glasses. She told me that she reads some poetry every day and how nothing bothers her really. She bends like a willow and lets this place wash over her.

★   ★   ★

The college is a gothic building with high windows and two green arched doors. It was impressive and silent on that still afternoon, and all around it was that Sunday quiet that I didn't know existed any more.

I walked up the long winding stairs to the first floor of the college and when I looked up I could see each of the four floors up above. The steps were narrow and some of the old tiles in the hallway were loose. It was Simone who had found the job. The college needed an English teacher, someone who could speak English fluently and look after the student applications and keep things on track during their stay.

The security man showed me to my little apartment. It was on the third floor overlooking the courtyard, a wide half-moon expanse covered with yellow pebbles and sun. The old building wrapped itself around it and when he had gone I opened the high double windows and sat with my chin in my hands. There were fourteen lime trees marking out the quadrangle and the clock in the tower suddenly rang out four chimes. I knew that there would be many days now when I would sit at these windows staring out and comparing Paris to home. In a matter of hours, this city had taken me in. It had not accepted me or welcomed me, but it seemed happy to let me slide quietly into its folds.

The room is at the end of the third-floor

landing and it carries the half-moon shape of the building. The main wall curves gently towards me and there are two windows that look out into the courtyard and another round window on the opposite wall where I can see the Jardin du Luxembourg. There is a kitchenette with a small two-ring hob, a fridge, a stainless-steel sink and, so far, one white mug. It was bought hurriedly on Rue Monge on that first Sunday night. There is a whistling kettle which, during a moment of loneliness, I christened 'Jean-Paul'. The walls in the kitchenette are painted pale blue and it has rounded into another curious corner to carry more of the building's shapes. There are two wooden chairs low to the ground just under the window and that's my sitting room, which is also my bedroom, and my bed is just behind the door. The floorboards are polished oak and with the red rug under the windows, this is my new home.

There were two students wearing shorts and carrying a ladder down the corridor. They manoeuvred it through doorways laughing and talking to each other and then looking up one of them said, '*Bonjour, madame.*'

'*Bonjour,*' I replied, but I knew he was Irish. He had pale legs and he was sweating and when I looked at him for a second longer

I could see that he was intelligent and gay.

So there it was, 'Madame' had found its way to me. With one word they could categorize me. When I met Audrey the following Friday she explained it all in detail.

'Mademoiselle is a little silly, girlish,' she said and then, 'Madame does not mean old, it means they have respect for you. Not that you have lived your life, but that you are living it now. There is nothing silly about madame — don't mess with madame,' she said then, nodding her head towards me, and she opened her notebook and wrote down a list of things I needed to see.

Saint Eustace — Sainte Chapelle — Les Halles — Sacré-Coeur.

'The Eiffel Tower,' she added, and she said this reluctantly as if to say, 'If you must.'

And then there was a little P.S. 'Let's ignore our mother's well-intentioned advice,' it said, and this meant nothing to me at all.

I told her I was worried about my French and she shrugged and said calmly, 'It will come,' and then, 'You must learn to go with it,' and she demonstrated by shrugging her shoulders and making a puff sound with her mouth.

'These are words too,' she said.

And that was how we met on that first Friday. Sitting outside in the late evening sun watching the Parisians walk up and down. There was red wine and a platter of cheese and we held out our first tentative words towards each other, and they dangled there as if they were on fishing rods.

★   ★   ★

When Audrey orders wine she consults the waiter. She holds the menu tightly and a little too close to her face. From time to time she listens to what he says and nods and then looks through the list again.

The restaurant is getting busier and they are not in any hurry at all. He says something that makes her laugh and she pulls a face and then points out her choice. She has created a small tight circle where only she and the waiter exist and I would like to know how she does that. She shows him that she has time for him. That there is nothing so important as this wine and this waiter — and he is busy, with the other waiters beginning to flap around us like birds, and he doesn't mind in the least. He shoots away then with the menu tucked under his arm and his face is happy and warm.

We sit for a moment without speaking and allow the working week to slide away. Audrey is wondering if there is something she has forgotten to do and I sit quietly and leave her to this thought. In a little while we will thaw and drink some wine and then curl into each other for what will have to be another very long talk.

'So how is life at the college?' she asks, and by now we are well into this bottle of wine and leaning more towards each other and beginning to smile.

'Oh, fine, we have some new undergrads you know,' I say and Audrey lifts her eyebrows. 'Last night they played football on the street . . . they've been sitting up in the kitchen till all hours drinking wine, you know.'

'Bastards,' Audrey says.

'Well, we've all been there.'

I had found them in the kitchen sitting around a table drinking wine with one candle in the middle lighting up each face. The window was opened wide and two girls were leaning out and calling on to the street.

'Three nights in a row,' I tell her, and in my mind I am planning to join them the next time they wake me up. 'You know what young guys are like,' I say then.

'Bastards,' she says again, and with her accent she makes it sound like butter spreading on bread.

'They have energy,' I tell her, and now we

are beginning to get drunk.

I have noticed them, I must admit. Even in my new sackcloth, my old self still lives. Especially Peter, walking into breakfast in his socks, looking all fresh and scrubbed. I have wondered how it would feel to place my hand on his shoulder or flat against his cheek. How he would look back at me, how warm his skin would feel, how much of his youth and energy would tingle up through my touch. I imagine that I would have to kiss him first because I'm older. I imagine it, because I'm older.

'Twenty-nine is a dangerous age,' Audrey says, and she lights her cigarette and shakes out the match. 'You can pass yourself off with anyone, the very young and the very old . . . young men are wonderful, but . . . they always leave you in the end . . . that much I know for sure.' She looks sad, but only for a moment, and then she brightens as a young man cycles past with a brown parcel on the carrier of his bike. 'No, they're wonderful . . . so long as you can keep your figure,' she adds then.

There is silence and she looks at me carefully. 'You must know it,' she says, and with one look her eyes travel the length of my frame. 'I am glad you eat such a lot,' she says, and then laughs smoke out of her mouth.

'Otherwise I would have to hate you — and I don't want to do that.'

When the waiter comes over she gives me another glance and she orders another bottle of wine. Then she offers me a cigarette, which I accept, and we order more bread and cheese.

'Food is important here,' and she spins the wine gently in her glass. 'I mean, let's face it, anyone who's picky about their food' — her face is beginning to curl in disgust and her head shakes slightly so that her soft curls move — 'you know, I'll eat a little of this and a little of that . . . someone who's picky like that,' and her words are offered out to everyone who would like to hear them. We don't look at each other, but talk staring straight ahead as if it doesn't matter at all and then she finishes this sentence. 'Someone who's picky like that . . . is bound to be a really bad fuck.'

The small Le Bon Marché bag is put on the table and I push it reluctantly towards her.

'I got this for you,' I tell her. 'It's just something small, to say thank you . . . for taking the time, y'know . . . '

Audrey places her hand flat on her chest and out of nowhere her eyes have suddenly filled with tears.

'For me,' she says, and I am worried now

because it is only a Diptyque candle.

Audrey lifts it out as if it is a precious bird and then smells it and lets the scent take her somewhere else.

'Mimosa,' she says.

Before we met I had a picture of her in my mind as a tall dark lady and in fact she is quite small with lots of curly hair and a beautiful face.

We have two more glasses of wine and then we must leave. I had forgotten what it is like to drink good wine and talk to another woman. I had forgotten the comfort of it. The locking in and locking out of the world that can be done. As strangers we manage to be completely kind to each other, as only two single women can.

Audrey gathers up her things and then puts the candle carefully into her bag.

'Tonight,' she announces, 'I am going to sleep.'

She stands and then kisses me on both cheeks.

'Yes,' she says, and her voice is happy. 'A pill and some sleep.'

★   ★   ★

On Monday morning there is a letter from Jacob and it arrives with a new kind of winter weather. The cold snap has moved on and the sky is dark and full of rain. One of the students rushes past me in a raincoat and he calls back over his shoulder, 'I'm off to the Louvre,' and he is gone then, out into the world, making echoing sounds on the stairs.

The others wander into the refectory quiet in themselves and blinking with sleep. One boy arrives in a dressing gown and as usual Peter pads in quietly in socks. The refectory is a long narrow hall with rows of leaded windows along each side. In summer every window is left open and the orange curtains are sucked out and they float outside in the breeze.

The students stack bread high on their trays and drink coffee without holding the handle of the cup. They pour too much milk into their cereals and then chase the Rice Crispies around with their spoons. They are talking about a Chinese restaurant on Rue Saint Antoine now and how you can get three courses for fifty francs. I enjoy their patter, their ability to talk as soon as they open their eyes.

Outside the sky has grown darker and after a single crack of thunder there is a sudden hiss and a downpour of rain. They fall silent then and eat their breakfast just staring out. The rain bounces off the cobblestones and then runs in little rivers down the street.

'That's more like it,' Peter says, 'there's nothing romantic about sun.'

★　★　★

Café du Marché is only a few minutes from the college and it is quiet in the middle of the morning. The waiters wear T-shirts and long green aprons and they stroll around casually and pick up used plates and cups. There are pistachio-coloured walls and orange globe lamps and pictures of primitive man drinking wine by the neck in many different poses. I don't understand the captions and some day I will ask Audrey what they mean. They leave me in peace here. There are no waiters in white coats waiting to swoop in. They lean over the counter and talk to their regular customers and drink coffee with them from a glass. They block the door with a lift that can be lowered into the cellar. They take their time and don't seem to care.

'*Pardon, madame*,' they say, and they smile and are not really sorry at all.

The owner is a handsome man called Claude. He is a short square shape and he has thick dark hair cut in one length just below his ears. He smiles kindly at me and begins to make my coffee. '*Bonjour, Hélène*,' he says, and I take my usual seat inside the window and watch the rain.

I have often sat here on my own and watched him talk to the staff and his regular customers. He jokes with them and then smiles into the mobile phone. He is always calm and in control of everything. He wears a ring on his right hand — and I guess that's how the men do it in France. I wonder then about his wife and what she might be like and how they make love. Two short square people who are not oafish and roll silently together like clouds.

The couple sitting opposite are in their own secret place. I can feel it now as the sky grows darker and I envy the tension they create. She is wearing a cream-coloured beret and her hair has not been brushed. He looks at her and smiles and then — as if he finds it somehow unbearable — he looks out the window and away. Across the table their fingers are touching and they do not need to speak. I can sense that they might need to make love at any minute or perhaps they already have.

I slide my thumb under the envelope and there are two sheets of cream paper covered in his neat old-fashioned hand.

'Now, Jacob,' I tell him with a smile and I begin to read.

6 December 1997

Dear Helen,
I hope you are well and enjoying your time in Paris. Things are very much the same here, the glass is low and we are having a cold snap.

I moved the grey mare into the paddock behind the house. She takes half a bale every day — and she would need it. This morning I had to break the ice in the tank. We are going to have a fall of snow any day now.

I was up at the old house on Sunday, and walked around it, in through the rooms, and made sure everything was all right. I found a mouse in the scullery, but I think I found the place where he came in.

Beth and Tom are still coming and going and everything has been packed away. It took four removal trucks in the end. One of them reversed over the back lawn, but there is not too much damage. Most of it went to Leo's. Do you know they cut the two big beech trees down?

[And here his words seemed to trail away and I can hear the disgust in his voice.]

I hope you are well, Helen, and that you will be home soon.
Much love,
Jacob

I can see him, of course. Washing his hands carefully at the kitchen sink, leaning a little over the water, his arms tanned and wiry and his sleeves rolled up over his elbows.

He would have taken the writing paper down from the top of the old dresser. He would have turned on the yellow light in his kitchen and stood there between the toffee-smoked walls. He would have left his coat hanging on the back of the door and then sat down to write. His cap was left on a chair and his silver hair combed straight back from his forehead. One hand held the paper steady and the other wrote carefully to produce his beautiful old-fashioned script. It was not rehearsed. He spoke into the paper and his hand copied the words down.

He had come to me in this envelope and I can hear his intonation on every word, where he would take a breath, and raise an eyebrow. Everything so honest and full of common sense. He gives himself to me and doesn't care how unsophisticated he might be in my new surroundings. And to me Jacob could fly up and sit on the roof of any of these old buildings and then look down on them, and it makes me sad now because really he is all I have of home.

I can feel that he is worried about the house now and that he is asking me gently to decide. Rue left all her furniture to Tom and Beth and she left the house to me.

She said I didn't need furniture, but that I did need a home, and why is it that everyone I know wants me to settle down under a roof? And in my mind I have taken her furniture into a forest and I am sitting on a green couch under more green trees.

I order a second coffee and read it again, wishing it was my first time to read it, and this time I notice other things. I can smell the sea on a cold dark morning and I can see the grey mare with her white mane lifting in the wind.

Claude leans on the counter and watches me for a moment.

'Will you have something to eat?' he asks kindly. 'We have quiche. We have omelettes,' and then he looks up as Audrey walks in. She glances briefly at him and seeing me she claps her hands lightly and pulls up a chair.

'Ah, you are here, I was hoping you would be,' she says, and she looks back at Claude who is suddenly busy drying glasses and he is careful now not to look around. Behind the counter he moves things left and right and then he moves them back again.

'That's a very pretty scarf,' I tell her, and she glances up from the menu and tells me that she bought it in a boutique in Les Halles.

Claude carries the coffees to the table and then looks at her.

'Your hair,' he says, and he pauses for a moment and I like to watch these Frenchmen take the plunge. It is all done so calmly, so easily, as if it is like everyday chat. She looks up quickly and then glances shyly at me. He makes a snip-snip movement with his fingers to show her that he knows she has had it done.

'Très jolie, Audrey,' he says, and his voice is sincere, and when he says her name it is sweet, and with his beautiful accent it makes me think of Crème Brûlée.

'Oh, merci,' she says, laughing, and she puts her hands lightly over her curls as if to smooth them down.

When he goes I whisper, 'It's a pity he's married.'

'Oh, he's not married,' she says and her answer comes back very quickly and then he is gone, his feet moving silently under the long green apron and leaving two pretty pink spots on her cheeks.

★   ★   ★

Two old ladies meet under a lime tree near Notre Dame. They are old friends and they do not kiss, but stand up formally and shake hands. What they have is old, like their black wool scarves and their sensible black shoes, an old friendship worthy of respect — and I believe some day this is how Birdie and I will meet.

On Saturday morning I walk beside the Seine. The bookstands are opening and they are hanging out their art nouveau posters and the framed pictures of the Sacré-Coeur and Tournée du Chat Noir. A girl wearing a pink-and-red scarf hands me a flyer telling me about a Chopin concert in the church of St-Germain-des-Prés. When I sit on a bench under the trees near Notre Dame there are spots of sunshine on the dry pebble paths. This is where people sit and watch Paris go by. There is always something worth watching, some part of life that needs to be seen. There is a young writer on the next bench and he scribbles into a Moleskine notebook. When he stops he looks around, the writer in Paris, and how history repeats and repeats itself.

Then a tall man sits down beside me.

'Hello,' he says.

'Hello,' I reply, and my voice is reluctant.

'I think your sunglasses are very nice,' he says.

'Thank you,' and I am looking down at the dried-out pebbles and wishing that he would go.

'Would you like to have a drink?' he asks then, and his voice tells me that this is all perfectly normal in his world.

'No, thank you.'

But he stays where he is, waiting calmly, watching my sunglasses, watching me, until I realize that I am the one who must get up and leave.

★　★　★

It was Beth who packed everything in the end, and when she called me and asked what I would like to keep I said, 'Nothing, nothing at all.' My voice was not hard, just sad and eager to escape. Our conversation was short and in the background her new baby was crying and Angel was making her first attempt at words. Beside me Audrey's voice flew lightly upwards in a free-flowing torrent of French. There was a long silence and Beth waited for me to say something and then she said goodbye and then with a little laugh, '*Au revoir*,' and she put down the phone. After that there were many more short conversations as Beth walked back across the vast hall and into the dining room, silent and gliding in pink-slippered feet.

She would call me with odd little questions — to see if the pink soup tureen had a lid or if there was a key to wind the dining-room clock. I was sorry that I had distanced myself from her then and that she needed these things as an excuse to say, 'Hello.'

She was not to know that every clue she gave me, every reminder of our old life, were like sharp little bones sticking into my skin. We mourned our losses in different ways. She packed boxes and wrote labels and used real things to fill up her mental space and after that she had her babies and Tom. I on the other hand took to wandering, thinking too much, searching for something that might not exist.

There are times when it creeps up on me. It is like a soft knock on wood. 'Hello there,' it says quietly and then out of nowhere I am falling apart and missing Rue. I have my conscience to deal with too, and there are nights when I have wanted to call Jim. When that happens I put on my coat and walk the long streets of Paris, always more romantic in the rain.

If I get outside, there is noise and the sound of tyres running through puddles and yellow lamps reflecting on the street. There is some comfort in aloneness. The sound of the rain on my umbrella, the noise my shoes make as they walk along the quiet streets. The faint music and voices coming from a restaurant, and as long as I notice these things and as long as they feel important to me I am not able to come home.

★ ★ ★

Beth has always liked the breakfast tea set and the paintings by our grandmother. Tom wanted the art deco pieces and the dining-room clock. Then they sent the old harmonium and the piano to Martha Penrose and the rest to Leo's for auction.

The removal men arrived on time and it took three whole days to fill the trucks and carry out every box. The grandfather clock was propped up in the horsebox with the old red armchairs around it and every cushion in the house to keep it steady. 'Three hundred and forty-three boxes.' Beth told me this proudly because she had packed every one. She never mentioned what she felt when she walked into my bedroom and found my wedding dress hanging there.

It was only when she went to the altar at the end of the first landing and lifted the statue of the Virgin Mary that Jacob stopped her in her tracks.

'Bad luck to take that out of here,' he said, and she looked at him without speaking and then she put it back, where it belonged, on the cream-coloured altar in front of the red stained-glass window with the kneeler beside it. There is a broken vase filled with faded plastic flowers in front of the statue and this is only part of our home left exactly as it has always been. When she told me about this, she was laughing a little, and I could see then that she was happy to be left in charge. I asked her how Jacob was keeping.

'Same as ever really,' she said. 'Just quieter, I think.'

★ ★ ★

I send Jacob another letter from Paris and I describe everything to him as if he is sitting across from me in his red armchair. Like the antique toys in the shop window and how they are older than any child will ever be. And the shop that only sells Japanese teapots. And how people here are. Respectful, polite, cool, never offering anything they may not really want to give.

I tell him about going to mass in Saint Eustace and how the stacked-up male voices reminded me of inlaid wood. And the trees of the Jardin du Luxembourg and how they look after a white frost, then I tell him I will come home — but that I am not ready yet.

★　★　★

Judith stands at the mirror in my bathroom. She puts on smoky eyeshadow and then fixes a red silk rose in her hair. 'There's something about Paris,' she says again, and every time she says it now she says, 'Pareee . . . '

'I can't wait for you to meet Brian,' she says. 'I would really like your opinion.' But I can see that it is already far too late for that.

We meet in the Burmese Bar and he is standing inside the door carrying a white plastic bag. He is tall and very bald and when he leans in to kiss her cheek I am seeing a golf ball gliding through the air. He shakes my hand and then tells us to follow him to the bar.

'It rocks in here,' he says, and I am thinking that Paris is beautiful because it never does that, because there is no French for 'rocks'.

It is hard to see where we are going, but when we make it to the bar we buy cocktails and then we talk.

Behind us there is a giant Buddha and we are standing quietly at his feet.

The American woman behind us asks us to

move away then. She is wearing a cowboy hat and she is rude. She has blonde hair and when she stands up in her white cowboy boots she is taller than each of us.

'We've booked these tables,' she says, 'and you're crowding us out,' and then she calls Judith 'trailer trash' and we decide to leave.

During this time Brian stands with a peculiar half smile on his face. He seems to float lightly over us and he ignores the American who's looking for a fight.

When he goes to the bathroom, I tell her that he seems really lovely, but we have both noticed that he didn't buy his round. When we are leaving he walks through the door in front of us and Judith just smiles and carries on and what is it about tight people that also makes them tight inside?

Judith asks him if they can walk beside the Seine, and in my mind I am seeing her walk with a cardboard box.

'It's the most romantic walk in the world,' she tells him, but he says it's too late and that he's already feeling cold.

'There's something about a man who carries a plastic bag,' I tell her later, and she looks at me sadly and nods her head. Then I tell her not to worry about the walk along the Seine.

'It's not going anywhere,' I tell her, 'and

you can save that great river for someone else.'

* * *

It is magical in the Jardin du Luxembourg after a hard white frost. Every tree and shrub and blade of grass is still and white. They cannot move until the sun comes up and even then they are frozen and still, like Lot's wife. I like the silence of it and how we all walk quietly through it, puffing out warm breath and speaking quietly, giving this place some sort of reverential respect. At lunchtime we move out of our offices and take a small green chair and eat lunch knowing that in the middle of a humdrum working day there is still something really beautiful to see.

* * *

When Beth comes to visit she asks me if we can go to the top of the Eiffel Tower and we decide to go late one cold night. In the restaurant she whispers that she thinks the waiter is very rude and I tell her I don't notice any more.

She walks up to the ticket desk in the Métro station and asks for two tickets to the Eiffel Tower in her best French. She is

363

small to me then with raggy blonde plaits and her Chopper bike lying near her on the ground. The woman behind the glass knows that she is a tourist, and she pretends she doesn't understand, and sometimes this is their idea of sport.

She makes a puff sound out through her mouth and rolls her eyes and looks away and Beth just stands there watching her. Then she turns to me as if to say, 'What should I do?' So I walk up to the glass and ask the woman what part of Eiffel Tower she doesn't understand.

It is cold at the top and we are already tired when we arrive. We take a photograph and walk around for a minute and then we queue up to get back down again.

* * *

The bistro is on Rue Monge which is a steep winding street that runs down to Boulevard St Germain. From its doorway there is a wiry sound of a trumpet and a girl's voice as she sings. The music is coming from a radio at the back of the bistro and there are candles behind red glass on almost every table. There is a blackboard menu hanging outside the door offering three courses for a hundred francs. You may have a starter and a main course or a main course and dessert. I am about to move on when the owner appears. He is tanned with brown eyes and dark silky hair.

'*C'est bon*,' he says, nodding his head back towards the restaurant and then he asks if I speak French.

'Only a little.'

'This,' he says waving towards the menu, 'is traditional French food. *Boeuf Bourguignon*. Onion soup . . . '

'Oh . . . I don't want onion soup . . . do you have fish?' and I'm not bothered if he thinks I'm an idiot.

'Yes,' he says happily. 'We have poisson. A fillet of cod — '

'I don't like cod,' but I smile now to soften the blow, and when I laugh I can feel my earrings swing from left to right. 'Do you have salmon?'

'Yes,' he says, 'we have sal-mon in a cognac sauce. It's very good.'

The restaurant is empty and warm. It is a small square room with only a few tables. None of the furniture matches, but there is a candle in a little red glass pot on every table now.

He pours a glass of Kir.

'This is for you,' he says, 'because you . . . ' and he stops then, waiting for a large word to surface. 'Accepted,' he announces. Emphasizing the letter 'A' and stretching his lips back over his teeth to pronounce the word. His teeth are small and tobacco-stained, but he is handsome and a little flirtatious and I'm thinking, 'Frenchmen and their cigarettes.'

'It is Kir,' he says, placing the tiny glass on the table. 'White wine with blackcurrants,' he adds, and he is really spoonfeeding me now.

He looks happy as he comes back across the room and points out the fish on the menu.

'If it is not in English, then we' — and he points to himself with both hands — 'can explain.' He waits then just for a moment and I still feel naked when I eat alone.

I order warm goat's cheese salad and sal-mon in cognac sauce.

'Only small portions, please,' I tell him, cupping my hands together to make a small circle on the table in front.

'You are not very hungry?' he asks sadly, and then walks away to place the order.

There is still no one else in the restaurant and he saunters by and then stops again to make conversation.

'This is not your first time in Paris?' he asks.

'No, but I've spent more time in the South. I've been to Nice a couple of times . . . so I

366

am just getting to know Paris.'

He smiles lazily and looks quickly at the door and then back to me again. He does not understand everything that I have said. He is not sure what to say next so I speak first.

'I have been to some restaurants here and they're not very good.'

He looks astonished and I can see that his eyes are laughing all the time now.

'Where?' he asks.

'Behind the Panthéon.'

'Ah,' he says, 'for the tourists.'

'Last week,' and I'm warming up now, 'I went to the Burmese Bar. Do you know it?'

He shakes his head.

My cheeks are feeling hot and I am smiling a lot more than before.

'Where is it?'

'On the right, fourteenth, I think.'

'And it was good?'

'So, so — I returned a cocktail because it was . . . ' and I am looking for a way to explain what I want to say. They had forgotten to add the Syrop de Gomme. The waiter was rude. It was like a bordello inside.

'It was not very good,' I tell him then.

'Why you go?' he asks, laughing now.

'It is supposed to be very chic.'

'Chic,' he repeats happily.

'Supposed to be,' I remind him, nodding

slowly in his direction and looking up into his eyes and laughing again, and then there is the look that says we could go to bed.

When he comes back he is carrying the warm goat's cheese salad.

'*Bon appétit*,' he says, and he is smiling all over me now.

He waits at the door with his back turned until I have finished, and then he waits a little longer.

I pretend to read my book, but can feel that we are drawn to each other now. In the small warm room with the red candles and the smoky music, we are giving ourselves some freedom, knitting some sort of thing together and then batting it over and back. The atmosphere is intense and over full and I am wondering what would happen if he were to close over the door and walk towards me.

'So,' he says, lifting my plate, 'you like?'

I like to look into his dark sparkling eyes and flirt a little and inside there is just one thought: 'French men are good lovers,' it says.

I put my knife and fork together and tap the corners of my mouth with one finger behind the napkin. He sees that some of my lipstick appears on the white cloth.

The woman on the radio is singing, 'I've got you under my skin,' in a mixture of French and English, and we are still the only people listening to the music and seeing the small melting candles.

'So you are on holiday in Paris?'

'Yes, but I also work . . . I really like it here . . . the people . . . ' And then I decide to toss a bigger ball towards him. 'The men are quite . . . direct.'

I watch him from under my eyelashes and wait for him to speak.

'And Irish girls are a little shy,' he says.

And then we are both laughing. The air between us feels beaten and pulled apart and I wonder when it will snap.

He thinks for a moment and then nods.

'Yes, French, Latins, Italians are very' — and he sends his hand gently through the air like a fish swimming towards me — 'direct,' he concludes.

'And where are you from?' I ask, but then a waiter from next door comes in and he must speak to him.

He asks the owner for some bottles of Heineken. He can see that he has interrupted something and looks quickly around the empty room and then at me.

'*Bonsoir*. Good evening,' he says.

'*Bonsoir*,' I reply.

The owner puts the salmon in front of me with a little flourish.

'*Bon appétit*,' he says again.

'Thank you. *Merci*.'

'Do you enjoy jazz clubs?' he asks suddenly.

'Yes, very much,' and I wait before taking up my knife and fork.

'There is one near here where I like to go,' he says, 'but you might be afraid?' and he looks down on me with a big wide smile.

'With music like this?' and I nod my head towards the speaker on the wall.

'Yes,' and he gives a happy sigh.

He brings the dessert menu.

'I would just like tea.'

He waits at the door and then turns to me again.

I like that he cannot stop talking to me.

'I'm sorry, you asked me a question . . . ' he says.

'Oh yes, where are you from? Are you from Paris?'

'No,' he says, and his smile is wide enough to cover all sorts of things. 'I am Algerian.'

'Oh,' and I smile back at him, and then look at the teapot, but only for a second.

'Paris is a lovely city . . . the pace is nice and slow. How long have you been here?' And the words come out too quickly and I'm smiling too much.

'Six years.' And he is not sure if it has changed just a little now, but because I am smiling he tries again.

'So the jazz club . . . would you like to go there, with me?' and he laughs a little over the last two words.

Frenchmen are good lovers.

'I don't think so,' I tell him, and my face falls into pieces on my plate.

I look at him sadly when I say these words, shaking my head slowly and making my earrings swing from left to right.

★　★　★

The little girl stands near the statue and holds a piece of bread in the air. She stays very still and when the adults see her they are amused. One by one the tiny birds begin to flutter in and then they land and eat from her palm. There are at least six at one time and they are small and buzzing like bees.

★　★　★

The old men of Paris play checkers in the sun. They smile with wrinkled faces and nod slowly, and they are always so quiet and calm. They sit in the Jardin du Luxembourg or along the banks of the Seine. They sit side by side, not speaking, just watching everything, even though they have seen it all before.

Last night I had that dream again: my father is walking ahead of me and he keeps walking when I call. Sometimes I wonder if he walks the streets of Paris with me. Sometimes I wonder if he is already dead.

★   ★   ★

On Saturday night Leo calls and when we talk I curl up on a chair and watch the rain. We talk about Laytown and Paris and then just everyday things. Sometimes he says he misses me and I wonder what he really means. He doesn't mention the old house. He is slightly embarrassed by it, and the old chairs and tables are thrown between us now like a handful of odd shells.

He is, as he has always been, my brave friend, Leo, and he is not frightened now to be the undertaker of my old world. He will just get on with it and only mention it if there is something I need to know.

He adds in daft little things too and tells me that Blondie is getting fat and that he's cutting back on her hot milk and Weetabix and making her run on the beach. And everything he says tells me that she is being looked after very well.

Then out of nowhere he is talking about my father's desk and he calls it the old writing desk because he doesn't know what it means.

He tells me that he has found an old photograph inside it and I ask him if it has a secret drawer. This is an old joke between us, since the day he told me that this was every antique dealer's dream.

'No,' he laughs, 'it had fallen down behind the drawers,' and then I see how he has managed it. Knowing from the start that it is important to me.

I see now that he has gently reeled me in.

'I think it might be a photograph of your father,' he says quietly. 'You're in it as well.'

And when I say nothing because I can't, he fills in the gap gently.

'I'll keep it for you,' he says.

We talk for an hour like this every Saturday night and sometimes I have to call him earlier, because there is something that won't keep. I miss him and his mischievous face I have to admit.

'He might grow on you,' Rue said once, and I dismissed it, and I've never liked the idea of a man growing on me. Perhaps I am worried now that I have also grown on him. Maybe we have somehow grown together or maybe just grown up.

*   *   *

Audrey tells me she is going to the cinema with Claude. They are going to see *Othello* at the little red theatre on Boulevard St Germain. 'Interesting choice,' I tell her, and I am already grimacing at the thought of Orson Welles with his boot polish face.

'It doesn't matter,' she says, and I can see that she is different now. She is paying attention to Claude and hoping that it will work.

'This is all beautiful,' she says then, and she sips her wine and looks out over the street, 'but sometimes it is nice to have someone to share it with,' and she looks at me then when she speaks.

Then she asks if I will go on a double date and my other half will be the owner of the gallery where she works.

'Frédéric Lemoine,' she says, and her voice is level.

'You are joking,' I tell her. 'He is at least ninety-five.'

'No,' she says calmly, 'he is not that old and he is a very nice man,' and then I ask why she is not going out with him herself.

But I go because it might make a difference to her, and even though it is their first date they are like a married couple compared to us. Frédéric, who does not wish to be called Fred, croons snatches of Frank Sinatra into my ear. He is bald and behind his ears I am able to see his brains.

Audrey is my friend and I would like to help her to get it away with Claude, the floating cloud. Afterwards she thanks me and says she is sorry, because she knows Frédéric is as mad as a brush.

★　★　★

The college closes on Christmas Eve and as the last cheerful footsteps fall away there is just an awkward silence left.

The security guard waves at me through his window and I wave back. We are old friends now. He puts his feet up on the desk and watches TV. He says very little and I know he must wonder about my life and why I'm here at Christmas on my own. When Beth asks me to go to their house I tell her I would like to, because I would, but I need to be here. I need to be able to do this now.

The forecast says, 'Rain and sleet, but no snow.' There are sixty English papers to be marked and four new books to read. And these are all things I use to fill my days. These are things to keep the black dog outside my door, but I am used to the idea of it now. I have learned that being organized and filling up my days is the best foil to being alone

— and like all sorts of dead old days, these ones will also pass. There is a part of me that wants to hang a stocking up or to leave my shoes outside the door as the French children do.

When it gets dark the rain begins to fall steadily and with every gust of wind the drops are flattened on the windowpanes. Outside there are fewer cars going up and down the street and when I look closely there is ice in every drop. It is as if the city is closing down now and everyone goes away to whatever kind of Christmas they will have.

Then there are footsteps on the stairs and a soft little knock on my door and as I get up I remember Audrey said she would drop by.

He is smiling as soon as he sees me. His hair is wet from the rain. He is not wearing gloves and his hands looks cold, but his cheeks still have that clear fresh country look. When he smiles he is like a bright light on a dark winter afternoon, his teeth are white and perfectly straight.

'Hello, stranger,' Leo says, and he laughs out loud and when he steps into my room he wraps his arms around me in a hug. His cheeks are fresh and cold and there are tiny snowflakes melting on his scarf.

'It's Christmas,' he says then. 'Us orphans need to stick together.' And I am shrinking down into a little Oliver Twist.

He steps around a little awkwardly. He is smiling a lot and not fully sure of himself and then he sees my face and hugs me again.

'It's good to see you, Leo,' I tell him, and I mean every word.

He admires my room and notices the floor and the shape of the windows. He even admires the Quaker chairs and then turns one over lightly in his hand. He seems different to me now. Older and wiser, I think. He tells me Blondie is misbehaving and eating things in the shop.

'A good Queen Anne chair,' he says, shaking his head, and he is pretending to be annoyed. 'I've despatched her over to Jacob,' he says. 'I've put her on ice.'

He asks me all about the college and Paris and gives me the gossip from our town. We drink tea and outside it is still raining and with Leo here now, it feels like a whole other kind of day.

We find a bistro at the corner of Boulevard Saint Michel and order *Bœuf Bourguignon* that comes in little red pots. We drink wine and the owner comes out and wishes us a Merry Christmas and then, in a quiet moment, Leo puts his hand into an inside pocket and takes out a small envelope.

'Here it is,' he says, and he is watching my

face carefully and I'm thinking I've waited seventeen years. He gives it over and I hold it in my hand.

The owner comes up to the table and asks if we would like more coffee. He is polite and says that because it is Christmas Eve they need to close. The staff are standing near the kitchen door and their long faces tell me they would like to go home.

The envelope feels thin and it is dried out and discoloured after so many years and inside I am sunken down, like heavy wet clay falling into an open grave. I can feel my head getting lighter and it is as if the other diners are turning into ghosts. They have gathered around us now and they're singing Christmas carols and then someone suggests singing 'Three blind mice'.

'Are you OK?' Leo asks, and his voice is full of concern.

'I didn't really know what to do,' he says then, and he looks worried, and I know my face is getting pale.

'I just knew that this might be important to you.' Here he stops and looks down at the tablecloth.

'I was thinking about you here on your own at Christmas, and I was going to visit, and then this . . . ' And he is searching my face all the time.

'Did I do the right thing?'

The photograph inside is of my father and me. We are sitting on a red-and-white-striped garden bench with our backs to the sea. He is wearing a shirt with a butterfly collar and a brown V-neck pullover. His hair is down to his shoulders and, although I can't see them, I'm pretty sure he's wearing flares. I had expected to feel something. I had hoped I would recognize him and understand. Until now there was just an outline and today there is a face. I am looking into dark eyes like mine and I don't know how to feel. So I trace my finger over his face and say the only words I can think of: 'I came from you.'

He is staring straight ahead and not smiling, concentrating on allowing the camera to take this image of him and me. I am wearing a kilt as usual and my buttons are done up wrong. I have a pair of red woollen tights on and instead of looking at the camera I am looking at them.

The kid in the photo has already got it. It looks like she already knew how to play the game. If she had looked up at the camera, her eyes would have told me that the trick was not to care.

He has written on the back and the pencil is faded.

'To Hélène. From your father,' and the

date is 12 September 1971, and there it is like a clear statement of fact.

'Thank you, Leo,' and he nods at me and smiles.

When we walk back to the college the streets are silent and wet and the rain can't seem to make up its mind. The Eiffel Tower is lit up in a million different silver lights and we stand and watch it from the Panthéon.

'What age would he be now?' he asks, and he uses each word carefully, as if he is afraid of breaking bones.

'Early seventies,' I tell him. 'Actually, he's exactly seventy, I think, and that's if he's still alive.'

'Ever thought about . . . ?'

'No,' I tell him, and I want to cut him off. 'There's no point now.'

He smiles at me and keeps watching me, so I trust him and give him the other answer with a smile.

'Only every day.'

★ ★ ★

The handwriting on the back of the photograph is ornate. It is written with a loose, confident wrist. 'Hélène,' it says, and it is like an old-fashioned love letter, written a hundred years ago and delivered now by hand.

380

Later I tell Leo that I think my father looks a bit like David Cassidy, and he nods his head and agrees.

★ ★ ★

We have Christmas dinner with Audrey and Claude at Café du Marché. Frédéric Lemoine arrives and competes with Leo, who has no idea what is going on. We drink champagne and have oysters and foie gras to start. Then Claude carries in a goose surrounded by chestnuts and apples. Then there is cheese, Vacherin, soft and tender, and Frédéric tries to feed me bûche de Noël from his fork. When I look around Leo and Audrey are trying not to laugh. Claude's mother sits at the top of the table and after dessert she stands up and sings like Edith Piaf. There are white fairy lights around the windows and now and then someone walks past and looks in at us there.

Audrey raises her eyebrows at Leo and I tell her he is just a friend.

'Please,' she says, and her voice is firm, 'between a man and a woman there is really no such thing,' and when she moves beside Claude now she glides like a swan.

Afterwards I ask Leo what he thinks of my new friends and he laughs. It is after midnight and Christmas is over for another year.

'It was a bit like the mad hatter's tea party,' he says.

I know I will miss him when he leaves now, but as he packs and walks to the taxi I am frozen to the spot. He glances up at the window and waves and I wave back and try to say something meaningful with my eyes.

★   ★   ★

Sometimes I imagine that the photograph of Jacques Fournier speaks to me and it is always in a crackling BBC radio voice. I carry him with me all the time now, so that if anyone asks I can tell people that I have a father too.

★   ★   ★

Audrey marries Claude at the end of August. They invite Leo and we gather outside the Registry Office near the Panthéon. She is wearing a simple white Chanel suit and he is wearing a black suit and one white rose. They have made it look easy, and it is as if they are both landing safely now and just coming home.

We walk together down to Café du Trésor and everyone claps when we walk inside. The waiters pat Claude on the back and find a table for four and we sit there laughing and drinking coffee and wine. We are surrounded by tourists who are fascinated by two people who have married with such style. There is no cake or photographs, but when a tourist asks if she can take a picture Audrey's face lights up and she agrees. There is something about fresh love that's just easy and nice.

Later she asks me about Leo again as she sips her wine, and it is not that she is teasing, or trying to match us up. She watches me carefully and then she glances over to where he stands at the bar with Claude.

'Why not?' she asks.

'I have too much respect for him.'

And she pulls a face. 'Well, that's a good way to start.'

'I wouldn't want to do anything to hurt him,' I tell her. 'I really think he sees us as friends.'

Then I tell her that my sabbatical is over next month and this weekend I need to make up my mind. When she answers she is still thinking about Leo.

'You never know where the feelings begin,' she says, and she looks out on the street and we don't speak again for a little while.

When Claude joins us she asks him what he thinks and most men are hopeless when asked questions like that.

'My track record isn't great,' I tell him.

'You're not a greyhound,' he says.

⋆ ⋆ ⋆

There is a house near a beach in Ireland. It stands firm like a lighthouse looking out to sea. There are faces inside every window. Faces that only I can recognize. There is an old man with silver hair. He checks the windows and sweeps the floors. Early in the morning he gathers seaweed on the beach. There is a small girl with blonde hair and she needs to be looked after. There is a woman who laughs and talks all the time. Her hair is sandy grey and she has red cheeks. Her voice rings out from every room. She says things about the shoes that I'm wearing and about who my latest boyfriend is. That's just her way. It's how it is. Sometimes she makes us all kneel down for the rosary. Sometimes she dances to make me laugh.

⋆ ⋆ ⋆

He is old and loose like a ragged sail. He wears a paisley jacket and an orange and gold tie. He decides who he likes and makes it clear and there is no logic or reason behind the choices he makes.

It is a quiet easy Sunday, the first day of September, and Leo and I are moving silently between the shelves. I want to show him the bookshops of Paris today, because I have shown him everything else. This one is tucked into a side street near the Jardin du Plantes and there is an old man sitting at the till who I have never seen before. He has an American accent and I stand in the dark corner of his dusty shop and keep a book open in front of me while all the time looking at him. Leo is amused by it. He asks me if I have made up my mind yet. He would like to know when I'm coming home. We have found an easy rhythm now and don't get under each other's feet. We avoid all the Paris sights and instead spend our time looking for the best hot chocolate, or the best surprise — which is usually a tiny narrow street with a couple of dusty cafés off it and chipped-paint signs.

The old man talks to a boy with a Rastafarian hat. They are close and reading a book together.

'Did you see the book I gave Ariel?' he asks. 'It's kinda light, y'know, but nice.'

'Yes,' the boy replies. 'I saw it, it had a picture of a girl on the cover.' His voice curls off and I can sense that he feels he is better than this book for Ariel.

'Hang on,' the old guy says, and he gets up from behind the till and pulls a skinny little book from the shelf.

'Now, there's no girl on the cover,' he says, 'it's light but very nice,' and he pushes it into his hands. He takes no money and they are easy around each other. I want to know what I need to do now to have this old guy be easy and nice around me.

We walk around and flick through some of the secondhand books and Leo is watching me more than them. I'm watching the old man all the time. And he's giving me nothing at all.

A fat man with his glasses sitting on his forehead steps up next and I can tell that he is a difficult and arrogant man.

'Looker,' Leo says, 'not a buyer,' and I laugh.

The fat man turns his mouth down when he reads and he has folded the book back too much. I can pick up the end of their conversation as I move past the classics section at the back of the shop.

'Are you a doctor?' the old man asks.

'No, I'm not. Actually, I've been published . . . long time ago now, long oudda print,' and the old man acknowledges what he has said with a humming sound.

'Could I borrow this?' he asks then, and Leo nods at me and gives a little laugh.

'This is not a library,' the old man replies, and his voice is brisk and he looks past him and straight out on to the street.

Later as we drink our hot chocolates Leo tells me that I'm miles away and I smile because in truth I am.

'Do you mind if I go back to that shop again?' I ask him then. 'There's a book I need to get.'

'Sure,' he says, and I tell him that I will meet him on the first bench down by the Seine.

'The one beside the red houseboat,' I call after him, and he nods and smiles.

There is a chance now. Just a faint one, but I think I heard something in the old man's voice. There is a chance that he might remember me, that I might be someone he knows.

He stares straight ahead when I come in. His eyes are cold and they avoid my face and all the time there is a small voice inside me and it's trying to shout out to him.

'Notice me. Notice me,' it says.

'Do you have *Out of Africa*?' I ask, and even now he keeps staring out the open door. I want him to look at me, but he won't.

'Karen Blixen,' he says, 'no — we don't have that today.'

And so I pick up another book and flick through it and listen to his voice.

'There's that September wind,' I hear him say as someone closes the door. 'It's like everything's going to change.' And he talks down into the plastic flowers near the till.

He ignores me and instead focuses on two Chinese girls. And he is giving them his full attention now.

'Where are you from?' he asks and, when they tell him, he says, 'Hong Kong, sure I've been there, I've been all over, spent nearly twenty years in New York too.'

And all the time he refuses to see me standing there.

'We also have a picture gallery upstairs — it opens at four,' he tells them, and it is as if he is coaxing them now.

It is only three o'clock and they laugh and smile as people who do not fully understand do. When they turn to look through the shelves he begins to hum a tune under his breath.

He watches me for a moment and when I look into his eyes he looks away and then down.

'Where are you from?' he asks then, and when he looks up at me it is as if my heart is losing its beat.

'Ireland.'

'Ireland?' he says.

I have often wondered what happens when your heart just stops and if there are loose half-finished thoughts left floating in an empty space.

'Never been,' he says flatly, and when he looks away he turns the corners of his mouth down.

And in the Sunday quiet of this little shop this old man tells me that he doesn't know me. I breathe slowly as I watch him and then my heart starts beating again. I realize now that without my father, it probably always will.

'The picture gallery opens at four,' he says, and he points one finger upwards, but I am already walking towards the door.

'You can wait here if you like,' and he picks up a newspaper and holds it towards me.

'Here,' he says, 'read the funnies while you wait.'

★　★　★

There are small spots of sunlight lighting up each side of the river. The glittering barges float by and the passengers wave and raise a glass. Leo walks slowly as if we have all the time in the world. Like time has slowed down for us. As if time is waiting and giving us a chance to catch up. We find a bench and sit there without talking and I'm wondering if he remembers it too.

Audrey said, 'You never know where the feelings begin.'

'Leo?'

'Yes.'

'I'm going to come home.'

He turns his face to look at me and without speaking he nods slowly and smiles.

Our faces are reflected in the water and we are, as we were, boy and girl again.

Acknowledgements

I would like to thank the following people whose wisdom, encouragement and support have been invaluable to me:

My agent, Faith O'Grady.
Patricia Deevy and Michael McLoughlin at Penguin Ireland.
My friends and readers Deirdre Harrington, Suzanne Costello and Juliet Prendergast.
Margo Tracey for encouraging me to write a long time ago.
Dave McGloughlin, Eamon Clarkin, Peter McPartlin and Johnny Donohoe at IIBBDO.
Helen Carey at Centre Culturel Irlandais in Paris.
Melanie, Olive and Yvonne for listening to it all.
And my family as always, especially David.

We do hope that you have enjoyed reading this large print book.

Did you know that all of our titles are available for purchase?

We publish a wide range of high quality large print books including:
Romances, Mysteries, Classics
General Fiction
Non Fiction and Westerns

Special interest titles available in large print are:
The Little Oxford Dictionary
Music Book
Song Book
Hymn Book
Service Book

Also available from us courtesy of Oxford University Press:
Young Readers' Dictionary
(large print edition)
Young Readers' Thesaurus
(large print edition)

For further information or a free brochure, please contact us at:
Ulverscroft Large Print Books Ltd.,
The Green, Bradgate Road, Anstey,
Leicester, LE7 7FU, England.
Tel: (00 44) **0116 236 4325**
Fax: (00 44) **0116 234 0205**